"My God, you wanted to divorce me."

"There were reasons, dammit—you know that!" Malik snapped, trying desperately to keep his temper in check.

Zakira rolled her eyes and turned her back on him. "Save it," she mumbled, doing an admirable job of keeping her emotions in check, especially when she hurt so much. It was killing her to know that Malik had obviously been getting his life back on track all this time while she had been going crazy missing him. Obviously he didn't understand that, judging from his laid-back attitude.

"You're still my wife, Zaki," he reminded her unnecessarily.

"And?" she retorted. "That's only because I begged Tree to stall with the divorce. I just want to know what you expect from me?"

"I expect you to act like we have a marriage between us," Malik firmly informed her as he stood from the sofa.

"You know, it's been so long, I've forgotten what that means. If you think we can just pick up where we left off…forget it."

Books by AlTonya Washington

Kimani Romance

A Lover's Pretense
A Lover's Mask
Pride and Consequence

Kimani Arabesque

Remember Love
Guarded Love
Finding Love Again
Love Scheme
A Lover's Dream

ALTONYA WASHINGTON

is a South Carolina native and 1994 graduate of Winston Salem State University in North Carolina. Her first contemporary novel, *Remember Love* (BET/Arabesque 2003), was nominated by *Romantic Times BOOKreviews* as Best First Multicultural Romance. Her novel *Finding Love Again* won the *Romantic Times BOOKreviews* Reviewer's Choice Award for Best Multicultural Romance 2004. She presently resides in North Carolina, where she works as a senior library assistant.

ALTONYA
WASHINGTON

Pride
AND
Consequence

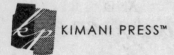 KIMANI PRESS™

ISBN-13: 978-0-373-86042-5
ISBN-10:   0-373-86042-0

PRIDE AND CONSEQUENCE

Dear Reader,

I thank each and every one of you for choosing to spend your valuable time with my work. As this is my tenth novel and a bit of a milestone for me, I thank those of you who have embraced me from the beginning with my first release back in 2003. It's been a wonderful ride thus far, and much of that enjoyment is due to you all.

I sincerely hope you've enjoyed the drama and passion of *Pride and Consequence*. As much as Malik and Zakira Badu's story intrigued and infuriated you, I hope it inspired feelings and thoughts on the power of honesty and communication, the allure of love and desire and the beauty of forgiveness.

Please share your thoughts, whatever they may be. Write to me at altonyawashington@yahoo.com and visit my Web site, www.lovealtonya.com.

Peace and blessings,

AlTonya Washington

My tenth novel—this is dedicated to my main guy. Mommy loves you, Masee!

Acknowledgment

I thank God for instilling in me my love of books and writing. I thank Him each day for providing the life, health and strength to create and for finding me a worthy recipient of this blessing.

Chapter 1

"Calm down, Zakira, just calm down."

The words replayed themselves again and again. She practically chanted the phrase in the silent hallway, lit only by the myriad of Christmas candles lining the walls.

For weeks, the terrible, yet familiar nightmare had intruded on Zakira Badu's dreams. There was no way she would get back to sleep anytime soon. She hurried down the black carpeted stairway, rubbing her hands across the sleeves of her short, pink satin robe. The kitchen was only a short distance away, and a cup of warm milk was always the perfect remedy for sleeplessness. Zakira's small feet padded the plush carpeting. Several tendrils of her naturally thick, waist-length hair were matted against her temple and neck. She tugged

at the clinging locks and sighed. The dreaded dream was
having the worst effect on her. The frazzled nerves and
edgy moods were both frightening and frustrating.

The lower level of the lovely Richmond, Virginia,
home was dark except for the electric holiday candles
arranged in every corner of the living room and along
the hallway that led to the kitchen.

The spacious state-of-the-art kitchen was void of any
light, but that didn't faze Zakira. She spent most of her
time in that portion of the house. In a matter of minutes,
she had the refrigerator door open, quickly selected a
carton of milk from one of the side shelves and kicked
the stainless steel door shut. From the overhead pan
rack, she grabbed a small gold-bottomed pot and headed
to the stove.

Once the milk was set to warm, Zakira leaned back
against the oak kitchen island. She hugged her petite
form and watched the stove burner turn orange from the
searing heat. Then, closing her eyes, she allowed her
thoughts to return to the disturbing dream.

The same nightmare had haunted her for weeks and
she could not understand it. The strange thing was that
the "nightmare" really wasn't that at all. It was more of
a vision. A recurring vision. In a candlelit room was a
man dressed in black and lying flat on some surface that
she could not make out. The man's identity remained a
mystery. The closer she moved to the unfamiliar form,
the more out of focus it became.

Uttering a low groan, Zakira pushed her hands
through her hair and massaged her scalp. She was so en-
grossed by her dark thoughts that she did not hear the

front door open and shut. The sound of another body moving around the house went unnoticed.

The milk on the stove had finally simmered long enough. Zakira removed it as though in a daze. She set the pot aside and was reaching for a mug, when a pair of arms extended out of the darkness to envelop her in a steely embrace. Zakira forgot everything and began to struggle as her captor lifted her from the polished hardwood floor.

Zakira's legs and arms flew wildly as she tried to wrench herself out of the iron hold. Her breath caught in her throat and prevented her from screaming. Her shock, combined with the pungent aroma from the man's leather jacket, overwhelmed her ability to fight harder.

The man placed her atop the wooden counter and, from there, Zakira bravely looked into the face of her attacker. When she spied the wide, white grin and shoulder-length dreadlocks, she raised her hand and placed a cracking slap to the man's face.

"You damn fool!" she breathed.

Surprised by his wife's actions, Malik Badu brought one large hand to the side of his handsome, dark face. He massaged his cheek, until the slight sting had vanished. "Zakira, what—"

"What the hell are you doing, sneaking in here like that?" she cried, pounding her fists against the front of Malik's jacket. "Do you know how much you scared me?"

Malik rubbed his hands along the side of Zakira's thighs. "Shh…baby doll, I'm sorry," he soothed.

"You should be! I really don't need you playin' 'Let's attack Zakira' tonight. Especially, when I just had one of those damn dreams," she finished, wiping a tear from her cheek.

Malik bowed his head, his long lashes closing over his grayish-black gaze. "Come here," he said softly, pulling Zakira against him and rocking her slowly. When her breathing had returned to normal, he pulled away and glanced behind him. "Is that what the milk is for?"

Zakira nodded. Malik's gaze narrowed as he cupped his wife's dark chocolate oval face and pressed a soft kiss to her full lips. He smiled, hearing her soft moan when the kiss became more heated.

Zakira tilted her head back and opened her eyes. Malik broke the kiss to trail his lips down the side of her neck. His hands ventured beneath the satiny material of her robe. She squeezed his shoulders when she felt his hands grasp her buttocks tightly as he lifted her from the counter.

"Forget the milk," he whispered in her ear and pulled her even closer. "I know a better way."

Instinctively, Zakira locked her legs around his lean waist as he carried her from the kitchen. Her hands pushed the heavy leather jacket from her husband's broad shoulders. It fell to the floor and was forgotten while they journeyed upstairs.

Only a few moments seemed to pass before Zakira felt herself being lowered onto the bed. Slowly and seductively, Malik unbuttoned her thin nightshirt and pushed it from her slender shoulders. His intense stare trailed across every inch of newly exposed skin, as though her nude body were a sight unfamiliar to him. His strong fingers curled around the waistband of the lacy panties she wore and he tugged them away.

Malik, however, had yet to remove his own clothes. He simply leaned across Zakira and massaged her soft skin.

"Mal..." she whispered, throwing both arms above her head and closing her eyes to savor his touch. The caress made her forget everything, except how wonderful she felt at that moment.

A sigh of disappointment escaped her lips when he ended the delightful massage. He replaced his hands with his mouth. Zakira moaned shamelessly beneath the touch of his wide, sensuous mouth gliding across her body.

Beginning with the column of her neck, he moved downward. Zakira still had her arms thrown overhead and gasped when she felt his lips pressing sweet kisses into the softly scented pit of her arm.

"Malik please..." she urged, as she tried tugging his sweater over his back.

In response, he pulled her hands away and pressed them to her sides. "Shh," he soothed, his warm breath fluttering against her skin.

She arched her body closer to his mouth. Long, heavy dreads grazed her skin when his lips touched the hardened tip of her breast. He released his grip on her wrists, and she instantly pushed her fingers through his hair.

Malik squeezed one breast as his lips feasted on the other. The simple, erotic caress robbed Zakira of her breath. She desperately wanted to feel his bare skin against hers. Once again, she moved her hands over his gray wool sweater. Suddenly, she requested that he undress by tugging at his broad shoulders.

A roguish grin touched Malik's gorgeous face and he again pinned Zakira's hands to her sides. He continued the caress, his lips moving onward from her breast to trail her flat stomach. Zakira's hips rose from the bed when she felt Malik's mouth touching the center of her body. Her lips parted as she pushed her head deeper into the pillows and enjoyed the caress.

The intensity of the kiss increased moment by moment. The expertise of the intimate caress was overwhelming. He knew exactly how his wife of three years liked to be touched. He never hesitated to give her what she wanted. In many ways, he played the willing slave in their bedroom. Every sexual request or fantasy was eagerly granted.

The soft groans expressed on Zakira's part soon turned to cries of pleasure. Malik never veered from his task and Zakira was soon experiencing an intense orgasm. He finally pulled away and watched her quiver from the incredible sensations coursing through her.

"Wipe that grin off your face," Zakira ordered later, without opening her eyes. She could envision Malik sitting above her, still fully clothed and smiling.

Of course, she was right. Malik continued to grin as he watched Zakira yawn before she drifted back to sleep.

Slowly and carefully, so he would not awaken her, he eased off the bed and headed to the bathroom. Once the door was closed behind him, he began to disrobe. Pulling the heavy sweater away from his chiseled torso, thoughts of Zakira filled his mind. Lord, how he loved that woman. She was his life, and he prayed he never lost her. Moreover, he prayed she never lost him.

* * *

A lazy smile brightened Zakira's face when she woke the next morning in her husband's arms. She was surprised that they had slept so soundly, especially when they usually woke in a tangle of covers, arms and legs. Not wanting to disturb the moment, she snuggled deeper into Malik's embrace and sighed.

Malik woke the instant he felt Zakira wiggling against him. When his grip tightened on her arm, she looked up.

"Morning," she whispered, pressing a soft kiss to the strong line of his jaw.

His haunting gray tinged stare narrowed. "Tell me about this dream."

"Malik…" she sighed, trying to pull away.

"Zakira…" he repeated in a warning tone, as he tightened his hold.

She grimaced and closed her eyes. "Baby, what does it matter now? I feel a lot better this morning."

"What about tonight?" Malik challenged, a slight frown beginning to form between his thick black brows.

She seemed to consider his question for a moment. Then she tensed and tried to sit up.

Malik, however, had made up his mind. He wasn't going to let her get away so easily this time.

"Let me go," she softly ordered when he pinned her beneath him on the bed.

His grip was unyielding. "Zaki, do you realize you were so caught up in that damn dream last night, that you didn't even hear me come in the house? Now we can do this the easy way or the hard way, but either way I'm gonna find out what's upsetting you."

Zakira's huge brown eyes searched Malik's narrowed darker ones. What she saw there convinced her he would not let up until she came clean. Finally, she nodded and he released his hold on her. She sat up in bed and focused her gaze on the burgundy-and-black comforter covering the bed.

"Um…it's really just a vision or…something."

Malik rolled his eyes. "Zakira…" he said once again. His tone warned her to be truthful.

She raised her hands defensively. "It is. I swear it. I see a man laid out, dressed in black. There're candles everywhere. Unfortunately, the closer I come to him, the foggier the scene becomes."

"And that's it?" Malik questioned as he propped himself on an elbow and watched her.

Zakira nodded. "That's it. I guess it freaks me out so much because it all just looks so eerie, you know?"

He shrugged one huge shoulder and pushed himself to a sitting position. "I think maybe you just saw a movie or something that scared you," he reasoned.

Zakira was not convinced. "I've never been spooked by a movie before. I don't see why that would bother me now."

"There's always a first time," Malik decided, watching Zakira consider the possibility. A small smirk tugged at his mouth and he leaned forward to press a kiss to her mouth.

"So, what time are we leaving on Thursday?" Zakira asked, turning on her stomach and resting her head on Malik's pillow. She watched him pull back the covers and get out of bed.

"Thursday?" he asked.

Zakira closed her eyes and grimaced. "The food festival? California?" she replied, her soft, melodic voice going flat.

Malik selected a black, long-sleeved shirt from his closet. "Damn, Zaki, I thought you were just teasing about that."

"Don't even try it, Malik Kuame Badu. You promised."

"Don't get excited," Malik soothed, waving one hand in the air before he once again disappeared into the closet. "We really didn't discuss it that much. I thought you were just making a suggestion."

Zakira toyed with a cotton-soft lock of her thick hair. "I suggested it because I wanted us to go. You agreed and said you'd take care of the tickets and everything," she reminded him in a weary tone. Getting away in the midst of the Christmas madness was a treat she was looking forward to.

"I'll get on it soon as I get to the restaurant," he promised, his deep voice muffled from the closet.

"Never mind," Zakira groaned, pushing herself up in the bed, "I'll handle it. This is the closest we'll probably get to taking a vacation. I don't plan on missing out."

"You're the best, Zaki."

"Mmm, so I've been told."

Malik emerged from the closet carrying a pair of wine-colored slacks and a matching jacket. He tossed them to the chair where the black shirt lay. "So what'cha got planned for today?" he asked.

Zakira swung her legs over the side of the bed. "Not much. I've got some things I want to try out in the kitchen, so I'll probably be there most of the day. After I handle our travel arrangements," she added pointedly.

Malik grinned. "You should bring that stuff into the restaurant when you get it together," he ordered, heading across the room to the bathroom.

Zakira shook her head. Her husband never passed on the chance to get her more involved with his business. Malik had just begun working on the restaurant when they met five years ago. Zakira had been interning for a Richmond consulting firm when he arrived one day for an appointment with a friend of his who also worked for the firm.

He had seemed hooked from the moment they met. The two began dating, and Zakira was very impressed by the smart, young, instinctive businessman. She was even more taken by Malik's fierce dark looks, his six-foot-plus height, his large, muscular build, and the thick dreadlocks which, at that time, only grazed his cheeks. When he smiled, his grayish-black, slightly slanted eyes crinkled at the corners and his smile instantly triggered deep dimples.

As Zakira got to know Malik, she discovered he was often viewed as intimidating and unapproachable. While his appearance unsettled most people, his wife felt just the opposite. Many marveled that such an overpowering soul could be with so gentle a soul as the sweet and kind Zakira.

For his part, Malik was completely bound to his wife. He didn't think he could ever become bored or disillusioned with her. Besides Zakira's fantastic looks, her mind was immensely intriguing. The intelligent twenty-nine-year-old woman had a quick mind for business and her savvy frequently rivaled his. That was one of the reasons he constantly encouraged her to take more of an interest in the restaurant. Badu's was Malik's creation, but he wanted to run it with his wife by his side. Perhaps one day, was her usual reply.

"Malik! The airport limo's here!" Zakira called, as she sprinted upstairs. When she got to the bedroom door, she almost collided with her husband.

"Ready?" he whispered, patting his hand against her waist.

Zakira smiled. "Mmm-hmm. I'm just gonna check and make sure we didn't forget anything."

"You mean make sure *I* didn't forget anything?" Malik teased, before kissing her neck and patting her waist once more. "Hurry up," he ordered.

Zakira headed to the picture window that overlooked the herb garden on the east side of the yard. She checked the side locks, then sprinted over to the bathroom door to take one last look.

"Uh-huh, just as I thought," she muttered, spying Malik's valise on the black marble counter. She grabbed the small piece of luggage and was about to head out, when she noticed a prescription pill bottle beside it. The label noted Malik's name, recommended dosage and the amount of available refills for a drug she had never heard of. Confusion etched on her face as she caressed the clear slender bottle.

"Zaki, let's move!"

"Coming!" she called, slipping the small cylinder into the valise before she rushed out of the bathroom.

San Diego, California

The eighth annual Restaurateurs' Retreat was being held at the Shepherd's Inn, a serene resort complete with lofty breathtaking views of the Pacific. Restaurant owners and critics alike were on hand for a weekend of sampling the latest, most creative and decadent dishes.

"Mmm…Malik, promise me we'll take a drive along the coast before we leave?"

"Whatever you want."

Zakira turned from their bedroom balcony. She watched her husband searching the tiny valise he had carried since they left the airport's limousine. She bit her tongue to keep from asking what he was looking for. She already knew. *Dammit, what are those pills for?* she silently questioned herself.

When Malik disappeared into the bathroom, she cast her suspicions aside and inspected the rest of the plush suite. The color scheme was an elegant white on gold, with thick ocean-blue carpeting throughout. Still, the heart-stopping view of the Pacific was what held her captive. The sight of the waves crashing against the huge stone boulders clustered along the west bank of the resort produced the most soothing sound. She closed her eyes and imagined making love with her sexy husband amidst the thunder of the ocean rolling across the massive rocks

"Stop it, Zaki," she ordered herself, stepping back into the room. In a matter of minutes, she had located the room service menu and ordered a small feast. She had just slipped into her favorite purple terry robe when Malik left the bathroom.

He offered no explanation for his obvious mood and went about changing into his own comfortable attire. Zakira ventured back out to the balcony with a copy of the festival's program in hand. She had browsed halfway through it, when Malik joined her outside.

"Damn," he whispered, as blown away by the view as Zakira had been.

She smiled. "I know, right? I could definitely get used to this."

Malik took a seat on one of the cushiony white armchairs and propped his bare feet against the white iron railing. "Don't tell me you'd trade East Coast livin' for this?"

Zakira set the program on the short iron table next to her chair and shrugged. "I think I could live here."

"California, Zaki?"

"What? It's beautiful."

"Yeah, *this* is beautiful, but the rest of the state…"

"Oh, stop, there are some very lovely areas here. Which is why I've often suggested that you expand your business here.

Malik's deep chuckles rose. "Remember what I said about you becoming more involved in my business? Forget it."

Zakira threw her head back and laughed. "Fair enough," she conceded, moving out of her chair. "I'm going to put my hair up. Room service should be here soon. I didn't think you'd be in the mood to go out tonight, so I ordered in."

Malik caught her hand when she stepped past him.

"Thanks," he said, pulling her to his lap. His big hands cupped her small face as his lips touched hers.

Zakira gasped, allowing him the entrance he sought. She kissed him with equal passion, arching herself against his wide, bare chest. Her nails grazed his flawless dark skin, and her legs trembled when his hand tested the softness of her inner thigh.

The doorbell sounded. Malik's eyes searched Zakira's face with an intensity that almost frightened her. Then, as though he were waking from a dream, he shook his head and smiled.

"I better get that," he whispered.

Zakira eased off his lap. "Um, I'll just be in the bathroom," she told him, praying her weak legs would carry her that far.

Zakira found the suite a bit darker when she emerged from the bathroom. The setting sun offered the only illumination. Slowly, she retraced her steps to the balcony.

"Malik..." she sighed, eyeing the seductive transformation.

A cozy round table set for two had been placed in the center of the balcony. Candles offered a golden warmth that seemed to intensify the fiery orange glow from the retreating sun.

"Thought we'd take advantage of a West Coast sunset," Malik explained, as he finished filling their wineglasses.

Zakira smiled and turned her eyes toward the sun. "I knew you were impressed."

Malik offered no response and simply walked over to hold her chair. When Zakira took her seat, his fingers brushed the nape of her neck in one fleeting motion.

"I'm glad you talked me into this."

"So, you're admitting I had to talk you into it, huh?" Zakira questioned later, as they ate thick slices of chocolate cheesecake in bed. The room was lit by the glow of the huge moon. In the distance, crashing waves provided a sound more romantic than the most heartfelt song.

"We needed to get away. I know *I* did," Malik admitted.

Zakira set her cake on the bedside stand and turned to rest her head on Malik's bare chest. "Is something going on with the business?" she asked.

Malik squeezed her shoulders. "What makes you think that?"

"You seem to be under a lot of stress. I thought maybe it was business-related."

The room was bathed in darkness, but Malik's frustration showed. "The business is fine."

Zakira heard the soft edge to his reply and debated whether to inquire further.

"Damn, this is so relaxing." Malik sighed, drawing Zakira more tightly against his powerful frame. "I wish we could stay longer than a weekend."

The quiet, peaceful tone of his voice robbed Zakira of her desire to mention anything that might ruin the moment. She pressed a kiss to one of his bulging pectorals and closed her eyes. The calming roar of the waves several feet below eventually lulled them to sleep.

* * *

"This is incredible. What is it?"

"Canapé Ricotta, ma'am."

"Come on, there has to be more than ricotta cheese in this thing," Zakira marveled and popped another one of the exquisite pastries into her mouth.

The young dark-haired man behind the red-and-white-painted boot, beamed. "It's actually a blend of several cheeses along with a butter and herb sauce. The flavor of the ricotta cheese is most pronounced, hence the name."

"Outstanding," Zakira complimented once more. "Baby, you should try this," she told Malik when he arrived at the booth.

"Hit me," he requested, opening his mouth for one of the canapés. "Not bad," he said as the pungent blend of herbs and cheeses triggered his taste buds.

"So, where were you?" Zakira asked, once they had moved on from the Italian food booths.

Malik's grin triggered his dimples. "There's a Louisiana soul food booth back there," he announced.

Zakira glanced across her shoulder. "You're kidding?"

"Mmm-mmm."

"Why didn't you come get me? I could go for a bowl of hot gumbo right about now," she said, pushing her hands inside her quarter-length olive-green sweater jacket.

Malik slipped one arm around her waist. "I thought we could go there for lunch—they've got a restaurant here at the resort."

"Sounds good," Zakira absently replied, her brown eyes widening as she spotted another interesting booth.

* * *

"Do you have room left for anything?" Malik asked his petite wife, watching as she scanned the menu of Louisiana specialties.

"Please," Zakira drawled without looking away from the menu, "I've been thinking about that gumbo since you told me about this place."

"Did I hear someone say gumbo?"

Zakira looked up and smiled at the cheerful young woman who had arrived at the table. "You sure did. I'd like your biggest bowl," she said, giggling when Malik uttered a soft mocking sound of shock.

"Great choice," the perky honey-complexioned waitress replied before turning to Malik. "And will it be the same for you, sir?"

Malik's slanting gaze narrowed a bit more and he pushed his menu aside. "Nah, I think I'm gonna pass."

Zakira leaned forward. "Baby, aren't you gonna eat anything?"

"Just bring me a glass of lemonade, will you?" he asked the waitress, who smiled and nodded before leaving the table.

"You must be hungry? You barely sampled any of the food out there," Zakira noted, watching Malik shrug. "Are you feeling all right?"

"I'm fine, Zaki. Don't start."

"I'm not starting, I just—"

"I'm going to the restroom. I'll be back." He interjected, leaving Zakira staring after him.

Lunch was a quiet affair. Malik's silence had unnerved and angered her so that Zakira managed to finish only half of the spicy rich seafood gumbo. She had the remainder of the lunch packed in a to-go container and told her husband she would see him later. She spent the rest of the afternoon visiting more booths, chatting with other restaurant owners and enjoying the vibrant beauty of the seaside resort. She adjourned to the suite much later that afternoon and decided to take a nap before the evening's scheduled gala.

Subtle tingles of sensation surged up and down Zakira's spine. She shivered in her sleep and snuggled deeper into the warm queen-sized bed.

"Zaki…"

"Hmm?" she moaned, slowly awakening when the pleasurable sensations grew stronger as they coursed through her body.

Malik's perfect teeth fastened to Zakira's earlobe and he whispered her name again. When her lashes fluttered open and her brown eyes focused on his face, he pressed a kiss to her mouth.

Zakira rolled her eyes in response. When she turned her head away, she could hear his deep chuckle in her ear.

"I'm sorry," he sang.

Zakira turned onto her back and fixed him with an unimpressed glare. "I know," she replied pointedly

Again, Malik chuckled. "Forgive me?"

Zakira laced her fingers together atop the crisp blue sheets. "I guess I could, if I knew what happened. We were having a great time, and all of a sudden you flip."

"I know, and I'm sorry."

"And that's it? You've been acting strange for a while now, and your only explanation is you're sorry?"

Malik fixed her with another devastating smile. "I don't want to talk about it," he declared, leaning over when she turned her face away.

The soft lingering kisses he dropped to her neck slowly melted the ice wall she had constructed. After a few moments, she turned and pulled him into bed with her. Malik's hands were everywhere, caressing, squeezing, fondling…. Zakira moaned his name as her fingers entwined in the long dreadlocks. Malik cupped her breasts in his wide palms and savored the taste of one, firm bud. The kisses journeyed upward, landing against Zakira's collarbone and along the smooth column of her neck.

"Mmm…" she moaned, encircling his neck as she arched into his chest. The fabric of his shirt grazed her bare skin with the most delicious intensity. Suddenly, the full force of his massive frame settled across Zakira's body and her eyes snapped open.

"Mmm…Malik, wait a minute…Malik…Malik?" she called, nudging his side with her knee.

There was no response and she began to shove against his broad shoulders. "Malik? Son of a…" she sighed, realizing her husband had fallen asleep while making love to her. When the sound of soft snores caught her ear, she braced all her weight against his and managed to push him away.

While Malik slumbered, Zakira stood next to the bed

and watched him. Her suspicions were raging, and the strange pill bottle was at the center of her thoughts.

"Forget this," she whispered. "I have a party to dress for." She headed for the bathroom while Malik's snoring gained volume.

"Actually, we've been having problems simply finding a venue for the event."

"Who wouldn't want to take part in something like that?"

Two women stood talking next to Zakira at the buffet table. The annual Saturday Night Gala had been in full swing when she arrived. The black-and-white affair offered dancing, wine tasting and, of course, an immense dinner buffet.

"You'd be surprised how fast people shy away when they find out something's for charity. Especially the businesses. All they care about is what type of fee they'll generate for renting out their establishment."

"Excuse me?"

The two women silenced their discussion and turned to face Zakira.

"I'm sorry to interrupt," she said with a smile. "I couldn't help but overhear. What is your charity, if you don't mind me asking?"

"No, of course not. It's the Richmond Children's Cancer Research Fund."

"Richmond? Virginia?" Zakira asked.

The woman who had spoken pressed one white-gloved hand to her throat. "Yes, it's really just a group of doctors' wives who run the organization. We have no ties with the hospitals or state agencies, but we've managed to collect over half a million dollars during our two years in existence."

"That's admirable," Zakira breathed, highly impressed by the group's success.

Suddenly, the woman shook her head and gave a nervous laugh. "Please forgive me. I don't know where my manners are. I'm Lydia Cartright."

"And I'm Jessica Black."

Zakira set her plate down on the buffet table and shook hands with both women. "Zakira Badu, I'm also from Richmond."

"Well, it's certainly nice to meet a home girl." Lydia noted before gesturing at their surroundings. "So, what brings you all the way to a California food festival? Pigging out like the rest of us?"

Zakira laughed. "Yes and no," she replied. "My husband owns a restaurant in Richmond. I don't know if you've ever heard of Badu's?"

"Badu's?" Lydia and Jessica cried, exchanging glances.

"Honey, my husband and I eat there all the time!" Jessica was saying.

"Same here. In fact, Badu's was the next restaurant on my list," Lydia softly mentioned.

Zakira's brown eyes narrowed. "On your list?"

Jessica cleared her throat and fiddled with the folds of her white satin evening gown. "Lydia's trying to organize the next event for the charity. We were thinking of renting a hall and hiring caterers, but then we thought it might be cheaper to rent a nice restaurant for the evening."

"Unfortunately, your other colleagues in town are making us want to consider a charity picnic," Lydia shared. "Bring your own food, of course," she added.

"Well, it sounds like a great cause. I'd love to help any way I can," Zakira offered, folding her arms over the square bodice of her black evening gown.

Jessica and Lydia were overcome with gratefulness.

"You can't know what this means for us," Lydia whispered as she squeezed Zakira's hands. "We're hoping to schedule the event two weeks before Christmas—hopefully folks will be a bit more charitable."

"We can't pay a lot," Jessica warned, "but we promise to come up with a suitable figure."

Zakira waved her hand. "Let's not discuss all that now," she said, searching her black clutch purse. "I'll need to speak with my husband, but I know he'll be eager to help. Here, hold on to our card and give me a call when you get back to Richmond."

Jessica's almond-brown face softened with gratitude. "This means so much, Zakira. Bless you."

"My goodness," Lydia suddenly breathed, her green eyes riveted on the tall, gorgeous man who had just entered the ballroom.

Jessica and Zakira turned in time to see Malik make his appearance. Zakira felt her heart flip at the sight of him in the stylish tux. He wore his long dreads in a ponytail and the style only emphasized his rugged, magnificent features.

"Who *is* that?" Jessica whispered, her dark eyes feasting on Malik who had stopped to speak with two gentlemen.

Zakira smiled and turned to face her new acquaintances. "Ladies, that's my husband," she announced, laughing at the friendly envy they allowed her to see. She glanced across her shoulder, her expression rueful. She had managed to forgive Malik's unexpected nap, but promised that she would not forget to ask him about it.

"All right, you two, please don't forget to call. I'll discuss this with Malik and we should be ready to start planning right away."

Again, Lydia and Jessica reached out to shake her hand.

"Thank you so much, Zakira!"

"We'll definitely be calling."

Zakira waved off the two women, grabbed her plate and went in search of her husband. By the time she reached Malik, he was shaking hands with the two men he had been speaking with.

"Did you have a good nap?" she asked, waiting for him to turn around.

Malik let his head fall back and he closed his eyes for a moment. "Zaki," he sighed, finally turning to face her. "Baby, I'm sorry about that."

Zakira nodded and focused her smoky brown eyes on her full plate. "I wish I could remember how many times I've heard 'I'm sorry' over the last two days."

"It's about all I can say," he whispered, bringing his arms around her waist. "That, and I hope you'll let me make this up to you."

Zakira selected a plump pink shrimp from her plate and popped it into her mouth. "Make it up to me, hmm? You'll probably fall asleep before you can get halfway through it."

Malik's low laughter rumbled forth. "That's not the only way I know how to make up, Zaki."

"I'm glad to hear that."

"You gonna give me a chance here, or what?"

Zakira decided to let up a little and raised her eyes to his. "So, what do you have in mind?"

Malik took the plate from Zakira's hands and set it on the tray of a passing server. "I'd rather show you," he said, pulling her close.

Zakira began to sway to the rhythm of the sultry Latin groove. "This had better be good," she warned him.

And it was. Malik was true to his word. At 6 a.m. Sunday morning, he was rousing Zakira from her sleep and telling her to hurry and get dressed. They hopped into a rented convertible and began their day.

Zakira thought the view of the ocean from her fifth-floor balcony was exquisite, but it didn't compare with the view from the passenger seat of their car. When the sun rose, Malik let the top down and Zakira reveled in the feel of the fresh sea air whipping through her long hair.

"This is incredible!" she shouted, acting like a kid on a roller coaster as her wide eyes scanned the natural beauty surrounding them—entrancing blue water, tall cliffs, towering trees that filtered the gorgeous sunlight and the never-ending curved road that grew steeper as it carried them to a higher altitude.

"When did you think of this?" Zakira asked later that afternoon. They were seated on the hood of the black convertible, with a food-filled straw basket between them.

Malik dipped his wheat cracker into a spicy cheese spread and shrugged. "When I woke up and realized I'd fallen asleep while making love to you."

Zakira tugged her bottom lip between her teeth and studied his gorgeous profile. She ached to question him about his behavior...and the pills. "Malik—"

"What was it you were wanting to discuss with me after the party? Something about a charity?" he interjected, obviously sensing that she was about to ask something he was not prepared to answer.

"Yeah..." Zakira sighed, deciding it was best not to bring up such a heavy subject. "I met two women from Richmond last night. They're trying to plan a charity function and are having problems with the venue."

"Mmm...financial problems?" Malik guessed.

Zakira nodded, as she cut a portion of aged sharp cheddar from the huge block. "They're offering to pay, but, of course, they can't afford much. I'm hoping we can work something out. I'd really like to help them," she said, brushing a speck of cheese from her snug pink V-neck sweater.

"I don't have a problem with it. Hell, it'll be tax-deductible."

"Malik!" Zakira chastised.

"What? I'm just stating a fact," he said, chuckling at her horrified expression. "Anyway, what's the charity?"

Zakira nibbled the cheese and followed it with a swig of the fruitful red wine. "It's the Richmond Children's Cancer Research Fund. The women I spoke with are doctors' wives, they..."

"Malik? Baby? Did you hear me?" Zakira said a moment later, noticing the hard, set look on his face.

"We better bounce if we want to make the inn before dark," he suggested quickly, jumping to the ground and repacking the basket.

Zakira watched him closely, but she did not argue. As the car continued its trek up the gorgeous coast, she decided she would get her answers that night.

"How is it?"

Zakira shook her head. "So good. I've never had clam chowder this good. I guess owning a restaurant on the ocean makes it easy to get the best seafood. And I've definitely had my fill of it this weekend."

Malik's expression reflected concern. "You're not eating much. Are you sick?"

Zakira swirled her spoon in the creamy pearl-colored chowder. "No, I'm not sick. Are you?" she asked, raising her probing gaze to his face.

He would not respond and a few minutes passed in silence. Zakira silently chastised herself for the question. She hadn't meant to approach the subject quite that way. Besides, the day had been so wonderful, she didn't want it to end on a sour note. Unfortunately, Malik's mood had her more than a little suspicious.

"I had an idea about the charity dinner."

Zakira forced a phony smile to her face. "Oh?"

Malik ran one hand though his dreads and nodded. "I was wondering if you'd consider working with the staff on the menu and presentation?"

Despite her reluctance to become more active with the business, Zakira discovered she was quite interested in the idea. "What do you have in mind?"

Malik leaned against the oversized wooden high-backed chair. "Well, I was hoping you'd come up with your own ideas and discuss them with the cook staff. We have a meeting every day, so…"

Zakira was nodding. Ideas for the menu were already entering her mind. Of course, she would discuss them with the charity's coordinators first. Still, she had the feeling this was going to be a very successful event.

"You seem pleased," Malik observed, taking note of the expression brightening his wife's pretty chocolate-toned face.

Zakira could not deny it. "It makes me feel good to be part of something so important. I just can't believe they've had a hard time finding a place to have the thing."

Malik shrugged, pushing up the sleeves of his lightweight navy blue sweatshirt.

"I mean, I can't imagine anyone not jumping to help them. Especially for a cause like this. Cancer in children, it's—"

"Zakira, do we have to talk about this now?" Malik suddenly snapped, his stare glinting with frustration. "We're supposed to be having a good time here."

"What the hell is wrong with you, Malik?" she snapped back, her mahogany brown stare ablaze. "If I remember correctly, you asked me about the charity dinner. You know, your mood lately has gotten progressively worse and I'm tired of it."

"Zaki—"

"Please," she stopped him, pushing her chair away from the table, "I already know—you're sorry. Why don't we talk when you have a little more to say?" With that, she stomped away from the table.

Malik braced his elbows to the table and clutched fistfuls of his dreads. "Baby, you'll get your answers as soon as I get mine."

Chapter 2

Although Badu's never opened until 3:00 p.m., Malik always arrived at 8:00 a.m. His routine was practically the same each day. Before heading upstairs to his office, he went to the kitchen for a morning meeting with the chefs. The cooking staff of eight arrived even earlier than their boss, despite the fact that ingredients for the day's menu had already been prepared. The staff never departed without having the necessary supplies for the following business day chopped, chilled and marinated.

Everyone immediately came to attention when they saw Malik. Though the employees of Badu's admired and respected the forceful young man, they often wished he wasn't so demanding.

"Just a heads-up. We're going to be hosting a charity

dinner for cancer research a couple weeks before Christmas," Malik declared at the end of the meeting, already shrugging into the stylish tan suede suit coat he had thrown across a chair. "I should have more specifics soon, but there will be plenty of time for you guys to get prepared."

The eight chefs exchanged weary looks across the table. They had no problems being on hand for the charity event. It was the time leading up to the dinner they could have done without. Their boss could become more than demanding, he could be almost tyrannical.

"I won't be working with you on the event, Zakira will," Malik announced, sensing the chefs' relief without even looking at their faces.

No one at the table could mask their joy. The boss's wife would provide a refreshing change from her brooding, unyielding husband.

"It's not that we dislike working closely with you, you understand?"

Malik grinned. "Sure I do, Jo Jo." He wasn't offended.

Malik never apologized for running a tight ship. He felt his people respected him more for it and believed that respect made his restaurant the success that it was.

"So, when is she gonna start coming in, Malik?"

"Well—" Malik began, a smile coming to his face, when he looked toward the rear of the dining room. "Speak of the devil. There she is."

Zakira was slightly breathless as she hurriedly approached the table. "Sorry guys, I wanted to get here before the end of your meeting. Do y'all have a few minutes?"

"Sure, Zakira!"

"Have a seat, darlin'."

"Can I get you some coffee?"

Malik rolled his eyes and reclined in his chair as he watched the eight stiff-lipped men fawn over his wife. Of course, he could never blame them. Zakira brought out something bright in each of his employees. He believed they would work round the clock for her if she asked them to.

"I'm fine," Zakira was assuring the chefs, as she set her maroon cashmere wrap on a vacant chair. "This won't take long. I just wanted to discuss a couple of things with you all. Did Malik tell you guys about the dinner?" she asked, watching everyone smile and nod.

"Great," she said, already reaching into the oversized black leather tote she carried.

Malik's smoldering charcoal-gray stare never strayed from his wife as she discussed menu ideas and timelines with his employees. He admired the ease with which she handled the group of finicky chefs. When they began to discuss the particulars, he stood and took Zakira's elbow in a light hold.

"I'm gonna head on up to the office, unless you need me to stay," he said, brushing his hand against the soft clinging cashmere of her pearl gray dress.

Zakira coolly extracted her arm from Malik's grasp, feeling her entire body tingle scandalously in response to the sweet gesture. "Mmm-mmm," she replied, with a quick shake of her head. "I'll be fine."

He smiled and turned to the table. "Talk to you guys

later." He could feel Zakira's eyes linger a bit longer than necessary on his departing figure before she forced her eyes back to the page she held.

Before he exited the dining room, he turned to cast one last look at her. The sight of his wife taking an active role in his business pleased him more than she would ever know.

The annoying beep of the intercom pierced the silence of the spacious corner office. Malik slammed his fist against the talk button with such force the machine jumped off the desk.

"What is it, Chanel?" he barked. Reading invoices and recipes, and going over the books for the better part of the morning, had taken a fierce toll on his mood.

"Sorry to bother you, Malik, but Tree's out here to see you," Chanel Levy informed her boss.

"Sorry, Chanel. It's all right. Send him in," Malik instructed, tossing the paperwork aside as he leaned back in his chair.

A slight frown crossed his dark face when his best friend and lawyer Trekel Grisani walked into the office. "What's wrong?" Malik asked the moment the door closed.

Tree's long black lashes closed over his dark eyes as he shook his head. "Everything's fine, man," he assured his friend.

Malik visibly relaxed and leaned back a little further in the brown leather chair. "So what's up? I don't usually get visits from lawyers in the middle of the day."

Tree grinned, lowering his massive frame into one of

the chairs before the wide desk. "You got a problem with me coming by?"

Malik shrugged. "Nah. You want me to have somethin' sent up from the kitchen?"

Tree waved his hand and grimaced. "Thanks, I'm cool." He propped the side of his face against his palm and waited. When Malik remained silent, he sighed. "I think we've done enough small talk, man."

Malik's heavy brows drew close. "Small talk?" he repeated, purposely misunderstanding.

Tree expelled a frustrated sigh and leaned forward. "Man, will you please give it up? Have you heard anything from Doctor McNeil?"

At Tree's mention of the doctor's name, Malik instantly tensed. "I only saw him two days ago," he murmured, his deep voice raspy with aggravation.

Tree pressed his fingers to the bridge of his nose and cleared his throat. "All right, so it's been two days. Shouldn't they have the results from your tests by now?"

Malik pounded his fist against his thigh. "I doubt it." He sighed.

"I don't understand why it's taking so long," Tree complained.

In spite of his foul mood, Malik managed to laugh. "We *are* talkin' about cancer here, man. I think Doctor McNeil wants to be sure when he tells me I'm about to die."

Tree realized how unnerving the situation was for his friend. He suddenly regretted having mentioned anything about the tests. "I think you're overreacting now, Mal."

"I'm not so sure after what happened," Malik admitted, shaking his head.

Tree's long brows drew together as a frown further darkened his extremely handsome face. "What happened with what?"

Malik rubbed one hand through his dreads and stared out the office window that overlooked downtown Richmond. "Zakira's been having a dream for the last few weeks. She finally told me that all she can see is a man laid out in black, surrounded by candles."

Tree's brows rose expectantly. "And?"

Malik turned and shot Tree a murderous glare. "Hell, man, that could be me laid out dead."

A smile brightened Tree's handsome face. "Man, I think you're letting this get to you too much."

Malik turned back to the windows and braced his hands on the dark paneled sill. "We both know that could be me. The only thing missing is the casket."

"Mal," Tree cautioned, but even he found it somewhat unsettling.

A few days later, Zakira opened the door and her smile widened at the sight of her stepsister. "Cold?" she teased the woman standing there with her arms wrapped around her slender form, shivering.

Edwina Harris rolled her almond-shaped eyes to the overcast sky before she rushed past Zakira and hurried into the living room where there was a fireplace.

"Dammit, Z," she groaned, stomping one stylish, hiking boot shod foot to the carpet. "Why haven't you made a fire yet, girl?"

Zakira stared at Edwina for a moment, a dumbfounded

expression on her face. Then she slapped her hands against her sides. "I never thought about it."

"Do you have any idea how cold it is outside?" Eddie calmly inquired, propping one hand on her slender hip.

Zakira shook her head and walked over to take her stepsister by the hand. "I've been in the kitchen all morning. Come on, I'll fix you some coffee."

Eddie held back. "Make it tea and you've got a deal."

"No problem," Zakira obliged, leading the way down the carpeted hallway.

The moment Eddie stepped past the arched doorway of the kitchen, her eyes closed and a serene smile crossed her lips. "Mmm…what are you making?"

Zakira's expression was filled with pride as she listened to her sister marvel over the fabulous smells wafting in the air. "What does it smell like?" she teased.

Eddie shot her a wicked glare. "It smells like something I want a piece of."

Zakira clasped her hands and rushed to the cupboard to retrieve a plate. A fantastic cook, like her husband, she always relished the chance to show off her culinary talents. Edwina, of course, didn't mind sampling the dishes.

"What is it?" Eddie asked, watching Zakira scoop out what appeared to be a miniature pie.

A surprised expression touched Zakira's face as she set a fork on the side of the plate. "I know you've had chicken potpie before."

Edwina nodded, accepting the plate. "I have, but none that ever smelled like this," she whispered, breaking the pie's flaky crust with her fork. A delighted gasp escaped her mouth when chunks of potatoes, carrots and chicken tumbled onto the plate.

"That's because I use fresh ingredients and the crust is seasoned," Zakira revealed smugly.

"Mmm," Eddie sighed, when she tasted the delicious creation. "With what?"

Zakira took a plate from the cupboard and served herself. "Herbs from our garden out back."

"Well, it's delicious," Eddie complimented.

Bowing her head, Zakira acknowledged the compliment. "Thanks. So, um, what brings you by today?" she asked. Hearing Edwina's long, dramatic sigh, she already knew the answer.

"Men," Eddie breathed.

Zakira shook her head as she listened to Edwina lament over her latest poor choice. Not wanting to treat her stepsister's problems lightly, Zakira still found it all somewhat amusing. When most people saw Edwina Harris, they figured she had her life in perfect order.

Besides having her own medical practice, Edwina was a leggy twenty-eight-year-old with a model's looks. She wore her hair in a boyish cut that flattered her lovely, dark face. The full lips and almond-shaped hazel eyes gave her a captivating exotic appearance. Men were drawn to her like helpless puppets. Unfortunately, these "puppets" usually turned out to be toads. Toads, who took Eddie through one trial or another.

"I mean, I just can't believe I fell for his crap."

Zakira lifted another forkful of the delicious chicken

potpie to her lips and savored the taste. "I'm going to make my usual suggestion, but I don't expect you to take advantage of it."

Eddie sat up straighter on the bar stool in front of the kitchen island and waited.

"Give all this dating a rest for a while. Stop looking so hard, and maybe the right man will find you."

Edwina rolled her eyes toward the ceiling in response.

Zakira took a sip of her tea. "Why don't you put more time into your work? That couldn't hurt."

"That's the last thing I need to do."

"Eddie, what the hell is wrong with you?" Zakira finally snapped.

"Z, you keep forgetting I'm a sex therapist. Now, if I'm gonna take a break from dating, sex is the last thing I want on my mind."

Zakira tried to keep her smile from breaking through, but she failed. In seconds, both she and Edwina were laughing uncontrollably.

"Well, what about this?" Zakira said with a sigh, once the high-pitched giggles lost some of their zeal. "Come to our charity dinner at the end of the month."

Edwina's lovely face looked blank. "What does a charity dinner have to do with my dating situation?"

"Nothing, and that's why I think you should come. Not to meet anyone. Just get out and enjoy some good food and stimulating conversation for a good cause. Not to mention the, um, hundred-dollar-a-plate dinner."

Edwina choked on her tea. "I knew there was a catch. You ain't right, Z."

Zakira tried to hide her smile. One look at Edwina's face made her burst into laughter again. Of course, Eddie couldn't help but follow suit.

"Now, you drive safe and remember what I said," Zakira told Eddie a few hours later as they shared a tight hug.

Edwina relished her sister's embrace a moment longer before pulling away. "I'll try. And don't forget to send me my invitation!" she called, already sprinting down the porch steps.

Zakira shook her head and watched Eddie race toward her car.

The phone rang the moment Zakira twisted the front door lock. She rushed into the living room to answer before the machine clicked on.

"Zakira Badu."

"Yes, ma'am, may I speak with Malik Badu?"

"He's not here right now. May I take a message?"

"Mrs. Badu, this is Doctor Sedrick McNeil. I will just try reaching Malik. I'll try his office."

A faint frown formed on Zakira's face. "Oh, uh, all right," she managed.

The connection broke soon after, but she still clutched the receiver. *Malik didn't tell me he had a new doctor.*

"Oh, Malik, wait!"

"What is it, Chanel?" Malik said, grimacing as he pulled off the heavy jacket.

Chanel hurried down the hall. "A Doctor McNeil

called. He wants you to get in touch with him." She handed her boss a pink message slip.

For a moment, Malik was sure his heart had stopped beating. He noticed Chanel watching him strangely and ordered himself to get hold of his emotions.

"Thanks. I'll make the call from my office."

Chanel only nodded, her hazel eyes tinged with worry.

Malik tossed his jacket to the sofa and headed to his desk. Not wanting to prolong the inevitable, he picked up the phone and entered the necessary digits.

"Doctor McNeil's office," a perky voice greeted after the first ring.

Malik hesitated for a moment, and then cleared his throat. "This is Malik Badu I'm returning Doctor McNeil's call."

"Oh, Mr. Badu," the secretary sighed. "Doctor McNeil asked if you wouldn't mind coming in."

Malik's long lashes fell over his eyes. He almost demanded to be told at that moment, but managed to keep a lid on his temper.

"I'll be there within the hour."

In an effort to forget Dr. McNeil's mysterious call, Zakira decided to make another sinful dish. This time, she selected a recipe for fudge-ripple-swirled cookies. She always added her own special touches to any dish that wasn't her invention. It was the mark of a true cook, her mother always said. Unfortunately, Zakira was so preoccupied by the call that her usual creativity was somewhat hampered. And it was amazing that the cookies were ever ready for the oven. Zakira could not stop herself from looking out the window each time she heard a car pass. Several times, she found herself staring at the phone and wishing Malik would call.

Of course, the doctor's call could have easily been something routine. If only it weren't for the other inconsistencies in Malik's behavior. Zakira knew she wouldn't feel at ease until she spoke with her husband.

The delicious cookies didn't take long to bake. When they were done, she rushed upstairs to change her clothes. The waiting and wondering had finally gotten the better of her. In half an hour, she was leaving for the restaurant.

"Zakira! Honey, I was just asking Malik if you were coming in this week."

A suspicious smirk touched Zakira's lips as she watched the older man at her side. "Why? More suggestions concerning the menu?"

Head chef Carlos Hamils gave the boss's beautiful wife a knowing stare. "I'm done making any more changes. I know the organizers of the event have it hard enough without having my dedication to perfection getting in the way."

Zakira pressed her hand to Carlos's shoulder. "We really appreciate it," she whispered.

Carlos round, dark gaze was already focusing on the basket Zakira carried. "So what have you got there?"

"Damn, you don't miss a thing," she remarked, having forgotten her reason for stopping by the kitchen.

"Nothin' gets by this," Carlos told her, pointing

towards his long, angular nose. "So tell me what you've been mixing up in the kitchen. And don't tell me you're about to stop sharing ideas."

Zakira threw her head back and laughed. "Please! I'm the one who should be asking you to share ideas."

Carlos pressed his hand to his chest and sighed. "You're so good for my ego."

"Mmm-hmm. Well, I did bring something for you guys," Zakira revealed, lifting the basket she carried.

"I knew it. What is it?" Carlos inquired, already taking the package.

Zakira clasped her gloved hands together. "They're chicken potpies. I used herbs from my garden to season the pastry. The vegetables are fresh, and the chicken has been marinated in an herb sauce, also courtesy of my garden."

Carlos closed his eyes in happiness. "I can't wait to dive in."

"Well, there's enough for you and the rest of the guys, so let me know what you think. We'll meet Friday morning to discuss some other things pertaining to the charity dinner."

Carlos saluted her and headed farther into the kitchen with his delicious burden. Zakira smiled and relished the welcome vibe she received whenever she visited the restaurant. She had always felt a sense of acceptance from the Badu's employees and since she'd started organizing the cancer fund-raiser, she'd experienced an even deeper sense of acceptance. The staff truly seemed to enjoy working with her on the event and they respected her opinions and ideas.

Zakira sighed before heading upstairs.

"Zakira!" Chanel called, a bright smile on her face. "If you're looking for Malik, he left."

"Damn," Zakira muttered, setting her purse on Chanel's desk. "Did he tell you where he was going?"

Chanel shook her head. "Sorry, he didn't."

"Do you know when he might be back?"

"I'm sorry, he really didn't tell me anything before he left."

Realizing she would just have to wait it out, Zakira spent a little while longer at the restaurant, then headed home.

As Zakira was leaving Malik's office, he was arriving at the doctor's. He shut the door to his black SUV, but leaned against the car instead of walking away from it. He knew none of what he would hear that day would be good. He stroked the strong line of his jaw for a moment, thinking of how his life was about to change. Then, taking a deep breath, he headed into the building.

Dr. McNeil was in the lobby speaking with his receptionist. He turned when the lobby doors opened.

"Malik! Glad you could make it on such short notice."

Malik's dark eyes narrowed, and he gave the doctor a humorless smirk. "Why prolong it?"

Dr. McNeil gestured in the direction of his office. "This way."

Malik's stride was rapid but steady as he followed the doctor. When the double oak-paneled office doors closed behind them, he turned and spread his hands. "Well?"

Dr. McNeil headed toward his desk. "Have a seat, Malik."

With a grimace, Malik watched as the doctor calmly took his position. He followed suit, choosing one of the cushioned chairs in front the wide pine desk. "How long have I got?"

"Malik…" Dr. McNeil faltered, trying to find the right words.

"Listen, Doc, can you please just get to it?"

Dr. McNeil studied him for a moment. Then, sighing, he removed his round, gold-rimmed spectacles and leaned forward. "The mass of tissue we discovered after the scan is a tumor. The tests showed that it's malignant."

Though Malik had assumed as much, the news was a shock. He felt a strange tightening in his chest, as though his breath were being shut off. Bowing his head, he buried his face in his hands and groaned.

"This isn't the end of things, Malik. There are treatments." Dr. McNeil informed him.

Malik leaned back in the chair and pressed his fingers against the bridge of his nose. "How did this happen?"

Dr. McNeil frowned. "The tumor?"

Malik nodded.

"Well, it's difficult to say," the doctor replied. "Actually, the cause of tumors is unknown."

Malik pushed his tall, athletic form out of the chair and paced the floor. "Dammit, you've got to have some clue!" he snapped.

"Malik, a lot of money and time has gone into studying tumors and their causes, but there's still no concrete piece of evidence that gives a satisfactory explanation. Studies have shown that cancer can be caused by viruses, forms of radiant energy, even heredity."

Malik shook his head and pushed his hands into his trouser pockets. "This hasn't happened to anyone else in my family."

"There's always a first," Dr. McNeil quietly pointed out.

"Thanks," Malik replied dryly, rolling his intense dark gaze towards the ceiling.

"There is the possibility of surgery," Dr. McNeil suggested.

"No way. No surgery." Malik firmly refused, his slanting eyes narrowing further.

Dr. McNeil stood behind his desk, obviously surprised by Malik's attitude. "You do realize that this could save your life?"

Malik waved his finger at the doctor. "Yeah, well, what if something goes wrong with the surgery, what then? This is my brain we're talking about. Can you guarantee that if I survive the surgery I'll be all there, mentally?"

Dr. McNeil sighed. "No, I can't. There is always a risk when surgery is involved."

"Well, Doc, that's a risk I don't want to take."

"Malik—"

"Doc, please." Malik interrupted, raising his hand. The stress of the moment had finally gotten the better of him and he dropped to the windowsill and sat there holding his head. "Believe it or not, all this scares the hell out of me. But surgery scares me more than the tumor."

"Malik, I can understand how this might be affecting you, but you should keep a positive outlook on this. The operation could very well be a success."

Malik's voice was slightly muffled beneath his hands covering his face. "I can't let Zakira see me that way, stuck in a bed. And I can't let her see me die."

By eight o'clock that evening, Zakira's nerves were in overdrive. After leaving Badu's, she took a long drive, did some Christmas shopping and visited a few friends. Feeling a little better, she decided to go home. When she called the restaurant and discovered Malik was not there, nor had he been home, she became worried again. Trying to keep an open mind, she washed her hair and braided the thick mass into two pigtails which she wrapped around her head. She even cleaned the already immaculate house in an attempt to keep from fretting over the whereabouts of her husband. So much activity eventually exhausted her, and she collapsed on the sofa for a short nap.

Malik's key scratched the lock some thirty minutes after Zakira fell asleep. He entered the house quietly, not wanting to frighten her if she was still awake. The tense, guarded look in his dark eyes turned softer when he found his wife fast asleep in the living room. He crept across the thick carpet so he would not awaken her. Easing his heavy frame to the sofa, he took a seat next to her.

Malik's exquisite charcoal gaze roamed Zakira's face as though he were trying to memorize her lovely features. Very lightly, he traced the soft line of her brow and Zakira instantly awoke.

Frowning a little, Zakira got her bearings before

glancing up. When she saw Malik leaning over her, she bolted up on the sofa. Her small fingers, curled around the lapels of his suede jacket and jerked him close to her.

"Where have you been all day? Why didn't you call me?" she asked frantically.

Malik pulled Zakira's hands away and held them tightly in his. "Shh. I'm sorry, I'm sorry," he whispered, pressing soft kisses to the tops of her fingers.

"Where were you?"

Malik shrugged and let go of Zakira's hands as he leaned back on the sofa. "There was someplace I needed to be."

"Like Doctor McNeil's office?" Zakira softly inquired.

Malik's narrowed gaze snapped to her face. "How'd you—"

"He called today, but you weren't here. It sounded urgent."

Malik ignored the faint pain near his temple. "It was just an exam. Routine."

Zakira propped her elbow on the arm of the sofa. "You didn't tell me you changed physicians. That's why I was worried."

"Damn, Zaki, does it matter?" Malik snapped. He desperately wanted to confide in her, but something wouldn't allow him to. The inability to be honest with his wife caused his already short temper to boil.

Zakira's eyes widened slightly at the outburst, but she chose to ignore his mood. "Why don't you come sample what I worked on today?" she asked instead. She knew Malik too well to believe nothing was wrong. She would just have to use a different tactic to get some answers.

Malik's gorgeous grin instantly returned. He leaned across her and lowered his mouth to the side of her neck. "Should I go to the kitchen or the bedroom?" he teased.

Zakira burst into laughter. "The kitchen, man!" she ordered, pushing away his heavy body.

A look of mock disappointment clouded Malik's handsome dark face, but he did as he was told. It took much longer than usual to reach the kitchen with his hands tugging at Zakira's blouse.

"Sit!" she ordered, when they finally reached the kitchen.

Malik got comfortable at the kitchen island while Zakira removed the light dinner she had prepared from the oven. There were the delicious chicken potpies, a mixture of broccoli, tomatoes and cucumbers marinated in a zesty wine vinegar and crushed herb dressing, and huge apple-walnut muffins. A light white wine topped off the tasty meal.

For a while, the only sounds in the kitchen were the clinking of utensils and glasses as they feasted on the dinner.

Several times, Zakira's wide gaze traced every nuance of Malik's face. She tried to search out any signs that something might be wrong. Of course, he looked as fit as ever.

"These dinners get better and better," he complimented, after taking the last swig of wine from his glass.

"Thanks, baby," Zakira whispered across the table, genuinely pleased by the compliment. "Did you have enough?"

Malik massaged the back of his neck and stood. "I'm just gonna get another drink."

Zakira's wide eyes followed him as he made his way to the counter. He lost his footing, just before he reached his destination. He had to grasp the edge of the oak counter for support.

"Malik?" Zakira called, rising from the table as well.

"I'm all right, Zaki," he said, hoping he sounded convincing. "I don't think I need another drink."

Zakira was not amused by his teasing. "Are you having another dizzy spell?"

Confusion etched on Malik's face and he turned. It was obvious that the comment took him by surprise. "What do you know about my dizzy spells?"

Zakira leaned against the edge of the table and regarded the handsome giant trying to put up a brave front. "I know you've been having them at least three times a week. But, of course, those are only the ones I've seen. I even know where you keep the pills."

The depths of Malik's eyes took on a darker tint and he looked as though he wanted to respond. Then, thinking better of it, he ran his fingers through his dreads and moved away from the counter.

"I'm goin' to bed," he mumbled, leaving Zakira alone in the kitchen.

The task of cleaning the kitchen turned out to be less time-consuming than Zakira anticipated. After she finished, she headed for bed.

Malik was still in the shower, when she walked into the bedroom. She decided to slip into her nightgown, since she had taken a shower just before starting dinner.

She was smoothing lotion across her skin when Malik walked out of the steamy bathroom. For a moment, he stood staring at her while drying the droplets of water from his chest. He tossed the towel to the dresser and headed across the room, stopping just behind his wife. He grasped her hips in a firm hold and pulled her back against him. Burying his handsome face in the crook of her neck, he inhaled her sweet scent.

"I know you're tired of hearing it, but I *am* sorry," he whispered, his deep voice sounding muffled.

The soft apology sent shivers down Zakira's back. She closed her eyes briefly and savored the moment. Then turning, she raised her face to his for a kiss.

Malik did not disappoint her. He pressed the tip of his tongue to the corner of her mouth, before tracing the lush full line of her lips. Zakira repeated the intimate action as she traced the wide sensual curve of his mouth.

When the kiss deepened, Malik lifted Zakira against his nude body and carried her across the room. Setting her down next to the bed, he lay back and pulled her down to him. With her straddling his huge form, Malik's large hands trailed possessively over her thighs and beneath the hemline of her gown.

Zakira threw her head back and moaned when she felt Malik's thumb caress the soft bud of her womanhood. The light circular motion of his finger soon had her wet with need. He removed his fingers and slid both hands around her hips to cup her full bottom. Lifting her easily, he slowly set her down over his throbbing arousal.

Zakira's hands caressed Malik's sexy, dark chocolate form, tracing his chiseled torso and abdomen. She rotated her hips and smiled when she heard him groan in response. Feeling his hard length inside her forced cries from her mouth.

Malik's touch traced every curve of her body, fondling her full breasts beneath the silk nightie she still wore. One hand reached up to pull the pins from her hair, before he unraveled the thick braids. When the black mass fell across Zakira's shoulders, he cupped her neck and pulled her down for a deep kiss.

Soon though, Malik wanted control and flipped Zakira to her back. He draped one of her shapely legs across his shoulder and deepened his thrusts....

"Malik?" Zakira whispered a long while later when they lay sprawled across the bed.

"Mmm-hmm?" he murmured, smoothing his palm against her flat stomach.

"Baby, if there were something wrong...you would tell me, right?"

Zakira never saw Malik squeeze his eyes shut as he answered. "I promise I would."

Chapter 3

Zakira woke early the next morning wanting to make love to her husband again. "Malik…" she sighed, reaching across the bed. When her fingers touched the cool sheets, she sat up and looked around the bedroom. Malik was nowhere in sight, but Zakira was certain he was still home since he never left without waking her.

Slipping into the wispy gown that had been tossed aside the night before, she went in search of her husband. The moment she stepped into the hallway, delicious aromas drifted upward from downstairs. Nose in the air, she followed the wonderful smells all the way to the kitchen.

Wearing nothing but a pair of burgundy silk boxers, Malik was at work in front of the stove. A wicked smile tugged at Zakira's lips as she crossed her arms over her chest and enjoyed the sultry view. After a moment, her eyes drifted to the dinette table and she noticed the spread. There were fluffy-looking, round pancakes, fresh orange juice, milk and seasoned hash browns.

Malik was a whiz in the kitchen. It had been his primary reason for wanting to open the restaurant. Unfortunately, there were now so many obligations involved with running Badu's that he spent little time cooking.

"Have a seat," Malik called from the stove without looking around.

Zakira did as she was told. She was about to serve herself when Malik walked over and set a mouthwatering broccoli-and-three-cheese omelet before her.

"Oh, thank you! My God, how long have you been up?" Zakira exclaimed, immediately digging into the omelet.

Malik shrugged and turned to the kitchen island. "I had to get up and get this," he said, pulling a brightly wrapped package from a side drawer.

"What have you done?" Zakira asked, as she set down her fork and took the gift. It only took a few seconds to tear through the wrapping. When she touched the gold velvet box, her brown eyes snapped to Malik's face. "What is it?"

Malik pulled one hand through his dreads and sat across from her. "Open it."

Sighing, Zakira opened the long case. Her loud gasp filled the room when she lifted a gorgeous diamond-encrusted tennis bracelet from the box. "Malik," she whispered, shaking her head at the extravagant gift.

"Think of it as an early Christmas present. Besides,

I wanted to make up for the way I acted last night when you asked about Doctor McNeil."

"I love this," Zakira assured him, gesturing at the sparkling piece of jewelry. "But all I want is for you to be straight with me."

"I know," Malik assured her, nodding his head quickly. He stood, but Zakira grabbed his hand before he could get too far. She tugged and waited for him to take the chair next to her.

"Malik, I've got an awful feeling about this and it has nothing to do with any dream," she said, cupping the side of his face in her palm. "It's scaring me."

Malik pulled her hand away from his face and pressed a hard kiss to her palm. He never answered, but Zakira could tell by the guarded look in his dark eyes that he was scared, as well.

Elegantly dressed couples filed into Badu's Restaurant. A long red carpet led from the establishment's entrance and ended at the edge of the sidewalk. Each guest felt like royalty as they clutched small white envelopes that carried Badu's logo on the outside and an invitation inside.

The restaurant had undergone a mild transformation for the event. Several extra dining tables had been set on the edge of the dance floor to accommodate the staggering number of guests. Several people took to the smaller dance space, eager to enjoy the cool jazz stylings of a local group. Others were more interested in the fantastic dinners that were served. Diners had their choice of three entrées: spicy roast duck basted in a fragrant white wine sauce with a delicious wild rice, broccoli and herb side; a hearty chicken, scallop and red onion sauté served on a bed of tender noodles; or grilled salmon steak with a fresh vegetarian stir-fry.

Malik watched Zakira mingling and smiling as she wandered through the crowd. Every aspect of the evening was so perfect he wanted the entire group to know who was responsible. Heads turned at the sound of a crystal goblet being tapped with a fork. Malik had requested the band take a break when he joined them on stage.

"Ladies and gentlemen, if I could have your attention. I have a small announcement to make!"

Zakira turned to watch her husband. Her cocoa gaze sparkled with love as she admired his smooth, handsome appearance in the tailored, three-piece beige pinstriped suit.

"Tonight, many of you have approached me with congratulations on coordinating such a successful event. I wanted to let everyone here know that the menu, the atmosphere and the luxurious setting are all my wife's doing. What you see before you tonight are the results of her hard work. Zakira, girl, you wanna come up here and take a bow?"

Applause filled the air as Zakira made her way toward the stage. She accepted Malik's hand, and he escorted her up the short stairway. She kissed his cheek, then turned to face the crowd.

"I'm sure we all wish there weren't a need for this type of event," she told the crowd, watching the group nod in agreement. "Since there is, I want to thank the committee for allowing me to be a part of it. I thank you for your compliments, but the real accolades should go to the women who lend their efforts each day to help fight this dreaded disease that affects so many children."

Zakira's graciousness and emotional words brought forth another round of applause. She stood smoothing her hands across the sides of the chic, ankle-length silver satin evening gown and waited for the crowd to settle down.

"In lieu of applause," Zakira was saying, "we here at Badu's would like to forward our fee for hosting tonight's event to the Richmond Children's Cancer Research Fund."

Deafening applause followed the announcement. Zakira bowed, and then nodded toward the band, who were preparing for their next set. She left the stage with Malik at her side.

"So are you glad you accepted the invitation?"

Edwina smoothed her hands over the chiffon sleeves of her cobalt-blue silk evening gown. "Oh, Z, I still get shivers thinking about what you did. That was a beautiful gesture, forfeiting your fee from tonight."

Zakira toyed with a curly tendril that dangled from the chignon atop her head. "I thought so, too. Raising money for any charity is hard enough without having to worry about another bill."

"Amen," Eddie agreed, her light hazel eyes scanning the crowded room.

"So, you didn't answer my question," Zakira said. At Eddie's frown, she rolled her eyes. "Are you glad you accepted my invitation?"

Edwina groaned. "Yes, I am. Despite the fact that I've seen two of my ex-boyfriends here with their new women, might I add."

"Please! I bet they drooled all over themselves when they saw how gorgeous you are."

Edwina brushed her hand against Zakira's bare arm. "I appreciate your kind words."

"Kind, hell, they're true. Edwina Harris, you need to let that mess go. It's their loss. Move on."

"Mmm…spoken like a woman with a handsome, sexy husband to go home with."

Zakira's cocoa eyes clouded with concern. "Speaking of which, I haven't seen him in a while."

"Hey," Eddie said, a questioning look on her face. "Is something going on with y'all? I mean, I wanted to ask you about it when I visited before, but I was caught up in my own drama."

Zakira reached for her stepsister's hand and squeezed it. "Sometimes I forget how handy it is to have a therapist in the family."

"You need to talk?" Eddie whispered, pressing Zakira's hand to her chest.

"Not here, okay? Lunch, tomorrow. Is that good for you?"

"Yeah, sweetie, it's fine," Edwina assured her, pulling her stepsister close for a hug. "We'll finish discussing it later. You go find Malik."

"Thanks, Eddie." Zakira whispered, kissing the woman's cheek before hurrying off.

As Edwina stood near the edge of the dance floor watching her stepsister, she had no idea she herself was being watched. Trekel Grisani had caught sight of Edwina shortly after he arrived at the restaurant. He had noticed her speaking with both Zakira and Malik several times during the evening. They all seemed exceptionally close, and he couldn't believe he had never seen her before.

Several people told Zakira they had seen Malik head upstairs. She found him in his office, sprawled across the dark brown leather sofa. Just as she was about to approach him, his eyes opened and he sat up. Zakira decided to stay put and watch him. Malik covered his face with both hands and took several deep breaths. Then, he left the sofa and walked over to the wide desk. He stumbled just as he reached the brown swivel chair and grasped the edge of his desk for support.

Zakira balled a fist against her mouth to prevent herself from crying out. She watched Malik search one of the desk drawers before he extracted the now familiar pill bottle. He swallowed one of the capsules, then took a seat and closed his eyes again.

The next day, Edwina sat her elbow atop the table and propped the side of her face against her fist. "Are you sure you're not overreacting?" she asked, giving her stepsister a doubtful look.

Zakira rolled her eyes toward the restaurant's high ceiling. "No offense, Eddie, but you weren't there. You didn't see the look on his face when he stumbled. He was scared. He's acting so strange. The dizziness I figured was because he's working too hard, but now there's the pills, this sudden checkup, a new doctor, he's stumbling around like a drunk…I can't help but be worried out of my mind."

Eddie smoothed her hands over her low-cut navy silk blouse and leaned back in her chair. "This worrying can't be good for you."

Zakira's stylish ponytail slapped her cheeks when she nodded her head. "I know. But it's not going to stop until I get some answers." She spotted Trekel Grisani heading toward the table.

"Hey, baby doll," he greeted, as he took her hand and leaned down to kiss her cheek.

"Hey, sweetie." Zakira replied, patting her hand against his cheek. "I'm surprised to see you outside that office of yours."

Tree smiled, revealing his striking white grin. "Yeah, I break out every now and then."

Zakira laughed, as she raised her hands above the table. "Tree, I want you to meet my stepsister, Edwina Harris. Eddie this is Trekel Grisani."

Tree's extremely handsome face registered surprise. "Stepsister? And I'm just meeting her now?" he scolded playfully.

Zakira shrugged. "Better late than never."

Tree turned and his pitch-black gaze narrowed the moment he saw the exquisite beauty who stared back at him with her gorgeous almond-shaped eyes. Tree stood uncharacteristically speechless. The lovely, delicate features that never failed to render men helpless succeeded once more. However, this time, it appeared that Eddie was just as captivated as Tree.

Zakira hid her smile as she studied Tree's entranced expression and Edwina's reaction to him. After a moment, she cleared her throat.

"Tree, would you like to join us?" she asked.

Tree hesitated for a moment. Then, shaking his head, he ran one finger across his wide brow. "Um…I'm sorry, Edwina, for staring," he apologized very softly, his deep voice sounding very raspy.

Eddie fiddled with the wide collar of her blouse and nodded. "It's okay," she managed, surprised by the apology. An apology, in fact, was very unnecessary when she was just as guilty. Trekel Grisani was unbelievably gorgeous. The close-cut wavy black hair, striking onyx eyes, wide nose and mouth made for an irresistible combination. Zakira had called him Tree and Edwina figured it was a nickname. A well-deserved nickname, in any case. The man had an awesome build, to say the least. Massive shoulders, a wide chest and back, lean waist and long legs…yes, *Tree* was the perfect name for him.

"Thanks, Z, but I'm meeting with a client," Tree explained when he turned around. "I just wanted to stop and say hello."

"Well, listen, if you have some time later on, could I stop by and talk for a while?"

Tree smiled and glanced at his watch. "That's fine. Maybe around three?"

Zakira smiled. "I'll see you then."

Tree leaned down and pressed another kiss to her cheek. Then, he turned, pinning Eddie with his intense onyx stare. "It was very nice to meet you, Edwina."

Eddie's sweet brown stare was practically glued to

Tree's handsome face. "It was very nice meeting you," she replied.

Tree stared for just an instant longer before he left the table.

Eddie waited a moment before she turned her head. Her eyes followed Tree's departing form.

A smirk crossed Zakira's mouth as she watched her stepsister. "Yes, he is."

Eddie frowned and turned to face her sister. She waited for Zakira to elaborate.

"He really is as sweet and thoughtful as he is gorgeous and sexy," she clarified.

Eddie shrugged. "That would appear to be true," she agreed, lightly.

"Sure seemed taken by you, girl," Zakira teased.

Edwina smiled. "You are imagining things."

"Ha! I'm not imagining the way your eyes were glued to him."

"Z! I don't believe you said that," Edwina replied, outraged. "And anyway, wasn't it you who said I should forget about men for a while?"

Zakira waved her hand. "Not when it comes to Trekel Grisani. I can't believe I never considered putting you guys together before. You couldn't tear your eyes away from him and he couldn't stop looking at you. Why deny it? The man is gorgeous and built. Unlike most of his colleagues, he's a good, honest lawyer, and he seemed very into you."

Eddie sent Zakira an exasperated look. "As if I don't have enough problems with men," she sighed, raising her hands.

Zakira leaned across the table. "What problems, Eddie? Tree is a very nice guy. He's sweet, gorgeous and intelligent. You don't come across a combination like that every day."

"I'm sure you're right. But Z, maybe you haven't realized that I only date black men."

Zakira appeared dumbfounded. Then, she realized what Eddie meant. "Honey, Tree is black."

Edwina leaned back in her chair and balled her fist beneath her chin. "Did we just talk to the same man? Tall, gorgeous…white?"

"Eddie, he *is* black. His father is Italian, but his mother is definitely a black woman. He doesn't have her coloring, but look at his features and you can tell."

Eddie shrugged, but still appeared uneasy.

"Edwina you can't deny that you were attracted to him."

"Maybe I can't, but I'm just not ready for another man right now. Any man," she said, sounding as though she were trying to convince herself.

"He told me to show you right in, Zakira," Carrie Shephard said as she opened the door to her boss's office.

Tree was on the phone when his assistant escorted Zakira inside. He waved to her and began wrapping up his call.

She walked around the impressive penthouse office located in a posh silver skyscraper in downtown Richmond. She had not visited in a while, but she was always amazed by the beauty of Tree's home. Everything was dark and oversized to accommodate his size. Still, both the office and the living quarters held an unmistakable aura of style and authority. She was studying a wall decorated only with pictures of Tree and Malik. If Trekel Grisani couldn't put her fears to rest concerning her husband, she didn't know who could.

"Hey, you." Tree said, as he headed over to Zakira. He leaned down to give her a warm hug.

"Hi," Zakira sighed.

A small furrow formed between Tree's sleek brows and he pulled away. "What's the matter?"

She came right out with it. "Tree, do you know what's going on with Malik?"

"What's…going on with him?" Tree replied, watching Zakira suspiciously.

"Mmm-hmm. He's been acting so weird for the past few weeks. I think he might be sick… Can you tell me anything?"

Tree managed to slip his mask in place before Zakira could see that he knew more than he was telling. He had warned Malik that Zakira's intuition was keen where her husband was concerned.

Zakira took a seat in front of Tree's desk and pinned him with her large chocolate stare. "Tree, I know Malik is your client, but I'm asking you as his wife…as your friend. I'd appreciate anything you could tell me."

Tree reclined in his chair and stroked the smooth curve of his jaw. "There's not much to say."

"You haven't noticed anything?"

"Sweetie, it could be business or any number of

things. You know how Malik is," Tree observed, hoping he sounded convincing.

Zakira appeared crestfallen. "Yeah, I know how he is. But Tree, I know something's not right with him."

Tree ran one hand across his close-cut hair and grimaced. "Z, maybe he doesn't want you to worry."

"See, that's it right there!" Zakira shouted, pointing a finger at Tree. "This may be something I need to know. I don't care what it is. I have to know. Wondering is driving me crazy."

Tree left his chair and walked around the desk. He knelt before Zakira and pulled both her hands into one of his. "Shh...stop this," he soothed. "You're starting to upset me."

"I'm sorry," she whispered, sniffling softly. "You're right. Maybe I am making a mountain out of a molehill."

Tree squeezed Zakira's hands. "Why don't you go home and try to calm down. Malik will come clean with you, if there's anything to tell."

"You're right," she said, nodding as she absently smoothed her hands across Tree's shoulders. "Lemme get out of here." Tree stood and pushed his hands into the deep pockets of his trousers. As soon as the door closed behind Zakira, he was dialing Malik's number.

"Doctor McNeil, I've got Doctor Douglass Burns on the line for you."

"Thanks, Simone," Dr. McNeil told his secretary. "Hey, Doug."

"Sed, it's been a long time."

"I'll say. I don't hear from you every day," Dr. McNeil told his old colleague,

Burns chuckled. "Well, I'm actually calling about one of your patients."

McNeil frowned. "Which patient?"

"Malik Badu."

"Malik Badu? How do you know him?"

"He called to get some information on our center here. He liked what he heard and plans on admitting himself."

"You're kidding, right?"

"I'm afraid not."

"He hasn't mentioned it to me," Dr. McNeil said, as though he were speaking to himself. Douglass Burns was chief of staff at The Enlightenment Center, a cancer treatment facility staffed exclusively by specialists. "I wonder if he's told his wife yet?"

"I'm not sure about that. The reason I'm calling is to see if you'll send me his medical records. I have his consent."

"Certainly," Dr. McNeil promised, still somewhat surprised. "I'll have my assistant get right on it."

"He seems to be quite a young man," Dr. Burns observed.

Dr. McNeil grinned. "You're right, but he's rather stubborn, full of pride, as I've told him several times."

"I agree. He was very adamant about not wanting to discuss surgery or treatment. It's almost as if he's afraid to get his hopes up."

"Malik Badu is a man who hates for anyone to see him down," Dr. McNeil noted. *Especially his wife,* he silently added.

* * *

Tree sighed as he reached for the phone. He had been trying to get in touch with Malik since Zakira left his office earlier that day. Unfortunately, he had been unable to contact his old friend.

Before he could pick up the phone it rang. "Yeah Carrie?"

"Tree, Malik is here to see you. Have you wrapped up everything?"

"Yeah, thanks. Send him on in."

Tree waited for Malik to walk in and close the door before he lit into him. "Your wife was here asking about you. When are you gonna come clean with Zakira, man?"

Malik raised his right hand and walked farther into the office. "I already decided to. Soon. But there are some things I need to take care of first."

A fierce frown clouded Tree's face. "Such as?" he asked, not liking the formal tone in Malik's voice.

Malik pushed his hands into his trouser pockets and bowed his head. "I had some arrangements to make."

Slowly, Tree stood behind his desk. "I guess you heard from your doctor?"

Malik nodded. "It's confirmed."

Silence fell over the room for several minutes. Tree bowed his head and massaged the bridge of his nose, before closing the distance between him and Malik. The two friends hugged tightly, sharing a quiet moment.

"Look, I need you to do something for me." Malik said as he stepped away.

"Spill it," Tree urged.

Malik sighed and ran one hand through his dreads.

"I'll tell Zaki about the cancer, but I can't die in front of her. I can't let her see me that way." He paused and took a deep breath. "I've decided to admit myself to a cancer treatment center out of the state. I've already booked myself there and taken care of my financial needs, as well."

The look on Trekel's face was murderous. "Man, are you out of your mind? I can't believe you came up with something this stupid!"

Malik winced, but his mind remained unchanged. "I know this whole thing sounds cold, but I refuse to let my wife see me crumble before her eyes. That'd kill me faster than this cancer."

"So you're just gonna go away to die and not let her be with you at all?" Tree asked, still not believing Malik could go through with the coolly developed, intricate plan.

"I just can't stay here, man."

"You can't stay or you won't? What about Zakira? You're not even thinkin' about her!"

"That's all I been doing!" Malik snapped, spreading his hands as he glared at Tree. "It would kill her to see me waste away like that."

Tree shook his head. "I think you're worried about how it'll affect your pride."

A humorless smirk crossed Malik's mouth. "I understand how you feel, but I made my decision. You can back me up or I can find somebody who will."

Tree sent Malik a sour look before shaking his head. Then he shrugged to give his consent.

Chapter 4

After leaving Tree's office, Zakira went home and changed into a comfortable fleece jogging suit. Then she left for the restaurant, figuring some time in the kitchen would do her good.

"So what's on your menu?" Brian Deangles, one of the chefs, asked, watching Zakira gather mixing bowls and spatulas.

"Well, I was thinking about a recipe for linguine, with a different type of sauce. To spice it up."

"What have you got in mind?"

Zakira glanced over her shoulder pretending to be secretive. "You've had mushroom gravy?" she asked, watching Brian nod. "Well, this is a sauce, a much creamier texture, but the taste has a very spicy flavor."

"Stop," he ordered, raising his hand. "I just had dinner and you're making me hungry all over again."

She laughed. "Well, I'll make sure to call you when it's ready."

"You better," Brian warned, leaving her to her work.

Shaking her head, Zakira began to prepare her sauce.

It was already growing dark outside when Malik returned to his office. The vicious frown etched on his handsome face put Chanel on edge the minute she saw him.

"Get Zakira on the phone," Malik ordered before his secretary could say anything.

Chanel stood and followed Malik into his office where he was shrugging out of his heavy jacket. "Zakira's already here."

"Where?"

Chanel pointed behind her. "Down in the kitchen. She—"

Malik didn't wait to hear anything more. He was already headed downstairs.

"All right guys, don't try being nice to me. I want your honest opinions," Zakira ordered, as she watched the men wolf down linguine covered with the rich, zesty mushroom sauce.

The kitchen door swung open just then and she looked up.

"Malik!" Zakira called, running over to her husband. She stood on the tips of her toes and pressed a kiss to his cheek.

In response, Malik's grip around Zakira's waist

grew unbearably tight and she gasped. "Sorry," he whispered.

"What's wrong?"

"Nothing. I was gonna ask you out to dinner. You haven't eaten yet, have you?" He asked, glancing at the table of feasting chefs.

Zakira looked over her shoulder and smiled. "Nah. I was just messing around in here. I could fix us a plate. I think you'll like it."

Malik slid both arms around Zakira's minute waist. "I'd rather go somewhere private," he whispered next to her ear before pulling the soft lobe between his perfect teeth.

Zakira's lashes fluttered close, and she almost moaned. Clearing her throat, she looked back at the chefs. "Guys, we're gonna be saying good-night!"

Malik and Zakira took separate cars home after leaving the restaurant. Malik arrived about ten minutes before his wife. When Zakira stepped into the bedroom, she saw a huge suitcase filled with his clothes lying on the bed.

Malik was in the master bathroom, about to start the shower when he heard Zakira calling his name.

"What's this for?" she asked when he emerged from the bathroom.

Malik saw her gesture toward the suitcase. "You need to throw a few things in there, too. We're going away for a long weekend."

Zakira propped her hands on her hips. "Just like that?"

"Did you have something else planned?" Malik

asked, unbuttoning the stylish cream shirt he wore as he walked toward her.

Zakira's eyes were drawn to the wide, dark expanse of his chest as she shook her head. "No, uh-uh. It's just kind of sudden. Christmas is only a week away, and it wasn't that long ago we took that trip to California."

Malik waved his hand. "That was business."

Zakira folded her arms across her chest and fixed him with a naughty look. "It wasn't all business," she reminded him.

"Well, this is gonna be all pleasure," he promised, trailing his index finger along the curve of her cheek.

"Mmm, this sounds a bit too wonderful." Zakira shivered when Malik's thumb began to stroke the pulse beating at the base of her throat.

"Best kind of trip, don't you think," he whispered, replacing his thumb with his lips.

A slight furrow appeared between Zakira's brows as she tried to figure out Malik's motive for the trip. When he pulled her closer and began to nibble at the soft skin below her earlobe, she forgot her suspicions. "I think it's just what we need."

By the time Malik was done showering, Zakira was packed and ready for her own shower. Beneath the warm spray of water, she once again questioned Malik's sudden need to get away. He rarely suggested leaving town so close to the weekend, unless it was business-related. She could only pray that this time alone would get him to open up about what had been bothering him.

The bedroom was empty when she stepped out of the

steamy bathroom. The case on the bed was gone, so she figured Malik was downstairs packing the SUV.

Dropping to the edge of the bed, she unwrapped the towel from her head and massaged her scalp. The phone rang a few minutes later.

"Hello?"

"Z, it's me."

"Hey Tree, what's up?"

"Is Malik around?"

"Well, he's downstairs packing the truck. He wants us to go away for the weekend. If you wait a minute, I can get him on the phone."

"No, don't disturb him. Just tell him to call me whenever y'all get where you're going."

"I'll tell him, but can I get you to do me a favor too?"

"Yeah, what?"

Zakira grabbed her purse off the armchair next to the bed and searched for her address book. "Could you give my sister Eddie a call and let her know we're out of town?"

The cozy, intimate bed-and-breakfast lodge Malik had chosen for the weekend had just been touched with its first hard snow of the year. Located in the mountains of West Virginia, it was the perfect getaway. The Cramer Lodge was built entirely of brick, but had a rain-washed look that gave it a rustic appearance. The addition of white holiday lights on all the trees and brush made the place even more inviting.

Zakira slept practically the entire way. When she finally awoke, she was too drowsy to notice Malik frowning from a terrible headache.

"Mr. and Mrs. Badu, we were wondering if you'd make it through the snow."

Malik managed a smile as he shook hands with Gordon Reynolds, the manager of the lodge. "It wasn't so bad, but I think it's starting up again."

Gordon nodded and offered Zakira his arm. "Well let's get you both inside and registered. Mr. Badu, I'll send someone for your bags."

Malik waved his hand. "That's fine. It's only one. I can handle it."

Gordon led them to the long mahogany desk located directly across from the entrance. He stepped behind the desk and located the reservation in the computer system.

"All right, Mr. Badu," Gordon said, ripping the reservation slip from the printer. "If you'd just sign at the bottom."

Malik took the pen Gordon offered and prepared to sign. Suddenly, the pain in his head became so intense, he almost dropped to his knees.

"Babe!" Zakira cried when she noticed him wobble. Everyone standing nearby rushed to help.

"I'm all right. I'm fine," Malik insisted, lifting one hand to ward off everyone's assistance.

The bellhop escorted them to a cozy room. Malik took care of his tip and closed the door. Unable to stand the blinding pain any longer, he removed his jacket and went to bed.

Zakira remained silent, resisting the urge to run to him. She closed her eyes and prayed he would confide in her soon.

* * *

Two hours later, Malik awoke to find that the pain had left. He waited a moment before opening his eyes. When he did, he saw Zakira seated next to him on the edge of the bed. She was beautiful and seductive in a devilish black teddy. Her eyes, however, were filled with concern.

Malik, on the other hand, was instantly aroused. His sensual gray stare narrowed as he reached for Zakira. As soon as his hands curled around her arms, she resisted. Frowning, he let her go. "What?" he asked.

"Malik, if you don't tell me what's wrong with you, I'm out of here tomorrow morning."

One of Malik's hands clenched into a fist. He tried to think of a quick lie, but one glance at the look on her face dissuaded him. He had not planned to tell her so soon, but after his near fainting spell it could not be ignored.

Sitting up, he vaguely noted that his clothes had been removed and he was under the covers. He drew his long legs upward and rested his elbows on his knees.

"I had it all planned how I'd get into this," he sighed, his baritone voice sounding grave.

Zakira frowned. "I don't give a damn about your plan. I want to know what the hell is going on with you."

Malik nodded as he took her hand in his and toyed with her fingers. "I started having these dizzy spells about three, maybe four months ago. I didn't worry about it at first, because they didn't occur very often. Then, they became more frequent and…more severe," he said, seeing Zakira's frown. "Anyway, I went to my doctor and he ran some tests, but gave me the pills because my blood pressure was up. A few days later, I got a call that they'd…found something, so I had to go in for more tests. That's when Doctor McNeil got involved."

"He's the doctor who called the house?" Zakira asked, not liking the tone of the conversation.

Malik nodded. "Yeah. He ran more tests and confirmed what was suspected."

Zakira cleared her throat. "And that was?" She noticed that Malik's grip was become tighter.

"It's cancer. A…it's a tumor." Malik's answer was slow. He averted his dark gaze, unable to look at his wife.

Zakira pressed her lips together, but that did not stop the tears that rolled down her cheeks. Pressing her fingers to her mouth, she forced back the sob that rose deep in her throat. "Where is it?"

Malik's heavy brows drew together. "Where?" he asked, misunderstanding.

Zakira squeezed her watery eyes shut. "The tumor, where is it?"

Nodding, Malik sniffed and looked down at the comforter. "My head. My brain."

"No. No, this…this can't be. It has to be a mistake. I mean, did you get a second opinion?" Zakira cried, hating the feeling of helplessness.

"Zaki, Zaki…" Malik soothed, pulling her close. His smile was full of pain as he felt her turn her face into the crook of his neck while she cried. "Baby, I did all of that. I've seen the tumor myself through X-rays."

Zakira pushed herself away and searched Malik's eyes with her own. She didn't want to believe it was happening, but the stony, solemn look she saw on her husband's handsome face convinced her. Taking a deep breath, she wiped the tears from her cheeks. "So, what's next? Can they operate?"

A guarded look crept into Malik's gray eyes. "There's too much risk of complications with the surgery, so—"

"But they can operate?"

"Zakira…" Malik sighed, hearing the hopeful tone in her voice.

"Oh, Malik, don't tell me you're not even gonna think about it?"

"Baby, listen to me," he whispered, sliding his hands over her arms, "we're gonna talk about this a lot more. I know you have a lot of questions, but right now, I just want you in bed with me, all right?"

"Malik—"

"Shh." His hands went to the wispy, satin ties on the bodice of Zakira's teddy. Unraveling them slowly, he pulled the material away and his eyes feasted on her breasts.

Zakira's eyes closed as she felt her nipples harden in response to the gentle caress. Malik bowed his head and pressed soft kisses to the smooth skin spilling over the top of the teddy's bodice. He tugged the straps from her slender shoulders in order to expose more of one breast. His hair fell against Zakira's bare skin to create the most sensuous friction.

"Malik!" Zakira gasped when she felt his fingers curl into the crotch of the lacy lingerie and pull the snaps loose. His fingers sank into a wealth of moisture.

He cupped one breast in his hand and suckled the

firm peak. He pushed Zakira back against the bed and practically ripped the rest of the delicate material away from her body.

Flesh to flesh, they were entwined in each others arms. Zakira pulled Malik's head away from her chest and thrust her tongue past his sensuous lips. He uttered a deep groan in response to the lusty kiss. His hands tightened around Zakira's waist, before they curved around her thighs and pulled them apart.

"Mmm…" they moaned simultaneously when their bodies connected. Malik's thrusts were unrelenting as he vented his frustrations through the sensual act. Zakira cried out as her hips rose to meet each powerful lunge of his throbbing manhood.

The erotic encounter lasted into the early morning hours. When they finally exhausted themselves and drifted to sleep, Zakira knew she would never treasure anything as much.

Edwina's hazel stare narrowed as she stared at the phone on the bed stand. She debated on whether to answer its ringing, since she was in the middle of reading a patient file, but realized it could be an emergency. Tossing the file aside, she answered the phone by the third ring.

"Hello?"

"May I speak with Edwina Harris?"

The deep, unfamiliar voice immediately grabbed her attention. "This is Edwina Harris."

"Edwina, this is Trekel Grisani. We were introduced the other day by your stepsister, Zakira."

Eddie couldn't suppress her surprised gasp when Tree

identified himself. "Uh…yes, yes I—I remember you. I'm, uh, sorry for asking, but how'd you get my number?"

Tree reclined in his desk chair and chuckled over the question. "Zakira gave it to me. She asked me to tell you she and Malik have gone away for a long weekend."

"Mmm, that sounds romantic." Eddie replied, in a dreamy tone.

"Yeah…romantic," Tree murmured, his easy mood vanishing.

"I wonder why Z didn't just call me herself. She didn't have to bother you with this."

Tree smiled at her perception. He enjoyed the low, soothing quality of her voice and believed he could talk to her all day.

"Tree?"

"It was not a bother, Edwina."

"Uh, call me Eddie, please."

Tree chuckled. "Anyway, Eddie, I got the feeling from Zakira that it was a spur-of-the-moment thing."

"So where did he take her?"

Tree sighed. "I'm not sure. I told Zakira to have Malik call me when they got…wherever."

"Is there something wrong?" Eddie asked, catching on to the sour tone in his words.

"Nothing" was the short reply.

Eddie frowned slightly and pressed the receiver closer to her ear. "Listen, I know we don't know each other, but I can tell something's wrong."

Again, Tree laughed. "Are you psychic?"

Eddie smiled. "No, I'm not psychic, but I am a psychologist."

"Well, there you go, then," he said, his words tinged with laughter.

Eddie pulled off her glasses and sat up. "All right, then. Since you think I'm such a psychic, I'll tell you that it sounds like you're not happy about Malik taking Zakira away for the weekend. Am I right?"

Tree was silent for a moment. "Zakira thinks Malik's taking her away for romance but there's a lot more to it."

"Sounds ominous," Eddie slowly replied, a frown coming to her face.

"It is, Eddie," Tree confirmed. "Malik was diagnosed with cancer. I think he's gonna tell Zakira while they're away."

Eddie's grip tightened around the receiver and she sat perfectly still for a moment. "Malik…" she whispered, her voice barely audible.

Hearing the shock and despair in Edwina's voice, Tree regretted his decision to say anything.

"Edwina? Eddie?"

Softly, she cleared her throat. "Yeah?" she replied, trying to sound normal.

Tree wanted to kick himself for upsetting her. "Honey, I'm so sorry."

Eddie sniffled. "That's all right, Tree. I'm glad you told me. I don't need to fall apart in front of Z when I see her."

Tree smiled, impressed by her attempt to be strong. "I'll let you go, all right?"

"Mmm-hmm…thanks for calling," she said, staring at the receiver for a moment before hanging up.

* * *

"No…" Tree groaned, when he heard the phone's low, yet annoying ring. Massaging the tight muscles in his neck, he headed back toward his desk.

"Trekel Grisani."

"Hey, man, it's me."

"What's up?" Tree asked, sitting on the edge of his desk.

"Have you had a chance to get started on the arrangements we talked about?" Malik asked.

Tree rolled his eyes and sighed heavily. "Mal, why don't you give up on this? Man—"

"Tree—"

"All right, all right," Tree said, raising his hand in defeat. "Yeah, I've gotten started on everything you asked for."

"Thank you. Look, I know you don't agree."

"I care about what this is going to do to Zakira. Have you told her yet?"

Malik was quiet for a long time. "I told her."

"How is she?"

"How do you think?"

"What'd you tell her?"

Malik knew what his friend was asking. "I only told her about the cancer. Right now, that's all I want her to know."

Tree ran his hand across his dark, wavy hair and frowned. "Mal, I hope you know what you're doing."

"I do. Thanks, kid."

The connection broke and Tree shook his head. He could see this whole thing turning into an ugly mess that Malik would regret having started. Still, he knew his friend was scared and he wasn't about to shut him out now.

Setting the receiver back to its cradle, Tree's thoughts turned to Eddie. He couldn't see her face when he told her the news. But her voice painted enough of a picture. She sounded as though the wind had been knocked out of her, and he hated having upset her that way.

After shutting off the desk lamp, he stood and headed to his office door. He strolled down the hallway toward his apartment, but stopped just short of the door and leaned against the wall.

Maybe I should apologize to her in person, he thought. Of course, he knew that really wasn't necessary. Though Eddie was upset, he could tell she was glad he had told her. In truth, he really just wanted to see her again. Hearing her low, breathless voice on the phone had only whetted his appetite to have her in his sights.

Pushing himself away from the wall, Tree continued his trek toward his apartment. A grin touched his wide mouth as he considered asking Edwina out.

Zakira stirred the rich, sour cream sauce into her hash browns before lifting a forkful to her mouth. Her large brown gaze rose to sneak a glance at her husband, before snapping back to the table.

She was still in shock over the news he had dropped the night before. Now, however, she was on a mission to save her husband's life.

"So have you and Doctor McNeil talked about treatment?" she asked, watching Malik refill his juice glass.

"What?" he replied absently.

Zakira's hand covered his over the glass. "Have you and Doctor McNeil talked about how you can fight this?"

Malik sighed heavily, before raising his gray stare to her face. "No."

A furrow formed between Zakira's delicate brows. "Well, are you going to?" she asked, watching as Malik shrugged. She leaned back in the cushioned arm chair. "Malik, what the hell is wrong with you?"

A sinister expression clouded his face. "You know what's wrong with me." He sarcastically replied, pushing the long dreads out of his face.

"Why won't you talk about this?"

"Zakira—"

"I mean, I've heard that a positive outlook has—"

"Will you stop it!" Malik roared, throwing the beaded juice glass into the fireplace.

Zakira quieted, watching him rise from the table and almost knock his chair to the floor in the process.

"I'm not about to let this change my lifestyle!" he told her, his features taking on a menacing appearance.

"Baby, I just don't want you to give up," Zakira quietly told him. "Malik?"

He rubbed his hand across his wide chest as though he were in pain. She toyed with one of the tendrils that had fallen from her high pin-curled ponytail. "Malik, do you remember me telling you that I was out of here if you weren't straight with me?"

Knowing his wife was dead serious, he crossed his arms over his chest and looked directly at her. "I'll leaving in a few months."

"Where—where are you going? Why?"

Malik rushed to Zakira and knelt beside her chair. Gathering her hands in his, he pressed soft kisses to the tops of her fingers. "It's a private cancer treatment center."

Zakira began to calm down somewhat. "A treatment center? So you do want to fight this?"

Malik couldn't look at her. "I'll do what I have to."

Zakira blinked her tear-filled eyes and took a deep breath. "So when do we leave?"

Malik's head snapped up. "What?"

Zakira shook her head. "When are we leaving for the center? I know you have a million things to take care of with the restaurant and all—"

"Zaki…" Malik sighed.

"What? Do you want me to help you tie up things?"

"I don't need you to do anything, all right?" he said, standing.

Zakira let out a breath. "Listen, I know I can be stubborn about going into the restaurant, but I really don't mind—"

"Zaki, please! Do you have to go on and on about this?" It killed him being unable to tell her the whole truth and he couldn't stand seeing the confusion in her eyes. He grabbed his jacket from the sofa and stormed out of the room.

"Shanice, I need to see about rescheduling two appointments. I forgot about that meeting next week."

When her secretary didn't answer, Edwina lifted her hazel stare from the folder she was studying. "Are you okay?" she asked, watching the young woman over the tops of her gold-rimmed, cat's-eye glasses.

Shanice gave Eddie a helpless smile and averted her brown gaze to the corner of the room.

Edwina pressed her full lips together in hopes of concealing a surprised gasp. She couldn't believe she hadn't noticed him as soon as she stepped out of her office. Trekel Grisani in her small reception area easily could have been compared to a bull in a china shop. Still, he carried his size with the utmost confidence and moved with the grace of a cat.

Shanice looked back at Edwina. "I was just about to call you," she whispered.

Eddie was speechless as she watched Tree approach her. Lord, he was even more gorgeous than the first time she'd seen him.

Tree stopped right before her and pushed one hand into the deep pocket of his black ankle-length leather trench. "I hope this isn't a bad time?"

Edwina tilted her head back in order to look directly into his deep onyx eyes. "No, no it's not a bad time at all," she said, managing a cool tone. She didn't want to appear too flustered in front of Shanice.

Tree stepped closer and took Eddie's wrist in a light hold. "Can I talk to you for a little while?"

With Tree's large hand holding her wrist and his cologne teasing her senses, Eddie feared she would swoon. Taking a very deep breath, she nodded. "My office is this way," she said, gesturing toward the corridor behind her. "Shanice, hold my calls," she instructed, without glancing in her assistant's direction.

Tree pulled the coat from his huge frame as he followed Eddie down the hall. His dark gaze turned seductive as it raked her slender form encased in the stylish sky-blue dress. It was made of a clinging cottony material that hugged every curve and only reached mid-thigh.

Tree expelled a deep breath, his eyes narrowing. He shook his head at the wicked thoughts running through his mind. Eddie opened her office door and waited for him to precede her. Instead, he laid his hand at the small of her back and urged her forward. Eddie stopped in the middle of the room and turned, waiting for him to close the door.

"Has something else happened to Malik?" she immediately asked, wringing her hands.

A small smile crossed his mouth as he set the coat he carried on the sofa. "Nothing more has happened," he assured, watching her relax. "I did want to apologize, though."

Eddie frowned. "Apologize?"

Tree nodded, undoing the buttons on his stylish maroon jacket as he walked closer. "I didn't mean to upset you when I called. I'm sorry."

Eddie could feel her mouth fall open, and it took a moment for her to regain her composure. "I, uh, thank you."

The sound of Tree's chuckling filled the air. "Don't sound so surprised."

"It's hard not to be," Eddie sighed.

One of Tree's wide shoulders lifted as he shrugged. "I don't know why."

Eddie's look of surprise, became suspicious. "Are you serious?"

"I mean what I say, Edwina," he assured her.

Edwina studied the tall, handsome giant for a long moment. "I'm sorry, Tree. You just seem to be a very busy man. Wouldn't it have been easier to call or, I don't know, e-mail me?" she nervously inquired.

Now, Tree appeared surprised. "Eddie, what type of men have you been around?"

"None who would come all the way across town to apologize because they think they've upset me."

"Well, that's how I am."

Eddie looked away. Taking a deep breath, she massaged the muscles of her neck and closed her eyes. If Tree wasn't out of her life soon, it would be impossible for her to resist him.

Tree's gaze became more intense as he noticed the uneasy expression on Edwina's face. He knew he had shocked her and that she was attracted to him. Now that he'd talked to her again, he couldn't help himself. Edwina Harris was lovely and exquisite, and he wanted her.

Meanwhile, Eddie tried to dismiss the electricity in the room but couldn't. Clasping her hands tightly, she gave Tree a dazzling, albeit shaking, smile. "Listen, I'm sorry if I offended you. I really appreciate the apology, even if it was unexpected. So, um, thank you for coming by and—"

"Have dinner with me tonight."

"What?"

Tree's long strides brought him closer to Eddie, and soon he was standing right before her. "Have dinner with me," he softly repeated.

Eddie tried to drown out the deafening tone of her

heartbeat in her ears as she spoke. "Tree, I—I can't have dinner with you."

"Why?"

"I just can't."

"Do you have a patient?"

"Uh, well, no."

Tree's dark stare narrowed as he studied her. "What is it, Eddie?"

Edwina leaned against her desk and fiddled with the chain around her neck. "I get done here very late and I just don't think—"

"I'll pick you up whenever you're ready."

"Tree, this may not be a good idea," she warned, smoothing her hands across her arms.

He braced his hands on either side of Edwina against the desk. "Well, we'll never know if you keep turning me down."

Eddie tried to look everywhere but at the gorgeous face inches away from her. It was no use; her almond-shaped hazel stare finally snapped to his face.

"I may look ferocious, but I promise you'll be safe with me."

Unable to control herself, Eddie laughed.

Tree's eyes followed her every move. "Does this mean you'll go?"

Eddie nodded slowly. "I'll go."

"I'll pick you up at seven," he told her, striding across the room to grab his coat.

"I could meet you."

"Forget it," he threw over his shoulder before the door closed behind him.

* * *

Zakira had been going crazy in the suite since the argument with Malik. She snatched her coat from the rack and ventured out for a walk around the lovely grounds.

During the night, a heavier snow had fallen. The already beautiful landscape now appeared like something on a Christmas greeting card. Unfortunately, the enchanting atmosphere had no effect on Zakira's mood. The weight of all her worries finally caving in on her spirit, she dropped to the snow-covered ground and began to cry.

When Malik finally returned to the room and discovered Zakira wasn't there, he searched the inn from one end to the other. Something told him to search the grounds and when he found her crying in the snow, his heart ached.

Unable to just stand there, he went over and knelt beside her. Pulling her small form into his arms, he rocked her slowly.

Zakira jerked when she felt the strong hands touching her. When she saw Malik, she dried her tears quickly and tried to put on a brave face. "Malik, why are you doing this?"

"Doing what?" Malik calmly replied, still rocking her back and forth.

Zakira pulled away. "You're cutting me out. I don't understand why you're being this way," she cried.

Malik couldn't look at Zakira. He knew that one glance into her soulful wide, brown eyes would be his undoing. "You know, maybe you should start coming to the restaurant with me," he suggested to change the subject.

Zakira shook her head. "Malik..."

A playful grin brightened Malik's fiercely handsome dark face. "You know how much they love you there. Plus, you need to start becoming more involved with the place."

A guarded look rose in Zakira's eyes and she stood. "This isn't something I want to talk about right now," she said before walking away.

Uttering a low sound of aggravation, Malik went after her. Zakira's steps were somewhat slowed by the deep snow, and he caught her easily, then whirled her around to face him. Zakira slammed against his chest, and they both fell to the ground.

After a few moments of being covered in the powdery snow, they began to laugh. Zakira gathered a handful of the icy creation and smashed it into Malik's hair. Her victory was short-lived when he turned the tables and flipped her onto her back. The glint in his exquisite gaze turned serious as he stared into her eyes.

"I love you, girl," he whispered.

"I love you, too, so much," Zakira breathlessly replied, her eyes shining with tears.

Malik lowered his head to kiss her. Their lips were less than an inch apart when they heard their names. Looking up, they noticed a short man and woman approaching them across the snowy yard.

"All right, all right, break it up!" Cecil and Melinda Furches playfully called.

Malik stood and pulled Zakira up, as well. Smiles brightened their faces when they recognized the Furches.

"Long time no see, man!" Malik said with a laugh, walking forward to shake hands with Cecil.

"Damn, I know." Cecil agreed.

"Zakira, how are you, girl?" Melinda Furches asked as she and Zakira held hands and kissed each other's cheek.

"I'm fine, but you look great. What are you doing?" Zakira marveled.

Melinda shrugged and smiled up at the sky. "Who knows? Chicago must agree with me."

Zakira laughed. "It must."

Melinda put her arm around Zakira's shoulders and whispered, "I think the colder the weather is, the better Cec and me get along."

"Oooo, girl, you're still crazy." Zakira gave Melinda a wicked look as they headed over to the men.

The Furches were a welcome sight and gave the Badus a chance to forget their problems. The four had a wonderful time catching up and reminiscing. Finally, they decided to enjoy lunch together.

The cozy atmosphere of the inn's dining room resembled that of a log cabin. The polished wood furniture, thick quilts covering the walls, plush carpeting and the delicious aromas in the air all created a relaxing environment. The area was spacious enough to give patrons a warm, intimate feeling, even when the place was filled to capacity.

The Badus and the Furches enjoyed coffee and hot cocoa before their lunch arrived. The mood was as cheerful as the conversation. Zakira, however, noticed Malik press a finger to his temple several times. She tried ignoring it, but couldn't.

"So, Malik, is your restaurant still goin' strong?" Cecil was asking.

Malik nodded and took a sip of his cocoa. "Better than ever," he finally said.

"Cecil, do you still rent out those old buildings?" Zakira asked, stirring her marshmallow filled cocoa.

"I sure do. In fact, I just bought an old warehouse in New York."

Zakira's brows rose. "Sounds good."

Cecil's face fell. "Unfortunately, I don't know what to do with it."

Malik's rich deep laughter sounded. "Not you?"

"Hmph. I think he wasted his money," Melinda chimed.

Everyone laughed. Cecil leaned back in his chair with a thoughtful expression on his round, honey-complexioned face. "I think I've just solved my own problem," he announced.

Melinda toyed with a lock of hair from her sleek, Chinese bob. "What now?" she sighed.

"Malik, have you ever considered branching out with your restaurants?" Cecil asked.

A frustrated look appeared on Malik's face, but before he could respond, the food arrived. Everyone had huge appetites, and the spread on the table proved it. There were heaping bowls of shrimp fettuccine in a rich, creamy sauce, fluffy sourdough rolls, delicious green salads and white wine to complete the meal.

"I mean, you've been in the business for what now? Three, four years? I think a Badu's in New York would be a big success," Cecil predicted as he dug into his meal.

"Oh, here he goes," Melinda drawled, rolling her

eyes toward the windows. "I truly believe if somebody cut Cec, he'd bleed numbers. Baby, can't you give the business talk a rest for a while?"

"Hell, Melinda, we don't know when we'll get the chance to hook up with these two again," Cecil argued.

Zakira could see that Malik seemed to be growing aggravated by the discussion. "Cecil, if y'all are going to be in Virginia a while, why don't you drop into Richmond? Why not for Christmas Eve? We can have dinner together and discuss it then. Maybe you can bring along photos of this great warehouse of yours."

"It's a plan," Cecil decided, a broad grin brightening his handsome round face. "Zakira, Malik, when you see the place, you're gonna fall in love with it. I don't think you'll have any doubts about expansion then."

Zakira's warm brown eyes sparkled with excitement as she watched Malik sprinkle a mound of Parmesan cheese to his fettuccine. It appeared that he wasn't as interested in the venture as she hoped. But she was becoming more interested in Cecil's proposal with each passing minute.

"Tree? There's an Edwina Harris on the line for you. Are you available or should I—"

"Put her through, Carrie." Tree told his assistant, shrugging out of his olive-green suit coat as he waited for the connection. "Eddie?"

"Hi, Tree. I hope I didn't catch you on your way home?"

Tree's deep dimples creased his cheeks. "Well, actually you did, but since 'home' is right down the hall, don't worry about it."

Eddie tried to laugh but only managed a shaky sigh. "Tree…"

The sound of her voice made him pause. Suddenly, he realized why she'd called. "Are you canceling out on me?"

Eddie closed her eyes. "I'm sorry, I just—"

"Hey, hey don't worry about it. Maybe another time? Call me?" he urged.

"I will," Eddie promised, thankful that he had made it so easy. "Goodbye, Tree."

The tone of finality to her words, brought a frown to Tree's face. "Good night Eddie."

"So, what did you think?"

Malik frowned and threw his jacket to the bed. "About what?" he asked, turning to look at Zakira.

"Cecil's proposal. You hardly said two words after he mentioned it."

A humorless smirk crossed Malik's mouth. "You seemed to have enough questions for us both. Wasn't a need for me to say anything."

Zakira ignored Malik's sarcasm and removed her jacket. "So, are you interested?"

"How the hell can you ask me that, Zaki?"

Zakira frowned. "I thought it would do you good to put your mind on something else," she reasoned.

Suddenly the pain that had been nagging Malik during lunch hit him hard. He pressed his hands against his temples and leaned against the dresser. Zakira rushed toward him, but Malik extended his hand, stopping her. Before his wife had roped them into plans for Christmas, he'd toyed with the idea of staying at the inn through the holiday. Now that was the last thing he wanted.

"You know, I thought a long weekend would give us time to relax and enjoy each other." Malik quietly stated, massaging the fading pain in his temples. "All we do is fight, so I think we should leave tomorrow."

"That sounds good to me." Zakira agreed.

Malik headed toward the bathroom but stopped in the doorway and looked at her. "I'm sorry, Zakira. I know you're trying to help. But I can't be thinkin' about venturing into a new level with my business when I won't be around to see it through."

The way he closed the conversation broke her heart.

Chapter 5

Zakira didn't see Edwina's car out front when she stopped by on Christmas eve. But she took a chance that her stepsister might be home anyway.

The moment Eddie opened the door and saw Zakira out front, she stepped forward and enveloped her in a tight hug.

Eddie nodded. "I'm sorry."

Zakira wiped her cheeks and sighed. "So am I."

"Come on in here," Eddie whispered, pulling Zakira inside the house. She hated the stressed look on her stepsister's face, but knew it could not be helped. "So, how's Malik?" she asked as they got comfortable in the kitchen.

"Malik's Malik," Zakira replied wearily.

Eddie pulled two mugs from the cupboard and prepared to make tea. "Is it hard talking to him?"

"Very," Zakira confirmed. "You know, even though

I suspected something was wrong, I never thought it would be something like this."

"Oh, honey, how could you have guessed this?"

Zakira shook her head. "I don't mean the sickness. I had a feeling it was something health-related, not cancer, but…I'm talking about my husband's plan to leave his life before this cancer…kills him."

Eddie handed Zakira a mug of hot tea with lemon and set hers to the table. "Leave?"

"He wants to go away and die. Can you believe that?"

"No. I don't get it."

Zakira pushed away her mug. "He's gonna check into some treatment center and spend his…last days there."

"Well, Z, maybe he's trying to spare everyone having to see him sick. Malik is one of those strong silent tough brothas, you know? He doesn't want to look weak in front of others."

"Edwina, I appreciate what you're trying to do, but Malik isn't being considerate. He's being stubborn, cold and thoughtless," Zakira declared.

Silence settled over the kitchen.

"I didn't mean to bring you down," Zakira finally said.

Eddie frowned. "What are you talking about? I love you and Malik."

Zakira propped her face in her palms. "When you answered the door, you looked like you were glowing." she noted.

"Please," Eddie sighed as she shrugged off the comment. Knowing where the conversation was headed, she didn't try to dissuade Zakira from talking about Trekel Grisani.

"So he came to see you in person, huh?" Zakira slyly questioned.

"How'd you know?" Edwina asked before she could stop herself.

Zakira's expression was full of delight. "I didn't, but thanks for telling me."

"You set all this up, didn't you?"

Zakira closed her eyes and nodded. "I wasn't sure if he'd come to see you or not. So? How are things going?"

Eddie propped one hand on her hip. "Don't you think that question is a bit presumptuous?"

Zakira considered the question for a moment. "I don't think so, Eddie. If there's one thing that man has a weakness for, it's a beautiful woman. I'm surprised he hasn't asked you out yet."

"Uh, he has," Eddie uneasily revealed.

Zakira sat up straight in her chair and watched Eddie expectantly.

"He came over to apologize for upsetting me when he told me about Malik. We talked a little, and the next thing I know, he's asking me out."

Zakira spread her hands. "And?"

Eddie stood from the table and rubbed her hands across her sagging blue jeans. "I said yes, but later I changed my mind."

"You *what?*"

"Z, please don't start," Eddie sighed.

"I just don't get why you'd turn him down."

Edwina dumped the rest of her tea down the drain. "Listen, Z, I'm not going to get into something with

Tree. I have enough problems with black men. I can't handle the pressure of dating a white one."

Zakira waved her hand in the air, but did not respond.

"I admit Tree is very sweet, and Lord knows he's fine, but I just can't. And this is my decision, remember?"

Zakira sat the cup aside and braced herself against the counter. "I know it's your decision. I just wish my problems with Malik were so simple."

Cursing silently, Edwina rolled her eyes toward the ceiling. She walked over to Zakira and pulled her close. "I'm sorry," she whispered.

"Oh, Eddie," Zakira sobbed. "I've really got to get myself together…especially now."

"Why?" Eddie asked, pulling away.

Zakira shook her head. "Malik doesn't want anyone at the restaurant to know about the cancer, so he wants me to participate more in the business. That means, I'll have to spend half the day pretending things are normal."

"Well, at least you won't have to pretend when you're at home since everything's out in the open," Eddie noted, her tone hopeful.

The look in Zakira's brown eyes was full of doubt.

Edwina had afternoon appointments and was about to leave for the office a few hours after her visit with Zakira. As she headed downstairs, the phone rang.

"Edwina Harris."

"Hey, Eddie, it's Malik."

Edwina sat on the arm of the sofa and her eyes grew wide. "Malik?" she whispered.

"Yeah. From the sound of your voice, I take it you know?"

"I'm sorry," she said, her hand going to her neck as she felt a sob rising.

"Not as sorry as I am," Malik teased.

Eddie managed a weak laugh. "So, how are you feeling?"

"Some days good. Some days, like crap. But, you know…"

"Yeah…" Eddie sighed, smiling at the brave tone in his deep voice.

"Listen, I didn't call to get you down. I'm trying to find my wife. Have you seen her?"

"She was here, but that was a couple of hours ago. Why? Do you need anything?"

"No, nothing like that. We're supposed to meet about the business. I'll still be involved with the restaurant of course but Zaki's gonna start going in more. And there are things she needs to know."

"Listen, Malik," Eddie began, realizing how defensive he sounded, "I know how strong you are, everybody does."

"Meaning?"

"Meaning, don't try to put on airs for anyone. All you'll do is wear yourself out."

"Thanks, doctor."

"I'm serious, Malik."

"So am I."

"Take care of yourself."

"I will. Thanks, Eddie."

Malik hung up the phone and thought about Eddie's words. She was right. He had been putting up a front for everyone, especially himself. Each day, he felt worse. His doctor had prescribed a medication to soothe the raging headaches. Unfortunately, they hadn't done much good. He knew the time was fast approaching for him to leave.

The phone buzzed, interrupting his somber thoughts. "Yeah, Chanel?"

"Malik, Tree's out here to see you."

"Show him in," Malik instructed, reclining in his chair.

The tense expression on Tree's face when he entered the office matched Malik's mood exactly. He knew Tree didn't approve of what he was doing, but he needed his friend's help. There was nowhere else he could turn.

"What's up, man?" Tree sighed, taking a seat in front of the desk.

"I guess I should be asking you that," Malik noted, raising his brows slightly.

Tree propped his elbow on the chair's padded armrest. "Everything you asked me to take care of has been handled. I even made the arrangements for your stay at that…treatment center." He glared across the room at Malik. "I still can't believe you're gonna go through with this crap."

"Tree—"

"What, man? What?" Tree snapped, standing out of the chair. "This is crazy. You should be here with your family, not runnin' off to some damn center!"

Malik stood as well. "I already told you to forget it, so…"

Zakira was on her way to meet with Malik when she heard the deep voices booming through the door.

She wasted no time walking into the office. "What are y'all doin'?" she called over the roar. The two men quieted instantly.

"Difference of opinion," Malik replied dryly.

Zakira wasn't convinced. "Well, I could hear you all the way outside," she told them, closing the door. "What could possibly be going on to make you fight like this on Christmas Eve?"

Malik became interested in papers on his desk, while Tree walked over to Zakira. "Sorry we disturbed you girl, I gotta get out of here," he whispered, kissing her before he left.

Malik could feel Zakira's brown eyes glaring at him. "What?"

"Are you gonna tell me what's wrong?"

Malik shrugged. "Difference of opinion, like I said."

Zakira shook her head, knowing she wouldn't get more of an answer.

For a moment, Malik's eyes narrowed as he watched her take off the heavy gray overcoat. Beneath it, she wore a clinging forest-green dress with a thigh-high hemline. The stretchy material molded to her small frame enticingly. Matching square-toed platforms completed the ensemble. Malik shook his head and tried to ignore how much his wife always aroused him.

Zakira turned and watched him strangely. "Malik? Are we meeting or what?"

"Yeah, yeah, we're meeting," he said, grabbing a folder off the windowsill.

"Cecil and Melinda called just before I left the house," Zakira mentioned as she strolled across the office.

Malik was busy gathering folders from his desk. "Oh yeah?"

"Mmm-hmm," Zakira murmured, clasping her hands as she watched him closely. "They were confirming dinner tonight. I was surprised to get your call about this meeting—I thought maybe you'd close a little earlier. Give your staff some extra time with their families…"

Scanning the contents of the folder, Malik offered a quick shrug. "I still have a business to run, Zaki."

"I know," she sighed, smoothing both hands across the comforting softness of the dress. "I was thinking about inviting Tree along, too. In light of everything that seems to be going on, it might be nice to get together for a relaxing evening, and I think he'd like Cecil and Melinda."

Malik finally looked up from the paperwork. His gorgeous charcoal-gray eyes raked Zakira's petite form with devastating intensity. "You're right," he finally replied, trying to dismiss the roguish thoughts ravaging his mind. "Shall we?" he gestured toward the other side of the room.

They took a seat on the suede sofa in the far corner of the office. Malik opened the folder that contained a list of suppliers and other information. The order of business that day was to familiarize Zakira with the people who helped keep Badu's running.

"Damn, I can't believe you deal with so many different people," Zakira exclaimed, surprised to see how many businesses were involved.

"Yeah, there's a lot," Malik replied, trying to keep his mind and his eyes on his work.

Zakira seemed genuinely interested, like a kid at a

zoo. Her eyes were wide as saucers as she tried to absorb all the new information being thrown at her. For Malik, on the other hand, with Zakira seated so close, it was virtually impossible to remain businesslike. She kicked off her shoes as she often did when preparing to settle in with reading material and got more comfortable on the sofa next to him. Her shapely, toned legs were close enough to touch.

Malik's long lashes closed as he gave an almost inaudible groan. Unfortunately, his wife seemed oblivious to his torment.

"So, do you have different suppliers for each item, or do some handle a variety of your needs?" Zakira asked.

Malik shifted and frowned at the list of names. "Um, it's a little of both," he informed her, putting check marks by a few of the listings. "A lot of these guys will try to pull anything if you're not firm."

Zakira sat on her knees and innocently rested against Malik's arm as she peered into the folder. "Are there any in particular I should watch out for?"

Malik shook his head and commanded his mind— and body—to focus on business. He managed to do an admirable job, highlighting a few names and giving Zakira some tips on handling the more difficult associates. He handed her the folder and, unable to resist another moment, began to fiddle with her hair. His gaze caressed every inch of her face.

"So everything in this folder should bring me up to speed with the functions of the restaurant?" She began thumbing through it.

"Mmm-hmm." He sighed, leaning back on the sofa and

watching her stand up. "That's just a list of suppliers and distributors, but those are the people I deal with most."

"Great," Zakira said, shutting the folder. "So is it okay if I take this home with me?"

"Yeah," Malik said, shrugging slightly.

Zakira tilted her head slightly. "You okay?" she asked, unaware how enticing she appeared to her husband.

Malik shut his eyes briefly. "Fine," he said with a smile.

Zakira returned the smile. "So what's next?" she asked, slapping her hands to her sides.

"That's all for today," he told her, knowing they wouldn't get anything more accomplished.

"Okay. Well, I'm gonna go home and study for a bit before dinner. Try and get in the holiday spirit."

Zakira tucked the folder beneath her arm and pulled her coat off the back of the sofa. Then, she bent down and pressed a soft kiss to Malik's cheek.

The instant Zakira's lips touched his cheek, Malik grabbed her arms and pulled her into his lap. Cupping his large hand beneath her chin, he tilted her head back and kissed her deeply.

Zakira gasped softly as the kiss intensified. Malik's tongue caressed the dark cavern of her mouth with fiery possessiveness. His hands moved from her arms and slid to the hemline of the short dress she wore. Effortlessly, he lifted her to sit astride his lap. Malik's rigid arousal nudged the most sensitive area of her body. In response, Zakira arched her back, bringing her breasts within inches of his mouth.

Malik began to push the dress higher over her thighs and she helped. Pulling the garment over her head, her thick hair cascaded down her back. Malik's sexy, dark gaze followed her every movement before they roamed her scantily clad body. Instantly, his fingers massaged her bare skin and slid up to unhook the clasp of her satiny bra.

He cupped the bare, dark chocolate mounds for his mouth. His tongue suckled the hardened tip, and Zakira threw her head back to enjoy the sweet sensations. Her slender fingers delved into his dreads and she pulled his head closer.

Malik didn't bother to remove his clothes. He did, however, undo his belt, the fastening of his stylish black trousers and the zipper. Zakira helped him free himself of the boxers he wore as he practically ripped away her panties.

"Malik," she breathed, when his strong hands took her hips in an unbreakable hold. Smoothly he eased her down over the impressive length of his rock-solid maleness. As he throbbed deep within her, Zakira moved in the most erotic manner. She succeeded in drawing deep groans from the sexy giant beneath her.

Malik rested his head against the high back of the sofa and closed his eyes. "Damn, Zaki," he whispered, all the while praying that she didn't make him lose control. He wanted the moment to last as long as possible.

As Zakira braced her hands on either side of his head and added more speed to her movements, their sounds of pleasure became more verbal. Aching for the closeness, they relished the steamy, erotic moment.

Chapter 6

Christmas Eve

"What'd I miss? What'd I miss?" Edwina yelled, as she ran back into the den.

Cecil Furches had just relayed another one of his outrageous, entertaining stories. Everyone in the room was rolling with laughter.

"Eddie, please don't make Cec repeat his corny stories," Melinda begged.

Cecil waved a hand toward his wife. "That girl has no appreciation for talent."

"Is that what you call it?" Melinda challenged.

"Was everything okay, Eddie?" Zakira asked from the bar where she was mixing drinks.

"Yeah, just a patient," Eddie explained, gesturing toward her cell phone. "Someone wanting to squeeze in before the New Year, can you believe that?"

"Sex therapy must be a really interesting field," Melinda observed.

Eddie folded her arms across the bodice of the burgundy V-neck cotton dress. "Well, it gets more interesting each year I practice. I've probably heard some things that would even shock Cecil," she teased, joining in when everyone laughed.

Melinda wiped a tear from her eye. "Now I know it definitely must be an interesting field."

"Anyway," Eddie continued, clicking off the phone, "I'm gonna go toss this thing in my car because I really don't want to be disturbed during one of Malik's great dinners."

"Why don't you just turn it off and put it upstairs somewhere?" Zakira suggested as she handed Melinda a frosty margarita.

Eddie was already headed out of the den. "Because I don't want to be tempted to use it."

It didn't take long to jog outside to her chocolate Mercedes parked next to the Furches' SUV. Eddie was about to place the phone in its holder when she decided to activate the voice service in the event someone called. That done she locked the car, turned around and almost bumped into Trekel Grisani.

"Hey, hey…" Tree soothed when Edwina screamed. He took her upper arms in a light grasp and gave them a reassuring squeeze. "Shh…I'm sorry. You okay?" He asked.

Eddie closed her eyes and nodded. She brought one

shaking hand to the base of her throat and took several deep breaths.

"What are you doing here?"

Tree's deep voice brought a smile to Eddie's lovely face. "Zakira...she invited me to a little holiday dinner with some friends of hers and Malik's."

Tree's dark eyes narrowed as he looked toward the Badu home. "That's what I'm here for."

After a moment of silence, they began to laugh. "I think we've been set up," Eddie guessed amidst their chuckling.

Once the laughter died, tension set in. Eddie couldn't bear to look up into the sinfully gorgeous face so close to her own. She wanted to explain why she had not called, but couldn't bring herself to form the words. When Tree suggested they head inside, her smile was a mixture of relief and sadness.

"Mmm, mmm! It smells good in here!" Zakira complimented upon walking into the kitchen.

"Thank you," Malik replied, though he was far from sounding modest. "Come taste this sauce I made for the fried catfish."

Zakira opened her mouth for the sample. She moaned when the light, creamy texture of the pearly white sauce settled against her tongue. It was spicy, but with a faint sweetness that she adored. "Fantastic, but you know at least one of those black people out there is gonna ask where the hot sauce is."

Malik burst into laughter. "Give 'em a little credit, Zaki," he said, reaching for the wooden spoon.

"Uh-uh." Zakira resisted, handing her husband a different spoon while she licked the remnants of the sauce from the other.

Malik leaned against the stove and watched her. When she kissed his cheek and complimented the sauce again, he wanted to hold her close. The intensity of his gaze encouraged Zakira to kiss him again. When her mouth touched his, Malik groaned and gave in to his need. The kiss turned steamy at once. Malik's hands caressed her hips before he locked her in a steely embrace. Zakira arched into his tall, chiseled form, her fingers disappearing into his dreadlocks. Malik's savage growls added more fire to the erotic kiss that deepened with every stroke of his tongue.

"Damn," he muttered suddenly and set Zakira away just as Tree walked in. Leaving her husband, Zakira went to greet him.

"Did you meet Cecil and Melinda?" she asked after they had hugged.

Tree fixed her with a knowing grin. "Eddie introduced us. I know what you're trying to do," he whispered, leaning close.

Zakira leaned back. "Do?"

"Setting me up with Eddie."

"Why Tree, I have no idea what you're talking about," Zakira replied, patting his cheek. "I need to go check the dining room." She left Malik with one last look before she walked away.

"Your wife is somethin' else, my man," Tree noted when Zakira was gone.

"Yeah, she is," Malik replied, busy with dinner.

"Malik, man, I'm sorry about that mess the other day in your office," Tree said softly, as he walked across the kitchen.

After a moment, Malik recalled the fight. He had been so consumed by other things that he had forgotten it. "Don't worry about it," he said, turning back to the stove. "You're only trying to help."

Tree folded his arms across the stylish mushroom-colored silk shirt and leaned against the kitchen island. "I don't suppose anything I said made you reconsider?"

Malik bowed his head and smiled. "Tree, man, give it a rest and help me carry out this food."

The dinner was set out on the buffet so everyone could serve themselves. There was golden fried catfish, stuffed baked potatoes, huge cheese biscuits and steamed broccoli.

"Hey, Malik, where's the hot sauce?" Eddie asked while everyone else raved over the homemade sauce.

Zakira, who was pouring wine, nudged Malik's shoulder. "Told ya," she whispered. "Look in the hutch, Eddie!"

Eventually, everyone took their places at the dining room table. The cozy, romantic setting was further enhanced by the soft jazz and candlelight. For a while, the group concentrated on the food and it wasn't long before the compliments began to roll in.

"So, Melinda are you and Cecil touring the East Coast or something?" Zakira asked in the middle of the meal.

Melinda giggled. "Actually, we're putting the finishing touches on our house," she announced, smoothing one hand across her shiny bobbed hair.

"House?" Zakira parroted.

"We just bought a place in Maine. Glou-Gloucester, is that right, Cec?"

"Gloucester," Cecil replied, using the correct pronunciation. "It's not really in Gloucester, but a few miles away."

"Damn. Maine." Tree was as impressed as everyone else.

Cecil waved his hand. "Please, y'all, that place has taken a lot of work. It was one of those handyman specials."

"Still, Maine," Edwina marveled.

"So when's the housewarming?" Malik asked.

Cecil snapped his fingers. "Glad you asked. We're having a housewarming weekend, inviting a few friends up to enjoy the place."

"And we want you and Zakira there, Malik," Melinda ordered. "Tree, you and Eddie are welcome, too. We'd love to see both of you."

Zakira smiled, noticing the soft looks exchanged between her stepsister and Tree. "So, when is this thing gonna be?"

"Have your schedules clear in two weeks," Cecil instructed.

"What's the weather like up there this time of year?" Malik asked.

"Honey, be prepared for anything," Melinda warned, and the conversation centered on the climate in that part of the country.

* * *

The annoying beep of the alarm clock stopped immediately when Zakira slammed her fist against the Sleep button. She snuggled against Malik and started pressing kisses to his wide muscular back. After a second or two, he turned and pulled her across his body. He ravaged the soft skin of her throat with his lips and tongue. His hands tightened on her waist when he moved to bring her breasts closer to his mouth. She and Malik had spent Christmas Eve, Christmas Day and the day after making love. She showed no shame in wanting the same turn of events that day as well.

Zakira played in his dreads and then let her head fall back. "Please, please make love to me," she whispered.

The instant the words were uttered, his entire body tensed. Zakira bolted up when he pushed her away.

"I got an early meeting," he said as he left the bed.

"Are we still going to meet at your office later to talk about the business?" she tentatively asked, watching him curiously.

Malik stopped and massaged his neck. "It'll be better to meet out somewhere. Let's try that new Chinese café downtown. Just meet me there," he instructed, leaving her alone in the bedroom.

"All right," Zakira whispered, her voice cracking.

"I'll have Carrie fax the affidavits this afternoon," Tree was saying into his cell as he caught sight of Edwina at the bar in the sports restaurant. "I'll catch you later," he finished, already heading to the bar where he could hear her haggling with a man behind the counter.

"Lightly toasted, not burned like it was before," Eddie was saying.

"Woman, haven't you ever heard of Cajun-style?"

Eddie burst into laughter. "Not when it comes to toast!"

The man was shaking his head as he scribbled on the pad he held. "Damn, you sex doctors are so picky," he complained.

"Eddie?"

When she turned and saw Tree, her smile grew even more dazzling. "Hi," she called, her eyes caressing every inch of his gorgeous face.

Tree glanced at his watch. "Is it so bad you have to spend your lunchtime at the bar?" he teased.

"Funny," Eddie replied, even as she giggled. "Actually, I'm waiting for a tuna on toast if Gordy would get the molasses out! Why are you here?"

"I met a client here." He explained, gesturing to the stools. "You got time for a glass of tea or somethin'?" He asked her.

Edwina set her leather carryall on a vacant bar stool. "Well, since it looks like I'll be here a while!" she said for Gordy's benefit. When the lanky, older man looked her way, she waved. "Could we get two iced teas over here if it's not a problem?"

Tree was laughing uncontrollably while Eddie and the bar's owner haggled mercilessly. After a while, she sobered and turned to face him.

"So, you seemed to enjoy yourself at dinner the other night," she noted.

Tree nodded, loosening the navy blue and gray tie he

wore. "It's been a long time since I've had such a good meal," he admitted.

"Mmm-hmm, Malik can surely get down in the kitchen," Eddie remarked, her expression displaying a bit of unease. "I, um, didn't have the chance to tell you on Christmas Eve that I was sorry."

Tree frowned and shook his head slightly. "Sorry?"

Edwina looked down at the bar's polished cherry wood surface. "I told you after I, um, turned down your date, that I'd call and…"

Tree waved his hand. "Eddie you don't have to apologize. Really, there's no need."

"Yes, there is. Thanks, Gordy," she said when their teas arrived. "I like to keep my promises and you were so nice about it, you deserve an explanation." She toyed with the mouth of her glass.

"Nice?" Tree said, with a laugh. "Eddie, you told me you didn't want to go out. I had to accept that. I mean, what was I gonna do? Hound you? Force you to go?"

Eddie smiled, her sparkling brown gaze relaying the intense attraction she felt for him. "I only wanted you to know that I—I've been dealing with a lot of stuff. A recent breakup," she explained. "It was pretty dramatic and I guess I just get a little spooked about seeing men right now. Even if it is just one date."

Tree nodded and took a quick sip of the cold tea. Eddie watched him closely, looking for some sign of aggravation in his gorgeous profile.

"Do you understand where I'm coming from, or do I sound like a total idiot?" she asked.

Tree turned and placed his hand across hers. "I know

where you're comin' from. But I think you should know that I'm still determined to know you and I hope you won't have a problem with that."

The confident, straightforward response brought a smile to Edwina's face. "I wouldn't have any problem with that."

Tree smiled. "So, are you gonna take the Furches up on their offer?" he asked, setting the lemon slice on the napkin next to his glass.

"The Maine weekend?" Eddie asked, squeezing the juice from her lemon slice. "My schedule's already clear. What about you?"

"Hey, it is Maine," Tree retorted.

"The coast," Eddie clarified.

"A *house* on the coast," Tree added, joining in when Eddie laughed. "So what would you say to us saving some gas and driving up together?"

Eddie tapped one nail to her chin. "I didn't even think about driving. I was gonna catch a flight."

"Ah, live a little. We could leave Thursday morning." Tree suggested. "Really see the sights."

Finally, Eddie nodded. "Okay, you've convinced me. It sounds like a great idea."

"Good," Tree said, deciding not to tell her how happy she had made him.

Malik and Zakira arrived at the Chung Palace at the same time. They exchanged quick kisses at the door before rushing inside out of the wind. The hostess promptly showed them to their table and left them with menus. Malik held Zakira's chair and waited for her to pull off the black wrap she wore. When he saw the confining wine dress beneath, he groaned and walked away before she took her seat.

At first, Zakira thought he may have been sick. Then, she saw the look he gave her before rolling his eyes.

"Malik, have I done something wrong?" she asked, setting her wrap aside as she pulled her chair closer to the table.

"No. Nothing," he curtly replied, his dark penetrating stare already scanning the menu. "What did you want to discuss first?" he asked without looking up.

Zakira shook off her concerns and focused on the restaurant. "I wanted to talk more about the suppliers," she said, pulling her chair around the table in order to sit next to Malik. "I wanted to know who you deal with the most and if you'd ever consider changing."

Malik hesitated before answering. Zakira's perfume was both hypnotic and seductive. When the waitress arrived to take their orders, he was finally able to concentrate on business....

"...I've been working with them about a year and a half," Malik said a bit later as they finished their food. "At first, they were coming up with some great menu and banner ideas. But the restaurant is becoming more noticed and I'm getting bored with their stuff, especially the advertising."

"So are you shopping for a new agency?" Zakira asked, pulling apart the egg roll she held and watching fresh cabbage and other ingredients spill to the plate.

Malik shrugged. "I don't know. They just don't seem to be coming up with anything different. I was thinking maybe you could take a look at their work and give an opinion about what you think we should do."

"Sounds good," she decided, polishing off the rest of the egg roll. When she pushed her plate aside, Malik signaled for the check.

Outside in the parking lot, she took Malik's hands. "Are you coming back home with me?" she asked.

"Why?" he replied, his expression blank.

Zakira fixed him with a wicked smile and stepped closer to ease her hands inside his champagne-colored suit jacket. "I was hoping this meeting would end like our others."

Malik clenched his fists when Zakira's mouth trailed his jaw. Finally, he stepped away and pretended to search his pockets for keys. "I really need to get back to the restaurant, but I'll see you later," he said, already walking away.

Zakira frowned to prevent her tears from escaping. She watched her husband settle into his SUV and speed out of the parking lot. The Navigator disappeared round the corner before she even moved.

The bathroom was silent except for the bubbly bath water swirling down the drain. Zakira stepped from the tub and went over to the lighted mirror. After securing the pins in her hair, she took a closer look in the mirror.

"Damn," she whispered, seeing that her eyes were still puffy and red from all the crying she had done that afternoon. Why would Malik push away from her physically? Especially now, when they should be closer than ever?

She chose not to harp on the issue, fearing she would lose control of her emotions yet again. She selected a bottle of coconut-scented lotion and left the bathroom. She was drying off when Malik walked into their bedroom.

Zakira didn't look his way, but she could feel his eyes on her. She finally glanced up to see him staring intently as she smoothed the lotion into her skin. When his smoldering dark eyes met her smoky brown ones, he looked away as though he were disgusted. At that point, Zakira lost her temper and threw the lotion bottle to the floor.

"What the hell is your problem?" she demanded, standing with her hands on her hips. Her expression was stormy and she was completely oblivious to her nudity. "Malik?" she called, when he only stared.

"Get dressed," he finally said, dragging his gaze to the floor.

Zakira raised both hands defensively. "Get dressed? Why? Do you suddenly have a problem seeing me this way? Every time I find your eyes on me, it's as though I've done something wrong. You look like you—like you disapprove or something. What the hell is goin' on with you?"

"Hell, Zaki! Dammit, I'm dyin' or have you forgotten that?" he raged, slamming one powerful fist against the wall. "I got more on my mind right now than playin' stud to you."

Zakira turned away before he could see the tears welling in her eyes. She grabbed her robe from the chair and slipped into it. At the bedroom door, her hand paused on the knob. "I'll sleep in the guest room. That way you won't have to worry about me taking advantage of you while you sleep!" she spat and let the door slam behind her.

Malik dropped to the bed, holding his head in his hands.

Gloucester, Maine

"So, what do y'all think?" Melinda asked, once the tour had reached its end.

"Well, I'm jealous," Zakira admitted, slapping her hands against her jean-clad thighs.

"Are you ever going to want to go back to Chicago? I know I wouldn't," Eddie said.

Melinda laughed. "I'll take your responses as compliments. Now, why don't you both go get settled? In three hours, there will be dinner and coffee served on the patio. We can enjoy the ocean view for as long as we like."

Zakira and Edwina stood shaking their heads as their energetic hostess bounced off. Then they headed toward the guest wing, chattering away.

"I couldn't believe it when I saw you and Tree arrive together. Anything I should know?" Zakira pried.

Eddie rolled her eyes. "Nooo. We just decided to drive up together, that's all."

Zakira knew there was more and enjoyed teasing Edwina. "Mmm. But neither of you brought a date?" she slyly noted.

Eddie folded her arms across the front of her fuzzy red sweater. "So?"

"Soooo?"

"So, we have our own rooms. So there."

"Ha!" Zakira blurted, her expression incredulous. "That only leaves more places to make love." She nudged Eddie's shoulder until they both burst into laughter.

When Zakira stepped into the bedroom, the lightness of her mood vanished. She and Malik had barely spoken since the more than three weeks prior. In that time, they had hardly seen one another. New Year's Eve and the following day had been a joke. Clearly, the fact that it could be their last New Year together was no motivation for civility. She made a point of waiting until he left the house before exiting the guest room in the morning, and she was in bed before he returned at night.

While Malik was busy unpacking, Zakira went to the closet. She found blankets and an extra pillow which she placed on the sofa.

"What are you doin'?" Malik asked, his hands stilling over his luggage.

"It'll raise too many questions to ask for a room of my own," Zakira replied, without turning to face him. "So, I'll have to make use of the sofa."

"That's not necessary."

"No? I disagree considering how distant you've been," she reminded him, finally turning to pin him with accusing eyes. "And Malik, that is something I can't even begin to understand."

"Baby, I'm sorry." Malik told her, running both hands though his dreads. "What I said to you before, I'm—I just have a lot goin' on."

"Well, news flash! So do I!" she snapped, slamming both fists to the back of the sofa. Before her emotions got her too riled, she turned away and grabbed her overnight case. "I'm going to take a bath. I should be done in about forty-five minutes. You'll probably want to be gone, so you won't think I'm trying to tempt you when I walk out."

On the beach, Tree and Eddie barely moved as their eyes feasted on the crashing waves.

"This is somethin' else," Tree remarked, tightening his hold around Eddie's waist.

She smiled and snuggled her face against the softness of his thick, black knit sweater. "I could stay like this forever."

Tree pulled away and looked down at her. "Just like this?"

Eddie nodded against his chest. "Exactly like this."

Tree trailed his index finger along her cheek and urged her to look up. When she did, he pressed the sweetest kiss to her lips.

Dinner was light, yet satisfying. The couples enjoyed music and the relaxing atmosphere. One by one, they wandered off to enjoy the privacy the place boasted. Zakira and Malik were last to leave.

"You coming up?"

Zakira retained her seat on the lounge and drew her knees close to her chest. "I'm gonna stay out a while longer," she said, smoothing her hands across the luxurious softness of her yellow sweater. "Don't worry, I won't disturb you when I walk in."

"Zaki—"

"Don't, Malik. Please don't make it worse by telling

me you're sorry again," she urged, closing her eyes as she silently prayed that he let her be. When he walked away, she released the sobs she had suppressed.

After a long beach stroll, Tree and Eddie headed upstairs.

"I'll see you in the morning," Eddie whispered, when they stopped between their room doors. She moved to kiss his cheek, but Tree cupped her face and kissed her mouth instead.

"I want you in bed with me," he growled during the deep kiss.

Eddie shuddered, caught up in the sensational kiss. She clutched Tree's shoulders when he lifted her against his massive frame and took her into his room. She felt herself being lowered to the king-sized bed in the far corner. Tree's lips trailed the softly scented column of her neck as his fingers ventured beneath the hem of her white sweater. A low groan slipped past his lips when his fingers grazed the side of her breast and he realized she wore no bra. Eddie pushed her fingers through Tree's hair and gasped at the luxurious texture of the thick, black locks. She felt his hands curve beneath her bottom as he settled more snuggly against her.

Suddenly, a tiny voice called to Eddie and she shook her head to ward off its unwanted warnings. Unfortunately, it would not be silenced and soon she was pressing against Tree's shoulders.

"Wait..." she whispered, even as she moved closer to his touch.

Tree uttered some muffled response, but did not veer

from his task. A moment later, he felt Eddie rise up from the bed and move away.

"I'm sorry," she called softly as she raced out of the bedroom without looking back.

Saturday was an event-filled day. The group ventured into a neighboring seaside town and visited the fresh markets while enjoying all the excitement of the marina. They indulged in the sensational food offered by the local eateries. That evening, there was a classical concert given by a local pianist. When the group arrived back at the house, they went to the beach and indulged in beers around a roaring fire. It was well past 2:00 a.m. when they all headed inside.

"To hell with this," Malik growled. He had barely been able to sleep without Zakira next to him. Refusing to spend another night that way, he took her off the sofa and placed her in bed. Zakira wiggled, but did not awaken as Malik's fingers trailed her collarbone before his lips followed the same path. Malik rested his head against her shoulder and simply enjoyed the comfort of having her next to him.

Early the next morning, Zakira found herself in her husband's arms. She noted that they were still clothed. No surprise, she sourly remarked to herself. After a long sigh, she quietly left the bed, dressed and set out for a walk.

The setting was exquisite—almost ethereal. At dawn, a mist settled over and around everything in its wake. It moved like a living thing, casting a calm, mellowing effect on the stunning environment.

Zakira found an isolated spot on a cliff overlooking the deserted stretch of beach. The area was shielded by towering trees, and she felt she could have stayed for hours.

It was some time before Malik found her. She was wrapped up in a thick red-and-black cashmere checkerboard blanket. He quietly stretched out beside her.

"Go away," Zakira ordered, without opening her eyes.

Malik turned and looked at her. "I can't do that until I apologize."

"Malik…"

"And explain," he added, watching her weary gaze turn expectant as she waited for him to continue.

"I'm dyin'," he began, pounding his fist to his palm as he spoke. "I'm dyin' and I'm angry. I'm mad as hell because soon I'm not gonna be able to do this," he said, trailing his thumb around the curve of her jaw. "Zaki, you don't know how hard it is for me to see you every day and know that soon I won't ever be able to see you again."

Zakira pressed her hand to his cheek. "I won't be able to see you, either. I'm suffering, too, you know?"

"I know," he acknowledged, covering her hand with his own. "But you'll still have your life…your memories. I won't ever have you again. I won't even be able to miss you, because I'll be dead."

"Well, baby, this attitude, this—this coldness," Zakira whispered, her throat constricting around the lump there, "this is killing me and I can't stand it. I want you to love me or play 'stud' to me, as you call it. Call me selfish, but I want as much of you as I can get. As much as you can give, until…"

"Shh," he soothed, when she began to cry. "I realize how wrong I was to do that to you. To us. I love you more than my life."

Zakira allowed her tears to flow more freely. "I love you, too," she whispered, laughing when his mouth settled to hers and he kissed her deeply.

They spent the rest of the morning in the private oasis, holding on to each other beneath the swaying trees.

Chapter 7

The next few weeks were like a roller-coaster ride for Malik and Zakira. Some days were wonderful. They basked in the love they felt for one another, and the nights became even more sensual. Unfortunately, for all the good days, there were those times when Malik was in such an evil mood, he barely said more than three words to his wife.

Through it all, Zakira was becoming more familiar with the business. She found that while cooking had been her passion, the business end of running a restaurant was just as fulfilling. There were times when Malik didn't want to come in to the restaurant at all. Fortunately, Zakira didn't mind picking up the slack.

Such was the case when Eddie came to visit one day.

Zakira had become a regular sight behind Malik's desk and was in the midst of haggling with a prospective supplier.

For a moment, Edwina stood just inside the door watching her stepsister on the phone. At first sight, the small woman might have appeared out of place behind the huge, mahogany desk, but that was far from true.

Zakira finished the call and waved Eddie closer. "Hey, girl, what brings you in here?"

Eddie smiled and stepped closer to the desk. "I'm on my way to my office. I just thought I'd stop in to see what was up."

Sighing, Zakira picked up one of the thick folders on the desk and waved it in the air. "Work, honey, work."

A small frown crossed Edwina's delicate features and she propped her hands on her hips. "Why do you sound excited about it?"

Zakira pretended to misunderstand. "How can anybody be excited by work?"

Eddie shrugged and smoothed her hands down over the clinging material of her short petal-pink miniskirt. "Well, Z, you sound pretty happy to be here in the midst of all this."

Zakira leaned back in the gigantic suede desk chair and closed her eyes. "I'll admit I love it, but I wish Malik was here to help me."

Again, Eddie was surprised. "To help you, but not to take over again?"

Zakira didn't respond, but she couldn't stop the smile that touched her mouth. Soft laughter between the two women began to fill the room, when the office door flew open.

"Man, Chanel wasn't at her desk, so I—" Tree was pulling gloves from his hands when he looked up. "Oh. Sorry."

Zakira stood behind the desk, smiling at the surprised expression on Tree's face. "I'm covering for Malik again."

Tree noticed, but his midnight stare had already found Edwina across the room. His pitch-black eyes narrowed, but he finally nodded in response to Zakira's words. "I'm sorry. I was supposed to see him today."

"Well, I can— 'Scuse me," Zakira said when the phone interrupted her. She resumed her seat behind the desk and answered the line.

Meanwhile, Eddie was studying the tops of her petal-pink platforms. She could almost feel Tree's onyx stare boring into her, and she hoped he wasn't planning to stay. Eddie had opted to take a plane back to Virginia after the weekend in Maine. She had not spoken to Tree since and she had given him no explanation for her strange behavior that night in his room.

"Sorry, guys, I gotta go down to the bar," Zakira announced as she grabbed a pad and made a hasty exit.

Eddie closed her eyes briefly. Then, she stepped away, placing more distance between herself and Tree.

"So, how are you doin'?" he asked after several moments of silence.

Eddie turned and managed a shaky smile. "I'm fine…and you?"

Tree nodded, pushing his gloves into the deep pockets of his navy wool trench. "I've been better," he admitted.

Eddie winced at the noticeable edge to his words. She

wrung her hands and took a few small steps toward him. "Oh, Tree, I'm so sorry. I feel like a damn heel for the way I acted."

Tree's dark brows rose slightly, he was surprised by her admission. Taking advantage of the moment, he held her exquisite hazel gaze captive with his smoldering dark one.

"Did I come on too strong?" he asked.

"No, no you didn't," Eddie immediately assured him.

"Then would you mind telling me what happened?" Tree queried, his slow stride bringing him closer.

Edwina smoothed her hands across the back of her stylish haircut. She leaned against the desk and raised her eyes to his. "I guess I'm still just really afraid to get close to anyone right now. I don't know, maybe I'm moving too fast. I've been doing a lot of…soul-searching since my last breakup. I guess the drama of that whole mess has affected me more than I realized."

Tree nodded, the subdued look on his face making him appear even more handsome. He followed Eddie to the desk and leaned down, bracing his hands on either side of her. "Will you let me take you out sometime? Nothing heavy…whenever you feel up to it?" he softly proposed, his gaze steady and intense.

Eddie managed a brief nod and a smile.

The dimples creasing Tree's cheeks deepened when he smiled. Then, the smile faded, and his expression became serious. His black gaze fell to her full lips and he was drawn to her like a puppet on a string.

Edwina's lips parted instantly and her lashes fluttered over her eyes in anticipation of the kiss she had dreamed of. His lips were a breath away and his hands were already cupping her hips to hold her steady.

"Guys I'm sorry about that!" Zakira burst into the office, apologizing. Her delicate brows rose as she witnessed her stepsister and Tree jump apart as though they had been burned. For a moment, she watched them suspiciously. "Did I interrupt something?"

Eddie rolled her eyes toward Zakira, but shook her head. "No, you didn't. Listen, I need to get going for an appointment, so I'll see you later."

Zakira simply waved her goodbye. Amusement brightened her vibrant brown eyes.

Edwina ignored the knowing look in her sister's eyes and turned toward Tree. "It was nice to see you again," she told him.

Tree nodded, the look in his midnight eyes full of desire. When the door closed behind Edwina, he sighed and turned toward Zakira. "I really don't understand her sometimes."

Zakira shrugged and headed to the desk. "Well, Eddie's crazy," she teased. "But she's very beautiful and sweet."

Tree's long black lashes closed over his eyes as though he were envisioning Eddie in his mind. "I won't argue with that," he murmured.

"So, what brings you into the restaurant?" Zakira watched Tree ease into a chair before the desk.

"I was looking for Malik. I thought he'd be here. I told him I'd stop by."

Nodding, Zakira pushed her thick hair behind her ears. "He didn't feel like coming in today. If you ask me,

I think he taught me the business to keep us apart. Now he can stay at home and not have me hovering."

A sympathetic look touched Tree's face. "Honey, I'm sure that's not true."

Before Zakira could disagree, the phone rang. It was the private line, so she answered immediately.

"How are you doin' over there?"

Zakira felt small shivers wiggle up her spine at the sound of Malik's soothing, deep voice. "I'm fine. Everything's smooth so far."

"Good, I'm calling to tell you Tree is supposed to stop by to see me."

Zakira smiled, glancing at Tree. "He's already here. Did you want to talk to him?"

Tree stood and took the phone. "Yeah, man?"

The strong tone Malik used with Zakira vanished the instant he heard Tree's voice. "How soon can you get here?" he asked.

Tree frowned at the uncharacteristically weak sound of his friend's voice. "Why?" he asked.

"I need you to get over here fast."

Zakira looked up when Tree slammed down the receiver. Before she could ask what the problem was, Tree was already headed out the door.

"Does Zakira know how bad off you are?"

Malik gave Tree a sour look. "Do you think she'd be at the restaurant if she did?"

Tree ran one large hand over his wavy hair and sighed. "You need her here with you, man."

"I don't need to hear this now."

"I think you do."

Malik raised his hand. "I need to talk to you about this party."

Tree's head tilted slightly as he blinked. "'Scuse me? Did I just hear you say *party?*"

Grimacing, Malik pushed himself off the sofa and walked over to the fireplace. He closed his eyes against the heat from the glowing flames. "I need this, Tree."

After a moment the confused scowl on Tree's face became one of understanding. "So, it's time, huh?"

Malik nodded. "It's time." He pushed his hands through the shoulder-length dreads as he turned. "You still with me?"

After a few moments of silence, Tree nodded. "Yeah. Yeah, you know I am," he said wearily. "What do you need?"

Malik went over the details for his "party" and Tree dutifully noted each request. As soon as Malik was done with the list, Tree left.

When the front door slammed behind him, Malik groaned. He gave a silent prayer of thanks that his old friend was there. Tree knew him too well not to know what the party was all about. It was time to say goodbye to family, friends…and Zakira.

"All right, what have we got here?" Zakira whispered to herself as she inspected the refrigerator. She had gotten home about 7:00 p.m. and headed to the kitchen to start dinner.

She chose long-grain white rice, crisp greens, a mixture of frozen vegetables and two thick sirloin steaks. While the rice was cooking, she chopped the greens and put them on to steam. Meanwhile, the frozen vegetables boiled as she prepared a sauce of butter, black and cayenne pepper and roasted peanuts. The steaks baked in the oven. They would be sliced, sautéed in an onion gravy and poured over the rice.

While everything simmered and baked, Zakira began taking off her work clothes. Too tired to even climb the stairway, she let each garment drop to the shiny, hardwood floor.

Malik had been in the den napping on the sofa when he heard what sounded like the clamoring of pots and pans. He decided to investigate and headed to the kitchen. When he walked in and saw Zakira removing her clothes, his heart ached for her.

Zakira whirled around when she heard the low groan behind her. She spotted Malik leaning against the doorjamb and rushed towards him. "You should be in bed," she softly chastised.

"I know," he absently replied, his gray stare trained on her barely clothed body. "I was on the, uh, den sofa."

"Well, let's get you back in there," Zakira murmured, placing her arm about his waist.

Zakira helped Malik back to the sofa, pulling a heavy afghan across him. When she made a move to leave, he grabbed her arms.

"Stay with me?" he softly asked, his grip tightening just slightly.

Happy that he needed her, Zakira smiled at the boyish expression on her husband's gorgeous dark face. "Okay," she said, slipping beneath the soft afghan.

The moment Malik had Zakira lying over him, his hands began to roam her seminude body with persuasive strokes. He massaged her back, his fingers dipping beneath the clasp of her bra to unhook the back.

Zakira shifted her position on top of Malik and gasped when she felt the extent of his arousal against her belly. She looked up, and her lips immediately parted for the deep kiss. Malik's tongue thrust smoothly into her mouth and they both moaned. Zakira cupped Malik's face in her hands and began to slide herself over his iron length.

Malik's hands slipped from Zakira's back, down her waist to the delicate lace panties. His long fingers dipped in to find her hot and very moist. He smiled, hearing her gasp. He deepened the kiss and the intimate caress below.

"Malik? Malik?"

"Hmm?"

Zakira broke the kiss and placed her hands flat on his chest. "I need to go check the food."

Malik's lips found the base of her throat to be irresistible. "The pots are fine," he assured her.

"I can't take a chance," Zakira replied, trying to move away.

Malik suddenly flipped Zakira beneath him. He continued the deep, slow caress between her thighs while his mouth feasted on her bare breasts.

The sensuous, double caress was her undoing. Zakira closed her eyes and arched her back, seeking more of his touch. Her soft cries filled the air, becoming louder until Malik pulled away.

"What's wrong?" she whispered, seeing him raise his head and look across the room.

"Something might be burning. You better go check." His gorgeous eyes were full of mischief.

Zakira slammed her fist against his chest. "You…jerk." She pushed him away so she could leave the sofa.

Malik's deep chuckle filled the room as he watched her race out of the room.

Thirty minutes later, Zakira emerged from the kitchen carrying a tray loaded with food and drink and wearing a short robe. Malik selected a steamy, erotic thriller to put in the DVD. In comfortable silence, they enjoyed the delicious meal. The movie proved to be as good as they'd heard it was and held their attention.

"Come over here." Malik called, watching from the sofa.

Zakira smiled, but kept her brown eyes on the television screen. "I want to finish the movie, Malik."

"I just want you close to me," he told her, his voice calm and very sexy.

Zakira finally looked at him. There was no way she could ignore the softly spoken words. Setting her plate to the coffee table, she joined him on the couch. Malik held her tightly as Zakira rested her head on his chest. With the sound of his heart beating beneath her ear and his large, strong hands stroking her skin, Zakira cursed her fate. *Why was this being taken away?*

"Malik! Malik?! Where are you? Malik!"

Zakira ran though the lower level of the house, frantically shouting and searching every room. Malik had called her at the restaurant and told her he needed her home…as soon as possible. Racing upstairs, she finally found him in the bedroom.

"Malik!" she called, gasping at the sight of her husband. He was standing near the bed running a thick towel over his glistening body. "What's wrong?" she asked, unable to take her eyes off his dark muscular frame.

"Get in the shower," he ordered, grinning at the look on her face.

Zakira was completely confused. "Are you okay?"

"I'm fine," he assured her, tossing the towel to his dresser and choosing cologne. "But we got a party to attend, so we better hustle."

"A party?" Zakira repeated, now confused and suspicious. Fortunately, the wicked smile on Malik's gorgeous face put her at ease. "I'll be ready in a few," she promised, beginning to undress.

"I thought we were going to a party. What are we doing back here?" Zakira asked, as Malik parked the SUV in Badu's parking lot.

"This is it," he revealed, getting out of the truck to come around and open her door.

Stunned amazement cast its glow on Zakira's face when she saw the grand transformation that had taken place. The restaurant appeared more exquisite than usual. Glowing candelabra were the main light source, and a long table was filled with every specialty on the menu.

Zakira racked her brain trying to recall a special date she may have overlooked. Of course, she wasn't the only one who didn't know what the occasion was. All the guests were in the dark.

Deciding not to worry herself over it, Zakira mingled through the crowd. There were old friends as well as family members in attendance. The evening promised to be something very special.

A light mist had just begun to fall as Eddie hurried inside the restaurant for the party. She took a moment to catch her breath, smoothing one hand across her stylish, short cut. She started to remove her coat. Just as she eased the garment over her shoulders, someone took over the task. Eddie gasped and turned to find Tree standing behind her.

"Thank you," she whispered, allowing him to finish the task.

Tree's dark eyes followed as the coat fell away to reveal a black, sleeveless double-strapped dress. "You're welcome," he assured her in a deep, slightly raspy voice.

She carried her cashmere coat to the cloakroom and waited for the attendant to hand her a claim stub. The next instant, Tree's hand curled firmly beneath her arm and he pulled her away with him. Eddie was sure she would have protested had she not been so fevered by his touch.

Tree wasn't about to let anyone infringe on his time with Eddie. He kept her by his side for most of the evening. They were dancing when Eddie squeezed her eyes shut, praying the annoying beep she heard wasn't for her, wishing she'd thought to leave the beeper in the car with her cell. She tried to ward off the aggravating sound by losing herself in Tree's arms again.

"Eddie?"

"Hmm?"

Tree smiled, loving the relaxed, trusting tone in the simple sound. Smoothing his hand across her back, he lowered his mouth to her ear. "You're beeping," he playfully noted.

Eddie gave a disappointed sigh and pulled away from Tree. He watched in utter fascination, his dark eyes narrowing as he waited to see where she had the beeper hidden beneath the skintight, short black dress. Edwina could easily read the look in Tree's eyes and was embarrassed.

"'Scuse me," she muttered and turned to walk away. As she headed to the pay phones near the restrooms, she gave a silent prayer of thanks that her weak legs supported her.

"So, was this your idea?"

Malik smiled down at Zakira as they swayed to the seductive rhythm of the music. "I had a hand in it."

Zakira smoothed her hands across the wide expanse of his back. "Well, what's the occasion?"

"Does there have to be one?"

Arching herself into the reassuring plane of his chest, Zakira sighed. "No, we can do this every night."

"Sounds good to me," Malik whispered, pressing a kiss to the top of her hair.

They tightened their embrace and wished the song and the dance could last forever.

Eddie stood by the wall for a moment clutching the phone to her chest. It made her so happy when her patients began to make progress, even if it cut into her profits.

With a sigh, she replaced the receiver and turned. "Oh!" she cried, pressing a hand against her chest when she saw Tree.

He didn't apologize for startling her. Instead, he pushed her against the wall. Eddie moaned softly and her thighs trembled as he pressed her into the secluded corner and kissed her deeply. His tongue slid smoothly past her full lips to stroke the sweet inside of her mouth. Eddie curled her hands over his massive shoulders and clung to him for support.

Tree was like a man starved for the taste of her. His kiss grew deeper and more forceful. Meanwhile, his large hands easily spanned her tiny waist before moving down to cup her full bottom.

Eddie gave in to her attraction for him as her tongue pushed past his and she kissed him back. With a will of its own, her leg rose to stroke the side of his huge thigh and long leg. She groaned in response as the grip he had on her derriere tightened and he lifted her closer to feel the extent of his thrusting ability.

Eddie tore her mouth away and leaned her head back against the wall. Tree's lips immediately sought the smooth column of her neck and feasted there. His strong perfect teeth tugged upon the delicate chain around her throat as he inhaled her soft, feminine scent.

The passionate episode was brought to an end when they heard deafening applause coming from the dining area.

Tree's head fell to Eddie's shoulder as he struggled to catch his breath, but he only succeeded in becoming more aroused by the feel of her breasts heaving rapidly against his chest. Placing his hand at her hip, he pushed away and closed his eyes.

Eddie's long lashes fluttered closed over her eyes as she took a deep breath. She settled shaky fingers to her bruised lips and pressed her thighs together in hopes of warding off the persistent tingling in her lower regions.

"We, um, better go see what's up," Tree whispered, his bass-filled voice rough with desire.

With effort, Eddie raised her light hazel gaze to his burning dark one. At her minute nod, Tree slid his arm around her waist and took them back into the party.

Toward the side of the dining room, next to the bar, stood Malik. Zakira was beside him, looking radiant, with just a hint of unease in her large brown eyes.

Malik raised his hands, immediately drawing silence from the crowd. "I know you people are wondering what the occasion is."

A low rumbling sounded among the guests as they all agreed.

A grim smile cast a rueful look to Malik's magnificent dark features. Taking a deep sigh, he clasped Zakira's hand in his. "The reason this beautiful lady here by my side has been in the restaurant so much is because I'm sick. I've…been diagnosed with cancer."

The low murmuring amongst the crowd grew louder. Zakira looked up at him in disbelief. Malik could feel her grip on his hand slacken. He knew she was confused and shocked, but there was no stopping.

"The reason for the party," Malik continued once the noise had ceased, "is to say goodbye to you all. I've talked to my doctors about surgery, but the chances that

I'd experience some mental loss during the procedure even if it helped the cancer are too great. I'd rather not go that way, you know?" he said with a short laugh.

The gasps of shock and surprised responses from the crowd continued as Malik dropped his news. The moment became so sad, Zakira could not stand it. Wrenching her hand from his, she ran from the room.

"Z!" Eddie called. She was about to rushed after Zakira, when she felt Tree's arms close around her.

"Eddie, let her go," he whispered against her ear, rocking her against his massive frame. Edwina's eyes blurred with tears, and she turned in Tree's embrace. She allowed him to comfort her, crying softly against his wide chest.

"Shh…shh," he soothed, pressing soft kisses against the top of her head. "I think Malik and Zakira just need some time alone."

Eddie nodded and looked up at him. "I can understand that. I don't think I can take any more of this, either. I just want to go home," she said, her voice soft and shaking.

Tree brought his powerful hands to her face and cupped her cheeks. "Will you be okay by yourself?" he asked.

Eddie searched the obsidian pools of his eyes and shook her head. "No."

Sighing as though he were relieved, Tree pressed another kiss to her forehead. Then, he looked around the room at the other guests still reeling from the news. He knew Malik and Zakira needed to be alone. Giving Eddie one last reassuring squeeze, he went to the head of the room and brought an end to the party.

* * *

Zakira's hair had fallen from the thick chignon she wore. The black mass flew behind her as she raced to Malik's office in tears. They flowed out of control and her heart threatened to beat out of her chest.

She stopped before the huge mahogany desk and pounded her fists against the polished surface. "Damn him!" she cried as more tears spilled down her cheeks.

Malik had followed Zakira to his office and now stood watching her from the doorway. His stomach churned painfully at the sound of her crying. Dammit, he raged. The last thing he wanted was to hurt her that way. But he knew that in the long run, it was for the best.

Zakira must have sensed his presence in the room, for she whispered, "I can't believe you just threw a party to announce your death."

Malik stood speechless for a moment longer. "I had to let people know, Zaki," he finally replied.

"You could've at least told me what you were going to do."

"Would you have still come?"

Zakira turned, the look on her face a mixture of confusion and surprise.

"Do you think your dying is something to be celebrated?" she asked, her tone furious.

Malik sighed and pushed his big hands through his dreads as he stepped into the office. "I thought it was the best way…considering it's time to leave."

Zakira's tears had flowed consistently from the moment she ran from the dining room. When she heard Malik's words, she dried her eyes and tried to pull herself together.

"When do we go?" she asked, frowning at the uneasy look she glimpsed in Malik's eyes before he turned away. "Malik?... Malik!"

He covered his face in his hands and groaned.

"Baby, what is it?" Zakira softly inquired, walking closer.

"You're not going with me," he said, his firm voice brooking no argument.

Zakira blinked as though he had slapped her. If her heart hadn't burst before, she was sure it was about to now. "So you'd just leave for treatment or...to—to die—and not let me be there?" she asked in disbelief.

"Exactly," he confirmed, though the moment was tearing him apart.

Zakira's legs went weak and finally gave out beneath her. The tears welled in her eyes, and she began crying all over again.

In an instant, Malik was beside her on the floor. "Baby, please understand this," he whispered, his voice hoarse with emotion.

Zakira's only response was to turn her cocoa eyes toward him. The look in the wide pools was clearly accusing.

Malik's expression hardened. "I'm not about to let you watch me die, Zakira. You can't expect me to do that."

Zakira shook her head and swallowed the sob rising in her throat. "That's what it means to be married, Malik. We're together no matter what."

"I can't do it, not even for you." Malik pressed a kiss to her head and started to stand.

Zakira's arms went around his legs and she held him to her. Malik went back to his knees and pulled her against him. They held each other for hours.

Tree pulled the keys from Eddie's shaking fingers. She gave him a grateful smile and waited for him to unlock the door and usher her inside.

Wringing her hands, she went to the living room and turned on all the lamps. The warm light gave the elegantly furnished room a cozy appearance. Tree appeared quite impressed. "I like it." He told her, shrugging his massive frame out of his overcoat.

Eddie managed a brief smile, before the unsteady feeling washed over her again. Now that Tree was there in her home, she didn't have the slightest idea what to say. She needn't have worried.

Tree tossed his coat to a high-backed, forest-green armchair and headed over to Edwina. He slid his long arms around her waist and pulled her close. One hand cupped her chin and held her still as he kissed her.

Eddie eagerly returned the kiss, moaning as his tongue thrust into her mouth. Her fingers curled around the lapels of his stylish sport jacket and she arched her voluptuous form into his body.

A voice in the back of Tree's mind cautioned him that it was still too soon for them to be intimate. He wasn't about to let her go just yet, though. The need to know she wanted him passionately and not just to keep her mind off her worries encouraged him.

His persuasive hands stroked her bare skin, his fingers slipping beneath the material at the small of her back. He caressed the swell of her buttocks and lifted her even closer. His mouth left hers to ease down the softly scented column of her neck. One hand cupped her breast, and he gently squeezed the full mound.

"Tree…" she sighed, lost in the mastery of his touch. It was as though he knew exactly where she wanted, needed the most attention. She never wanted him to stop…

A shudder racked Tree's massive frame when he felt Eddie's hands slip beneath his coat to massage his back. Suddenly, the urge to have her beneath him became overwhelming. Gripping her bottom, he lifted her high against him and carried her to the sofa.

Eddie's willingness and the soft, seductive tone of her voice when she sighed his name made Tree's heart pound at breakneck speed. When she was beneath him, he slid one hand up her thigh and under the raised hemline of her dress. His sensuous strokes against her skin were so steady and sure, he had her dress and stockings removed in no time.

"Eddie…" Tree groaned as his midnight stare feasted on her lovely dark form. Her bare breasts heaved uncontrollably and beckoned his mouth. He filled himself with her, his tongue swirling around the firm peak of one breast as he suckled mercilessly.

Eddie knew she should have protested in some way, but she didn't want him to stop. When Tree's fingers slipped beneath the lacy edge of her panties and into the creamy center of her body, she screamed her pleasure.

Tree's long fingers thrust more deeply as Eddie responses grew more vocal. She was as lost in the feel of his clothes rubbing against her bare skin as she was in the feel of his fingers teasing the extra-sensitive bud of her womanhood.

Tree rested his head against her shoulder and enjoyed the sound of Eddie's passionate cries in his ear. Her body moved erotically, enjoying every thrust and circular movement of his fingers.

"Tree…Tree…don't stop…please…" she shamelessly begged as she experienced an incredible orgasm.

When the movements of her body slowed, he raised his head. He made an attempt to take some of his considerable weight off her. Edwina's hands tightened around his arm and he stopped.

"Stay…" she asked, sounding completely exhausted.

Tree granted her request. He didn't leave until she had fallen asleep.

Zakira's eyes popped open and, for a moment, she was deathly still. Then, shifting, she tried to get a sense of her surroundings. She finally realized that she was on the sofa in the office at Badu's. It was the next morning, and she was alone.

Bolting upright, she slapped her hair away from her eyes and ran out of the office. Chanel was putting away her purse and shrieked when Zakira raced into the hall.

"Gosh, Zakira, you scared—"

"Can I have your car keys?"

Chanel frowned, not liking Zakira's disheveled appearance or frantic words. "Are you okay?"

"I'm fine," Zakira hurriedly assured her as she took

the keys that dangled from Chanel's fingers. "Thanks. I'll return your car as soon as I can!" she called, running down the hall.

Zakira ignored the strange sense of déjà vu that washed over her when she burst into the house, shouting Malik's name. Silence answered her crazed calls.

Taking a deep breath, she pressed her fingers to her lips and began walking through the house. She looked into every room on both levels. She didn't feel the tears pressuring her eyes until she walked into the bedroom. Every piece of clothing and all personal articles belonging to Malik were gone. The only thing he left behind was a letter on her pillow.

For what seemed an eternity, Zakira stood staring at the lone sheet of paper. Pulling herself together, she sat on the bed and snatched up the note.

Zaki,
I know you don't understand any of this. All I can say is that it's something I have to do to preserve what little sanity I have left. Don't ever doubt that I love you more than my life. I just can't die in front of you. I'd rather have you hate me than pity me. Tree will be in touch almost every day to make sure you're okay. He'll let you know when I'm gone. Take care of Badu's; it's yours now. Stay lovely, Zaki. Know that every day and night my mind will be on you.
I'll love you forever. Malik

Pressing the letter against her chest, Zakira bowed her head and cried. Her sobs gradually turned to loud wails that filled the entire house.

Sometime in the late afternoon, Zakira woke. She hadn't realized she had cried herself to sleep until she saw the tear-stained note lying next to her on the bed.

Like a zombie, she dragged herself from the tangled mass of covers. Deciding to take a shower, she pulled the long, satin evening gown from her shoulders. It was hopeless to think she was all cried out since she spent the entire time sniffing and wiping tears from her face. In the shower, she just hugged herself and rocked slowly back and forth beneath the warm, steady spray of the water.

Afterward, she slipped into a warm, comfortable old pair of pajamas and wrapped her long, damp hair in a towel. She was headed downstairs to fix herself a cup of tea, when the doorbell sounded. She walked past the front door as though she didn't hear it.

In no mood for company, she prayed whoever it was would leave her alone. At first, she thought it could be Chanel coming for her car but she had taken care of that earlier in the day. One of the waiters had taken a cab out to the house and picked up the car. She had left the key beneath the Welcome mat at the front door.

Shrugging, she continued on to the kitchen. But the doorbell continued to ring and Zakira continued to pray the person would just give up. She tried to concentrate on preparing her tea, but the annoying buzz of the bell was too much. She slammed a mug to the counter and stormed out of the kitchen. Her brown eyes blazed with fury and aggravation when she whipped open the door. When she saw Tree standing on the other side, that fury intensified.

"What the hell do you want?" she sneered.

Tree gave a grim smile and briefly bowed his head. "Malik made me promise to watch out for you. I'd planned to do that anyway."

Zakira just shook her head. "Malik told you to watch out for me? It seems he told you a lot, hmm?"

"Z…"

"What? Why didn't you tell me?" she asked, the tears beginning to well in her eyes again.

Tree stepped into the house and shut the door behind him. "Honey, I wanted to tell you, but Malik made me promise."

Zakira willed herself to calm down. "Okay, look. It was Malik's place to tell me about the cancer. But this plan of his to leave…God, Tree…you could've at least warned me."

The muscle in Tree's jaw danced wickedly as he struggled for the right words. Damn Malik, he thought, leaving him to look like the villain. Zakira looked as if she hated him.

"Tree?…"

"Listen, Z. I didn't really…know what—"

"Stop! Just stop it!" she snapped, pushing his hands away from her shoulders when he tried to comfort her.

"Zakira—"

"No! You flat out lied to me! I know Malik is your boy, but I thought I was your friend, too!"

Frustrated, Tree ran a large hand over his wavy hair and shut his eyes tight. "Zakira, I was in the middle here. You just don't understand."

"You're so right, I don't understand," she snapped, turning her back on him.

The dark depths of Tree's eyes were filled with sadness; his entire body ached. He knew Zakira was hurt and too angry to hear him. Stepping closer, he squeezed her arms lightly and pressed a kiss to her cheek. "I'm so sorry," he whispered. Realizing it was too soon to get through to her, he left.

The Enlightenment Center was a forty-bed cancer treatment facility located just past the Virginia/West Virginia border. A twenty-doctor staff specialized in experimental methods of treating the sickness, and they were making great strides.

Malik had driven all night and arrived at the fortress-like structure nestled in the mountains around 4:00 a.m. After checking into his suite, he went right to bed. The restless five-hour slumber did him no good, however. His mind was tortured by dreams of Zakira. The two of them together loving each other…making love…

The next morning he was in the midst of unpacking, when a knock on the door interrupted him. After a brief silence, the door opened and Malik's physicians, Dr. McNeil and Dr. Burns, entered.

"Malik, how are you settling in?" Dr. McNeil asked, walking across the room to shake hands.

"All right," Malik replied, meeting him in the middle of the room.

"You know Doctor Burns?" McNeil asked, glancing behind him.

Malik's smile was grim. "Yeah. How are you, Doc?"

Burns nodded. "I'm fine, but our concern is you."

Sighing, Malik returned to his unpacking. "I won't be a concern to anyone in a few months."

The doctors exchanged uneasy glances, before Dr. Burns stepped forward. "Malik, you should remember that here at The Enlightenment Center, our first concern is to promote positive thinking. It's been the key to many remissions."

A small light of hope appeared in Malik's midnight-gray eyes just for an instant. It disappeared, though. "You've got your work cut out for you," he warned them.

"Well, in addition to the need for a positive outlook, there's something else you should know," Dr. McNeil stated.

Malik was silent as he waited for the doctor to continue.

"We want to discuss operating."

Instantly, Malik began shaking his head. The long dreads brushed his wide shoulders as he did so. "I already told you that was a route I didn't want to take."

Dr. McNeil clasped his hands together. "Listen, Malik, Doctor Burns and I have consulted on this and we believe operating is something you should consider."

Malik's gaze searched the doctors' faces. "Do you remember telling me there could be devastating complications during surgery?"

"Malik, you *will* die if you don't have the surgery," Dr. Burns said, as he too stepped forward. "There's no question that it's risky. But Doctor McNeil and I feel that this would be successful. We've consulted on your case and we both believe you can come out of the surgery with no residual brain damage."

Malik closed his eyes and ordered himself not to take hope in the doctor's word. He had already resigned himself to the fact that his life was over. The tone in the men's voices however, was breaking through the wall of coldness he had tried to build. Excitement was already surging through his body at the thought of beating the cancer. A silent prayer repeated itself over and over again in his mind before he turned to face the doctors.

"All right, where would we begin?" he asked.

Chapter 8

"Come on, Z…" Eddie whispered in a panicky tone as she rang the doorbell. She had decided to give her stepsister a few days alone. Unfortunately, she had called several times to check on her and there had been no answer. Knowing Zakira always came to her with any problem and was now shutting her out worried Eddie.

She had been pressing the bell a good three minutes, but there was no answer. Deciding to investigate, she went around back and found Zakira on the patio curled up on a chaise lounge.

"Hey, girl," Eddie called, lightly placing her hand on her sister's shoulder.

Zakira jumped at the contact, but didn't bother to look up.

She placed a soft kiss to Zakira's forehead and sat next to her on the lounge. "How are you?" she asked, hating the way her best friend in the world appeared at that very moment. It was obvious that Zakira was still devastated over all that had happened.

Zakira finally raised her weak, brown gaze to Eddie's face. "If all I had to deal with was Malik being sick, I think I could've handled it."

Eddie smiled and rubbed Zakira's hand. "Baby, I know it's a lot to deal with."

"Hmph, I wonder if you really know."

A hurt look crossed Edwina's delicate dark features. "I just want to help, Z."

Zakira kissed Eddie's cheek, realizing how her words must have sounded. Pushing herself off the chaise, she shoved her hands beneath the thick mohair sweater she wore. "What I mean is, all these months I've been trying to deal with Malik's cancer and trying to figure out what else was going on with him. I even went to Tree for some answers that might have made all this…just a little easier. He knew everything the whole time and he wouldn't tell me."

Eddie tilted her head to the side. "Who knew? Tree?"

"Mmm-hmm."

Edwina stood up and smoothed her hand over the soft hair at the nape of her neck. "Well, I'm sure Malik felt he could handle the news about the cancer better—"

"Eddie, he knew about Malik's stupid plan to leave me alone and not tell me anything. Tree knew Malik was going to go away to die."

Eddie stood speechless for a moment.

Zakira held her head back in an attempt to ward off the tears pressuring her eyes. "I'm in no mood to talk about Tree any more, much less my loving husband."

Meanwhile, Eddie wanted to kick herself for being so caught up in Trekel Grisani. She wasn't even in a relationship with him, and he had already disappointed her.

The elevator doors closed behind Edwina. She let out a breath and leaned against them for a moment. Her visit to Zakira's had been unsuccessful, and Eddie feared her sister would remain bitter and angry indefinitely.

Deciding not to let her worries affect the work she had in store for the day, she took another deep breath and pushed herself from the elevator wall. When she stepped into the corridor leading to her office, her assistant looked up.

"Trekel Grisani is waiting in your office," she announced.

Eddie frowned and glanced in the direction of her office. "Shanice, didn't you tell him I might be in late?" she asked.

Shanice nodded as a smile tugged at her full lips. "I sure did, but he said he didn't mind waiting as long as it took."

"Oh," Eddie disappointedly replied.

She cleared her throat and headed to her office. When she opened the door, she spotted Tree standing near the windows.

Tree turned the moment he heard the door open. He studied Eddie with his intense, dark eyes and instantly noticed the wary look in her eyes. He knew at once that

We'd like to send you two free books to introduce you to our new line – Kimani Romance™! These novels feature strong, sexy women and African-American heroes that are charming, loving and true. Our authors fill each page with exceptional dialogue, exciting plot twists, and enough sizzling romance to keep you riveted until the very end!

KIMANI ROMANCE ... LOVE'S ULTIMATE DESTINATION

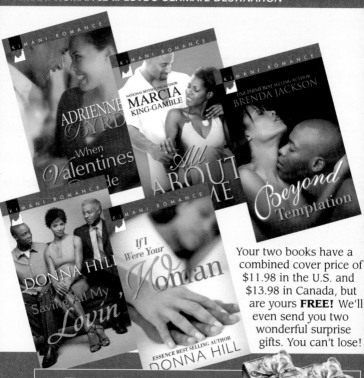

Your two books have a combined cover price of $11.98 in the U.S. and $13.98 in Canada, but are yours **FREE!** We'll even send you two wonderful surprise gifts. You can't lose!

2 Free Bonus Gifts!

We'll send you two wonderful surprise gifts, absolutely FREE, just for giving KIMANI ROMANCE books a try! Don't miss out —
MAIL THE REPLY CARD TODAY!

www.KimaniPress.com

THE EDITOR'S "THANK YOU" FREE GIFTS INCLUDE:

▶ Two NEW Kimani Romance™ Novels
▶ Two exciting surprise gifts

YES! I have placed my Editor's "Thank You" Free Gifts seal in the space provided at right. Please send me 2 FREE books, and my 2 FREE Mystery Gifts. I understand that I am under no obligation to purchase anything further, as explained on the back of this card.

PLACE FREE GIFTS SEAL HERE

168 XDL ELWZ   368 XDL ELXZ

FIRST NAME

| LAST NAME |

| ADDRESS |

| APT.# | CITY |

| STATE/PROV. | ZIP/POSTAL CODE |

Thank You!

she had talked to Zakira. "What are you thinking?" he softly questioned.

Edwina bowed her head and walked to her desk. "I don't see how you could keep something like that from her," she grumbled, looking through a small stack of folders.

"You don't understand."

"Hmph, you're right. I don't."

A grimace clouded Tree's handsome face. He remembered Zakira uttering those same words. It angered him more to hear them coming from Edwina. "Listen, Malik…he needed me."

Eddie rolled her eyes. "So did Zakira."

"Eddie, please!" Tree snapped, his deep voice growing raspier as his frustration mounted. He raked one hand through his wavy, dark hair as his grimace turned into a murderous glare. "I hated being put in the middle of this. But, I had a job to do. Malik came to me as a client and I had a responsibility to respect his wishes." Tree took a deep breath, and raised his intense gaze to Eddie's face. "I think you can understand that, being a doctor."

Eddie pressed her lips together and began to nod slowly. There was no way she could argue with him in that regard. "I'm sorry," she finally said. For the first time, she could see how much he was hurting. He loved Malik and Zakira as much as she did.

Trekel lowered his tall frame into one of the chairs in front of the desk. He covered his face in his hands and groaned.

The pain-filled sound weighed heavily on Eddie's

heart. Ignoring the voice that told her not to get any more involved, she stepped around the desk, knelt before him and pulled his hands away from his face. She gave him a tight hug, turning her face into the side of his neck as she inhaled the crisp, clean scent of his cologne. When she pulled away, Tree cupped her oval face in his palms.

Eddie's eyes lowered to his wide, sensuous mouth, and her lips parted slightly for his kisses. She gasped, allowing his tongue full entrance, but she did not resist the delicious caress.

Tree's brows drew close as the sweet kiss all but consumed him. "I want you so much, Eddie," he whispered into her mouth as one of his hands slid from her face to massage her breast.

Eddie melted beneath his touch and at the deep emotion in his words. Her slender fingers curled around the lapels of his jacket and she wished he would never stop.

"Have dinner with me tonight?" he asked, showering the dark column of her neck with countless kisses.

Eddie's entire body felt like water, she was so weak with need. She nodded.

Tree stood, taking Edwina with him. He pushed her against the desk and brushed his mouth next to her ear. "I'll pick you up at seven. And tonight I won't let you cancel on me," he promised in a soft tone that was too sweet to resist.

Edwina closed her eyes and took several deep breaths after Tree walked out of her office. No, canceling was the last thing she wanted to do.

* * *

Zakira stared at the answering machine with a wary expression on her face. She had planned on taking a break from the phone for a while. She knew Malik could have been trying to call, but he'd made her feel like such a fool, she didn't even want to talk to him.

It was 6:30 in the evening and she'd decided it was time to check in with the outside world. The fact that Malik hadn't called would've made her cry had it not been for the nine messages that had been left. Besides three calls from Eddie, there were six from the restaurant. They needed her.

"Badu's," a cheerful voice greeted.

"Chanel, it's me. What's going on over there?" Zakira asked, deciding to forget her personal woes and focus on business.

"Oh, Zakira, thank God!" Chanel exclaimed.

"What is it?"

"Well, Connoisseur Wines hasn't delivered the scheduled shipment, and we're extremely low. We've been getting the runaround from them for most of the day. I tried to wait as long as possible before calling you."

"It's okay. Give me the number to the supplier."

After assuring Chanel that she would handle everything, Zakira dialed the number for Connoisseur Wines's head of shipping.

"Brantley Carlisle," a brisk male voice answered.

"Mr. Carlisle, this is Zakira Badu. Badu's Restaurant."

Brantley cleared his throat. "Yes, yes Mrs. Badu, I'm very happy you called."

Zakira frowned. "You are?"

"Yes ma'am. Unfortunately, we may have given your staff a rough time earlier today."

"Yes. In fact, that's why I'm calling."

"Mrs. Badu, let me first apologize for the mix-up with your shipment. We realize the mess we must've caused, but another company will be handling the delivery."

Zakira nodded at the explanation. "Any idea when we'll receive it?"

"Any time within the next two hours. I am so very sorry about this. Please, if there's anything we can do to make up for our mistake—"

"Mr. Carlisle, the first thing you can do is to call me Zakira," she said, trying to ease the man's nervousness. "Now, as long as we get the shipment and it's not late again, then we won't have a problem."

"I can assure you we won't have the problem again." Brantley instantly replied. "Just to prove I mean it, the next shipment will be no charge to you."

Zakira smiled and shook her head. "That's very considerate of you. But your word that it won't happen again is good enough for me."

"It is?" Brantley replied in surprise.

"Well, shouldn't it be?"

Brantley gave a nervous laugh. "Of course. Of course, Mrs. Badu, it's just that…"

Zakira frowned. "Just that?"

"Well, excuse me for saying this, but Mr. Badu is never quite this forgiving. He'd want free shipments plus our heads on platters."

Zakira laughed, agreeing with the statement. "Well, Mr. Carlisle, my husband has fallen ill, so you'll be dealing with me from now on. I accept your apology. And your word that the shipments will be here shortly is good enough for me."

Brantley sighed in relief. "I must say that this is a surprising turnaround. We always have such a hard time pleasing Mr. Badu."

"Mr. Carlisle, don't get me wrong. I expect top work from your organization, as well. If I don't get it, I won't want your heads on a platter. I just won't do business with you again. Do we understand each other?"

"We understand each other perfectly, Mrs. Badu," he said, with respect in his voice.

"Damn!" Edwina muttered, as she raced barefoot down the carpeted stairway. An appointment with a patient had run past the scheduled time. It was just her luck that Tree rang her doorbell promptly at 7:00 p.m.

"Hi," she breathlessly greeted him when she whipped open the front door.

Tree's dark eyes narrowed when he saw Edwina standing before him in her bare feet. For the first time, he realized how much shorter than him she was. It wasn't a great difference, but he noticed.

"Come on in. I just need to put on my shoes," she invited, waving him inside her home.

Tree nodded and watched Eddie as she raced back upstairs. Taking a deep breath, he turned and strolled into the living room. Like the rest of the house, it had an elegant classy look. The sofa done in forest-green, trimmed in gold and surrounded by tall lamps of the same color, sat on a plush gold-toned carpet. The rest of the rooms in the lower level were done in colors just as warm and created a soothing, mellow atmosphere. Tree thought that it suited Edwina's character perfectly.

"Tree? Tree, where are you?"

"In here," he called from the den.

A light, lovely smile crossed Eddie's mouth when she found him lounging back on the sofa in front of the television. "Comfortable?" she inquired.

He smiled serenely and hugged himself. "Very."

Edwina shook her head and reached for his hand. "Come on."

Tree took her extended hand, but pulled her down to his lap. "Ooops," he said, a playful smirk casting a devious element to his dark, good looks.

Eddie's lips trembled slightly as her nervousness grew more pronounced. "What are you doing?"

Tree cupped her cheek in his wide palm and pulled her face close to his. His tongue slid into her mouth and he smiled when he heard her gasp. "I'm kissing you," he whispered.

Raising her hand, Eddie stroked the slightly rough side of Tree's face. Tentatively, she kissed him back. In response, she heard him groan and surround her in his iron embrace. She thrust herself closer to the hard, masculine body. She could feel every chiseled inch of his torso and thighs through the feathery softness of her chocolate cashmere dress.

Tree uttered a tortured groan and pulled away.

"What is it?" Eddie asked, unaware of the breathless quality of her voice.

He was pushing himself off the sofa and taking

Edwina with him. "I better get you out of here while I still can."

Eddie closed her eyes and prayed that her heart would slow its beating. She nervously smoothed her hands across her dress and tugged at the scooping neckline. Tree was behind her with both his hands at her hips. He nudged her slightly and began to walk toward the front door. In minutes, they were pulling out of her driveway in his car.

"You must know a good restaurant here?" Eddie asked as they were headed downtown.

Tree clutched his hand more tightly around the steering wheel in an effort to keep it off Eddie. He cleared his throat and nodded. "I know the best restaurant in town," he confirmed. "My place."

Edwina's hazel gaze widened as she stared straight ahead. Lord, she had no idea...

"Here we are," Tree announced, as he easily backed the fierce-looking Hummer into a reserved spot.

After a moment, Edwina's gaze focused past the passenger window. She blinked in surprise upon seeing the stark, imposing high-rise set against the night sky. She was eyeing the building in awe when Tree opened her door.

Trekel watched her intensely, smirking a little when he felt her tremble beneath the slight pressure of his hand cupping her elbow. Ignoring that, he pulled her arm through his and escorted her inside.

"Wow," Eddie breathed, as her hazel gaze wandered over the elegant, plush surroundings. Though the building housed mostly law offices and insurance firms, its furnishings gave a different statement. The decor was comfortable, yet professional.

"I can't believe how beautiful this all is," she remarked, as the elevator doors slid closed with a mellow hum.

Tree leaned against the paneled wall and pushed his hands into his pockets. "Yeah, it's gorgeous," he agreed, his pitch-black eyes trailing Eddie's form with unmasked appreciation.

Eddie turned to face Tree. "So, how many people live here?"

"Just me."

"Excuse me?"

Tree leaned his head against the elevator wall and smiled. "This is an office building...law offices, insurance people. One of my clients designed this place and since I was his lawyer, I got first choice."

"Mmm...convenient," Eddie slyly noted.

Tree bowed his head. "Very."

"So are we having dinner at your office, or..."

"My offices are on one wing and my home is on another," Tree smoothly explained.

Edwina swallowed past the lump that had suddenly lodged itself in her throat. "Oh," she croaked.

A soft buzz sounded, signifying their arrival on the penthouse floor. Tree pushed himself from the wall and stepped over to Eddie. "This way," he whispered, laying his hand flat against the small of her back.

Eddie nodded and followed his request. They made a left turn out of the elevator and headed toward the wide, oak double doors at the far end of the corridor.

While Eddie waited for Tree to locate his house key

and unlock the door, she took a moment to admire him. Lord, he was too much the way she would have him. *Intelligent, successful, thoughtful, not to mention, incredibly handsome, sexy and built like a weight lifter. If only...*

"Here we are," he announced, when the door was unlocked and opened. "I left dinner baking in the oven, so I better check on it first."

Edwina felt as though she were walking through a castle. *The man has to have a staff of twenty housekeepers,* she thought. The surroundings were so exquisite and pristine, they appeared to be taken right off the pages of a dream homes magazine. The living room was spacious, but filled with framed pictures and a mural that covered the far wall. Trekel Grisani was obviously a man proud of his mixed heritage. There were countless beautiful African hangings, masks and statues, as well as artwork of Roman origin. The furniture was comfortable-looking and oversized, which wasn't surprising considering his size. The place made Edwina want to curl up in a fuzzy sweater with a mug of herbal tea and listen to the classics.

"Eddie!" Tree bellowed from the kitchen.

"Yeah?" she returned his call.

"Make yourself at home and I'll give you the grand tour!"

Eddie pulled off her short, leather coat and hung it on the brass rack near the living room entrance. "Does the rest of the place look as beautiful as the living room?" she asked in a teasing voice.

"That depends on what mood my cleaning people were in," he answered as he walked into the room.

Eddie laughed. "That's good to hear."

Tree frowned, removing his watch and massaging his wrist. "Why's that?"

"Well, if you knew how to keep house that would make you too incredible." Her eyes were wide as she realized she must have spoken aloud.

The two of them stared at each other, their gazes practically sparkling from the sexual attraction they had yet to test completely. Edwina wanted so much to be touched by Tree again, but she warned herself to cast that from her thoughts.

"We better get started," he was saying, waving his hands toward the long stairway located through a doorway at the back of the room.

To Eddie's delight, the rest of the penthouse was as lovely as the living room. The decor was basically the same, but with subtle changes in color scheme and artwork. Each room had a personality all its own. The tour ended in the dining room where dinner would be served. Eddie trailed her fingers along the polished mahogany surface and noticed the far corner of the table had been set for two.

"Oh, Tree, this whole place is gorgeous. I'd never want to leave if it were mine," she admitted, turning to find him standing right behind her.

The look in Tree's incredible dark eyes said he wouldn't be averse to that in the least. He stepped closer to Eddie, causing her to retreat until she brushed up against the table.

Tree placed his hands on either side of her and lowered his mouth to the side of her neck.

"Don't…" she tried to resist as her thick lashes fluttered close.

In response, Tree's mouth slid along the soft line of her neck and across her jaw to her parted lips. He kissed her deeply, thrusting his tongue in the most delicious, erotic motions.

Eddie groaned and returned the kiss with passion. Her hands stroked his bronzed forearms, visible beneath his upturned shirt sleeves. He leaned closer still, until she was lying beneath him on the table.

Their hands roamed over each other's bodies in wild abandon. The passionate kiss was filled with need, as were the words they whispered.

Tree's huge frame shuddered. Desire for the lovely woman in his arms took over his entire being.

"Tree?…" Eddie finally whispered when the delicious aromas from the kitchen drifted below her nose.

"Mmm?"

"Your food."

Despite his need and almost painful state of arousal, Tree managed to pull away. He took a moment to catch his breath before standing and heading to the kitchen. Eddie pressed her hand to her racing heart and prayed for an end to the erotic tingle coursing through her body.

Malik dropped the stack of pamphlets on the desk and leaned back in his chair. Dr. McNeil and Dr. Burns exchanged glances as they watched him finish with the reading material.

"So, what do you think?" Dr. Burns asked, clasping his hands together.

Malik rested his head back against the chair, his grayish-black stare focused on the ceiling. "I still don't know what a lot of those long words mean, but I have a better idea about my condition."

"And the surgery?"

Malik pushed himself upright in the padded dark green chair. "I was hoping to read that it's going to be guaranteed one hundred percent successful."

Both doctors smiled sympathetically. Then Dr. McNeil stepped forward and slapped Malik's shoulder. "It's important that you believe the operation will be a success."

"That's right," Dr. Burns agreed. "You've gotta want to fight this thing. Your mind-set plays a big role where the sickness is concerned."

Malik drew one hand through his dreadlocks before he shrugged. "So what's next?"

Dr. Burns turned and walked behind his desk. "First, we have some tests to run. Once the results are back, we'll proceed from there."

"Will you be calling your wife?" Dr. McNeil asked, folding his arms over his chest.

Malik was silent for a moment, before he looked up at the doctor. "No."

"Damn," Eddie whispered furiously. She'd dropped her fork for the fourth time since they had started eating. She'd always prided herself on her cool demeanor, but that night it had deserted her. That was the last thing she needed to have happen with Tree sitting so close.

Tree decided not to comment on Eddie's obvious agitation. He couldn't blame her, since he had been fighting against losing his "cool" more than once that evening. He intended to make love to her that night. Perhaps she sensed that. He could only hope she wouldn't refuse him.

Eddie cleared her throat and sent Tree a dazzling smile. "I can't get over how good this is," she said, complimenting him on the delicious salmon steaks.

"Thanks, I'll be sure to tell my cook," he said, a grin brightening his handsome features.

Eddie shook her head. "I thought you'd take credit for it."

"Ha! No, I wouldn't joke about something like that!"

"Why?" Eddie asked, melting at the sound of his deep, infectious laughter.

Tree wiped a tear from his eyes. "Because the next time, you might ask me to prove my culinary skills."

Edwina tensed a little at his mention of "next time." Luckily, Tree didn't notice.

"I can't cook to save my life," he said. "The woman I marry will have to have skills in the kitchen or we'll both die."

Eddie laughed. "That's what restaurants are for."

Tree took a sip of his beer and nodded. "True, but I prefer eating at home. More privacy."

The grip Edwina had on her fork tightened instantly at the suggestive comment. After a moment, she glanced up to see his dark, deep-set gaze trained on her. The message she read there told her it was time to go.

"Tree—"

"When you're done with dinner, we can have dessert in the den," he suggested, crushing all hopes Eddie had for a quick escape.

"So what's for dessert?" Eddie asked when they walked into the small cozy den. Tree had followed her into the room without a tray or any sign of food.

"All I want is right here." Tree told her. The wicked smirk on his lips cast a devilish light to his incredible features.

Of course, Eddie had no doubts what he meant. She began to back away, her eyes darting from left to right as she struggled to find something to say.

Tree, however, had wanted the sweet, dark chocolate beauty too long not to give it his best try.

"I don't think this is the right time," Eddie whispered, hating the shaky quality of her voice.

A crooked smile caused the corners of Tree's smoldering midnight eyes to crinkle adoringly. "Edwina…"

"I just think maybe we should hold off a while, you know?" she reasoned, wringing her hands nervously. "Just until we know each other better."

"Can you honestly tell me that you don't want this?" he asked, the deep mellow sound of his voice resembling a low growl.

Eddie's lashes fluttered over her eyes, as she tried to block out the image of Tree's powerful form filling her view. Oh how she wanted him, but…

"Eddie?"

"All right, all right!" she admitted in nervous anticipation. "I do want this. I want you. But I just—"

Tree didn't give her the chance to finish. He took her hand and pulled her toward him. Edwina gasped at the smooth, easy movement. Tree crushed his mouth against hers and kissed her deeply.

Her hands curled into small fists and she pounded them weakly against his unyielding chest. "Wait," she pleaded beneath the masterful kiss.

"I can't" was his tortured response. He loosened his grip on her hand and slid both his arms around her slim frame.

Eddie's fists slowly uncurled and she softened in the protective embrace. Then slowly, with just a hint of uncertainty, she kissed him back. The force of the kiss subsided just a little when he felt her tongue gently caress his but his embrace tightened as he sought to bring her closer.

Eddie surrendered to the intense attraction she had for the man who held her so passionately. Her lips, swollen from the pressure of the kiss, trailed the strong wide column of Tree's neck. She inhaled the clean, masculine scent of his cologne as her fingers sank into his black, wavy hair. All of her inhibitions fell away to leave a shocking passion she desperately needed Tree to satisfy. Wanting to feel more of him, her fingers went to work on the buttons of his shirt.

Tree's large hands covered hers and stopped her. Edwina's hazel gaze snapped to his handsome face and, for a moment, she memorized his dark, deep-set eyes, the long black brows, the angle of his nose and the sensuous wide mouth. Somewhere in the back of her mind, a warning bell sounded. It told her to think about this and to remember all the times she had been hurt. This time, however, Eddie wouldn't let the more sensible side of her nature take over. She wanted this man too much not to take what he was offering.

Slowly, possessively, Tree's massive hands spanned Eddie's waist before they curled around her hips. Easily, he lifted her before him and buried his handsome face in the crook of her neck. As his lips nibbled at the soft skin there, Eddie threw her head back and eased her arms about his neck. She kicked off her chocolate pumps and locked her hips around his lean waist. A delighted cry escaped her when she felt the incredible bulge against the front of his trousers.

Tree smiled and continued to ravish her throat with tiny, erotic kisses. The need to have her naked beneath him became unbearable and he carried her upstairs.

Tree took only a few long strides into the darkened bedroom, before he set Eddie down next to the bed.

"Would you take this off for me?" he asked. His hand gently touched her dress and his dark eyes narrowed as they watched her.

Eddie almost swooned beneath the rush of sensation she experienced. Her pulse beat over every inch of her body as her hands moved to the nape of her neck, and she fumbled with the gold zipper there.

Tree pulled her to him and turned her around. Slowly and very gently, he tugged the zipper down the length of her back. The cashmere parted to reveal her flawless, dark skin. He couldn't resist trailing one finger down her spine and caressing the skin hidden from his view by the thin satin bra straps.

Eddie tilted her head back and was about to lose herself beneath the simple caress. Before that could happen, Tree pushed her away. It was evident by the coolly expectant look in his dark eyes that he expected her to finish undressing. He stood back on his long legs and pushed his hands into the deep pockets of his trousers.

Tree's casual stance belied the pulsing wave of desire that threatened to drive him mad. Patiently, he waited. His eyes never left Edwina as her slender hands went to her shoulders. *Damn, she's unbelievable,* he thought, watching as the cashmere peeled away. Greedily, his gaze sought and clung to every new inch of exposed skin. Though he had seen the loveliness of her body before, knowing she would be his that night made the experience completely new.

The dress finally pooled around Eddie's ankles. She stood before Tree wearing nothing but a wispy pair of black panties and matching bra.

A wicked smirk crossed his mouth and he stepped closer to her. All he wanted was to pull her to him and quickly satisfy the arousal raging within him. He controlled himself, though. Eddie was far too special, and he cared too much about her to rush anything that night.

Eddie raised her eyes and her breath stopped in her throat when she looked into the smoldering gaze that followed her. She caught her lower lip between her teeth, when the back of Tree's hand brushed her bare stomach. The caress was soothing, slow and possessive.

He lowered his mouth to the side of her neck and traced the length of her collarbone with his tongue. Meanwhile, his hands massaged her back before cupping her bottom.

Eddie's own hands stroked the firm, muscled length of his arms and marveled at the unleashed power.

When his fingers slipped beneath the waistband of her panties, he found the part of her that was moist with need for him.

"Tree…" she moaned, her legs shifting farther apart to allow more room for his fingers to explore. Sliding her hands over his abdomen, rigid with muscles, she raised her lips to his.

He didn't disappoint her, but smiled and kissed her. The pressure increased as his tongue nuzzled within the sweetness of her mouth. The intimate treat pushed her desire to a fevered pitch and increased the moisture Tree felt against his fingertips.

Edwina helped him unbutton his shirt. The crisp material fell away to reveal his chest, chiseled and smooth as a marble statue. Her eyes widened slightly, then narrowed as they traced each toned inch of his torso. Her hands cupped and caressed him as though she were sculpting his incredible frame.

After a while, Tree could stand no more of the teasing. He moved forward, forcing her closer to his bed.

A surprised cry escaped her when she tumbled back against the magnificent king-sized bed. Tree followed her down, his mouth blazing a possessive trail down her neck. Eddie arched her body in response, moaning when he caressed her breast and covered the hardened tip with his mouth.

"Tree…" Eddie breathed, her legs shifting apart for him.

Tree was in no condition to respond to her weak cry.

His hands were everywhere and finally reached the waistband of her panties again. Her hips rose from the bed as the wispy lingerie was pulled away. When she was totally nude, Tree stood and removed the rest of his own clothes. While doing so, his black stare glided across the seductive picture she made lying there in his bed. A low groan sounded in his throat as he covered her supple, slender body with his heavy, smooth one.

"You don't know how long I've needed this from you," he whispered in her ear, before his teeth nipped at the lobe. His body shuddered in response to Eddie's nails raking his back. Unable to wait any longer, he reached for protection on the nightstand and put it in place, then lowered his hands to her thighs and pulled them apart. His hips lunged forward, thrusting his length deep within her.

The instant erotic pleasure Eddie experienced weakened her so that she couldn't even cry out. Her body immediately began to move to meet each of Tree's powerful strokes. The increased sensation was overwhelming.

Eddie closed her eyes and Tree watched as she grasped her full lower lip between her teeth. A smile of pure male confidence touched his mouth as he watched her enjoy the feel of him inside her. She was everything he wanted. He had no intention of stopping until he took complete possession—until she was his…body and soul.

Chapter 9

"Chanel, can you just take messages for me over the next two hours? I need to finish going over these furniture books if I'm ever gonna get started redecorating this office."

Chanel nodded and smiled at Zakira. "No problem. I may step out for lunch in a little while, though. I'll let the machine pick up, if that's okay?"

Zakira waved her hand, already turning toward the office. "That's fine," she called over her shoulder.

Once the door closed behind her, Zakira headed right to the massive, polished mahogany desk. She picked up the thick furniture catalog, filled with stunning office ensembles. Leaning back in the brown suede chair, she studied the pages intently.

During the last two weeks, there had been a gradual change in Zakira's demeanor. She spent the majority of her time at the restaurant. Days off were nonexistent. Not that she minded, since home was the very last place she wanted to be. Of course, she was in the process of changing that. She knew that the main reason she spent so much time at the office was because she saw Malik in every corner of the house. She was, however, about to rectify that. Besides redecorating her home, she had also started remodeling Badu's. At the restaurant, Zakira's business sense and savvy was turning a lot of heads. Unfortunately, because of her dedication to the business, her social life had suffered. She rarely, if ever, got together with friends. It was as though she didn't notice…or care.

"Well, well, this is something I don't see very often," Eddie called across the office when she caught Zakira indulging in a rare moment of relaxation.

Smiling, Zakira set the furniture catalog aside and stood. "Eddie," she greeted, moving from behind the desk and enveloping her sister in a tight hug. "What's up, girl?"

"A lot and I don't have a soul to talk to about it." Eddie admitted in a sarcastic tone.

Zakira's bright smile faded just a little, before she turned away. "Well, I'm glad you decided to stop by. I need your help deciding on this furniture."

"Z, why don't you cut the act?"

Zakira whirled around, her large brown eyes widening. "You don't approve of helping me find new furniture?"

Eddie folded her arms across her chest. "You know what I mean."

"No, I think you better explain it to me," Zakira insisted, tossing her thick hair over her shoulders.

Eddie smoothed her hands over her wool sweater and stepped closer to Zakira. "This act you're putting on. Pretending not to miss Malik. Shutting yourself away from your family and friends. Hiding behind the restaurant. You can stop me anytime."

Zakira laughed, disbelief in her warm, brown eyes. "You know, as a psychologist, I thought you'd agree with me moving on with my life."

Eddie leaned her hip against the desk. "I would, if you were moving on in a healthy way."

"Healthy?"

"Z, it's not healthy trying to wipe out all evidence of the man's existence or shutting out the friends who know you both," Eddie cautioned.

Zakira bolted away from the desk. "That's not what I'm trying to do."

"From where I stand, it is."

"Well, you're not standing in my shoes!"

Eddie followed Zakira across the room. "I don't have to be in your shoes to see you trying to forget Malik was ever in your life! Redecorating the house, this office, the restaurant."

"Eddie, please," Zakira hissed, her voice suddenly soft.

Edwina walked closer to Zakira, enveloping her stepsister in a hug and pulling her back against her. "It's okay."

"Lord, Eddie, he's hurting me so bad," Zakira admitted, bowing her head as tears rolled down her cheeks.

"Honey, he thought what he did was for the best."

Zakira shook her head. "But shouldn't he be able to see we should be together?"

Eddie pressed a kiss against the back of Zakira's head and remained silent.

"You know, if I didn't still love him and miss him so much…"

"What, Z?"

"I could actually hate him," she replied and walked away from Eddie.

"Sweetie, you know he was only trying to prevent you from having to see him at his worst."

Zakira leaned her head back and stared up at the ceiling. "That's what marriage is about, Ed. Malik was just being thoughtless and selfish. As usual."

"How can you say that?"

"Because I know him."

Eddie shook her head, her clear hazel gaze full of sympathy for her stepsister. "Have you heard anything from him?"

Zakira shrugged and rolled her eyes. "He hasn't tried to call. I think the only person he's interested in talking to is Tree."

"I'm sure that's not true," Eddie disagreed, instantly rushing to Tree's defense.

"I am. It's just as well. I mean, if Malik wants to keep secrets, Tree's the perfect one to help."

"He's in your corner, Z," Eddie said, trying to sound reassuring.

Zakira's expression was doubtful. "Well, Eddie, unfortunately he's in Malik's corner, too. This isn't a situation where a person can play both sides against the middle."

Sadly, the more Eddie tried to change her sister's opinions, the more aggravated Zakira became.

"How you doin', man?" Tree whispered as he and Malik shared a tight hug.

Malik gave Tree's shoulder a hearty clap before he pulled away. "I'm good. How's Zaki?" he questioned, the gray-black depths of his eyes full of concern.

"I guess she's good," Tree replied, raking one hand through his dark wavy hair. "I really don't know, Mal. I'm concerned about how she's pullin' away from everybody. All she thinks about is the restaurant. Most of the time, she's there working."

"Can't Eddie help?" Malik asked, a frown causing his handsome dark features to appear fiercer.

Tree sighed. "Z hasn't made much effort to talk to her. Eddie wanted to give her some time, but now she's worried. I think she was going to visit Zakira at the restaurant today."

Malik squeezed his eyes shut and tried to fight the wave of guilt that crept into his heart. Knowing that he was responsible for tearing Zakira's world apart made him angry enough to hit something. "Listen, Tree, I'm going to have the surgery."

The worried expression on Tree's face disappeared. "Man, that's the best thing I've heard in a long time. So, are you gonna call Z, or tell her in person?"

Malik shook his head as he walked away from Tree. "The procedure is high-risk."

Tree propped his chin on his fist and nodded. "Well then, the sooner you tell Zakira, the better."

A muscle jumped wickedly in Malik's cheek as he gnawed the inside of his jaw. "I can't do that," he murmured.

Tree tilted his head as his dark eyes narrowed. "You can't do what?"

Malik slammed his fist against his palm. "I can't have her waiting like that."

Malik's words slowly settled in. "Would you mind tellin' me what the hell you mean?"

"I mean, if this surgery isn't successful, I could wind up in a coma or totally mentally incapacitated. If that happens... I want you to...to draw up divorce papers on my behalf and have them served to Zaki." The look in Malik's eyes added certainty to his words.

Tree's tall, huge frame visibly tensed. "No way in hell I'm doin' that to her," he growled.

Malik looked away, but pointed a finger in Tree's direction. "I know how this sounds, but if you think about it, you'll see it's the best thing to do."

"This cancer has totally eaten away your damn brain, hasn't it?" Tree raged, glaring at his best friend.

"Maybe it has," Malik slowly agreed, closing his eyes in regret. "But Tree, man, it's the only way I can face this surgery. I have to know that if I don't come out of it one hundred percent, that Zaki won't be hanging on, thinking I'm coming back or that things will be the same."

Tree was wholeheartedly against carrying out Malik's

wishes. However, with everything his friend was facing, he couldn't see any choice but to grant what could easily be a final request.

"Mr. Grisani, would you like a cup of coffee or something else while you wait?"

Tree favored the nurse with a warm smile as he shook his head. "No thanks. I'm fine."

The nurse returned the smile and then headed back to her station.

An entire week had passed. Tree found himself back in Maryland, this time for Malik's surgery. He cursed the fact that during the last seven days, he had been unable to talk his friend out of going though an operation without the support of his wife. Still, Malik needed someone there rooting for him, and Tree refused to let Malik go through the ordeal alone.

Again, Tree's thoughts settled on Malik's request to divorce Zakira if he slipped into a coma. *Lord, things are already tense between me and Zakira,* he silently noted. When he dropped this news on her, it would kill her.

Even if Malik came through the operation with no complications, it would be discovered that Tree had kept the information from Zakira and he would be hated by her, not to mention Edwina.

A hard look darkened Tree's striking features, and he grimaced. He was determined not to lose Eddie, especially not due to someone else's pride. Taking a deep breath, he scanned the waiting area for the phones.

"Mr. Grisani?"

Tree was on his way to call Zakira when he heard his name called. Turning, he saw Dr. McNeil walking toward him.

"How is he?" Tree quickly asked, his heavy brows drawn together in worry.

Dr. McNeil clasped his hands together and regarded Tree with a steady gaze. "The operation was a success. The tumor has been completely removed."

Tree raised his eyes to the ceiling and said a silent prayer. "Can I see him?" He asked, already heading in the direction the doctor had come.

"You can. But you should know that Malik slipped into a coma shortly after the surgery was complete."

Tree was not prepared for how much the sight of seeing his friend in a comatose state would affect him. Slowly, he curled his hands around the bed's chrome railing. He bowed his head, a low ragged sigh filled the room.

"Well, man, you did what we wanted you to do and look where it got you," he muttered, his voice a mixture of anger and sadness. As he looked down at his friend, it practically tore his heart out. Tree knew there was no way he could let Zakira go through that kind of pain, especially when it could go on indefinitely. He cast one last look at Malik, and seconds later, he was gone from the room.

Eddie set her mug of cocoa on the den coffee table, then tightened the belt around her old red chenille robe. She couldn't wait to settle beneath the warm, fuzzy blanket and relax in front of the fire. Unfortunately, before she could snuggle on the sofa, the doorbell rang.

"Damn," she whispered, pausing for a moment as she debated whether to answer.

Deciding the bell wasn't producing faster results, the person decided to knock. The thunderous pounding against the front door started Edwina's heart to racing.

Aggravated and more than a little frightened, she headed to the foyer. Peeking outside, she squinted to adjust her eyes to the dark. Seeing the gray Hummer in the drive brought a sigh of relief to her lips.

Tree stood leaning against the doorjamb, looking incredible sexy and very frustrated. A smile brightened Edwina's lovely dark face.

"This is a surprise," she greeted, taking his hand and pulling him inside the house.

Almost absently, Tree leaned down and brushed his mouth across Eddie's cheek. Then he walked past her, a deep frown etched between his long brows.

Tilting her head to the side, Eddie slowly followed him across the foyer. "What's wrong?"

"I didn't mean to bother you here," he replied when he walked into the den and saw the cozy setting before the fireplace.

"What's wrong with you?" Eddie asked again, propping her hands on her hips.

Tree squeezed his eyes shut and massaged the back of his neck. "Malik…he's…" he said, speaking as if the words pained him.

Eddie shook her head slightly and walked closer to him. "Malik's what? What are you trying to say?"

"He's divorcing Zakira!" Tree dropped to the sofa, covering his face with both hands.

A soft gasp from Eddie filled the room. For a moment she stood there, taking in the terrible meaning of the words.

Tree finally looked up at her and raised his hand, palm outstretched. Eddie didn't hesitate to accept it.

"I'm sorry," he whispered, pressing a hard kiss to the center of her hand. His grip tightened as he pulled her closer.

"When did this happen? Does Z know?" Eddie couldn't stop the flurry of questions as her eyes grew wide with expectancy.

Tree leaned back on the sofa and shook his head. "He, um, messengered the request from the clinic this afternoon, asking me to draw up the papers."

Eddie massaged the back of her neck. "Does Z know?" she repeated.

Tree's dark gaze followed the movement of his hand as it smoothed the supple length of Eddie's thigh where it peeked out beneath her robe. "I haven't been to see her yet."

"I better go now," Eddie decided, starting to get up.

"No, you don't," Tree snapped. The soft touch he applied to her thigh, tightened instantly.

"Baby, she's got to be told," Eddie reasoned. She didn't take Tree's foul mood seriously, understanding he was very upset over his best friend's decision.

Tree's hand clenched into a fist as he struggled against the wave of hatred he felt for Malik at that moment. What a stinking mess Malik had left for him to clean up, Tree thought. Still, he knew it was imperative, now more than ever, to play it cool. Especially if he didn't want to lose everything he had.

Opening his eyes, he slid his onyx stare over Eddie. Her clear hazel gaze followed his every move.

"I'll take care of this," he said, leaning his huge body over Eddie. "I'd rather tell Zakira myself, all right?"

Eddie simply nodded, concerned by the desperation she saw in Tree's eyes.

He smiled, his fingers pulling the robe's belt loose from Eddie's waist. "Thank you," he murmured against her skin. His lips trailed lower as his hands pulled the robe further apart.

A soft smile graced Eddie's mouth as she surrendered to Tree's sweet touch. His lips grazed the swell of her breast as his hand briefly tightened upon her hip. The feathery soft caresses grew more insistent as Tree grew more aroused. Edwina felt it, too, and arched closer.

Reluctantly, Tree fought against the desire that surged through him. There was something he had to do and he could put it off no longer. With great effort, he pulled away from Eddie. She frowned slightly, but didn't question him. Tree pressed one last kiss against her neck before he left.

Zakira rushed downstairs, checking the posts on her diamond stud earrings. She had a meeting with her accountant at the restaurant in an hour, but decided to enjoy a cup of tea before leaving. The doorbell rang, stopping her in her tracks, and she changed directions.

The last person Zakira expected to see when she pulled open the front door was Tree, but there he was, a look of uncertainty on his face. Obviously, he expected the door to be slammed on him.

Slamming the door, however, was the last thing on Zakira's mind.

"Hello," she softly greeted as he walked into the foyer.

"Sorry to bother you like this," Tree said.

Zakira shook her head, causing the thick curls to dangle wildly. "You're not bothering me. I'm glad you came by."

Tree couldn't hide the surprised expression that fell over his handsome face. "You're glad I came by?"

Zakira smiled in spite of herself. "I am. I missed you, boy, and I don't want this crap with Malik to mess up our friendship."

Tree's warm smile was a mixture of relief and happiness. He laughed and pulled Zakira against him. The two of them hugged tightly, overcome with happiness that the tension between them was dismissed.

"I'm glad I didn't put off coming to see you tonight," Tree whispered, squeezing his eyes shut tightly as he relished the hug.

Zakira nodded, her face pressed against his chest. "Me, too."

Arm in arm, they walked to the living room and sat on the sofa.

"I was just about to have some tea. You want some?" Zakira asked, already easing off the couch.

"No. Zakira—" Tree caught her arm and stopped her.

"What's wrong?" she asked, a frown beginning to mar her lovely face.

Tree covered both her hands in his and absently

toyed with her fingers. "I hate to talk about this when we just made up."

Instantly, Zakira knew the visit had something to do with Malik. "What happened?" She asked, grimacing at the anxious tone of her voice.

Tree's black gaze searched Zakira's face for a full minute before he spoke. "Malik…I got a request at the office today. He wants a divorce, Z. I'm sorry."

Tears immediately filled Zakira's eyes and spilled onto her cheeks. She could feel her chest tighten as a sob welled in her throat. Finally she cried. The loud, tortured sound came from deep within her body and was filled with pain and regret.

Tree didn't know if Zakira would accept comfort from him, but he knew he had to offer. Pushing aside his reservations, his hands closed around her arm and he brought her close.

Zakira didn't resist. She grasped the lapels of Tree's jacket as the shuddering sobs racked her tiny body. "Does he hate me this much, Tree?"

Frowning, he pushed her away and stared into her teary brown eyes. "What are you talking about?"

Zakira could barely speak past her crying. "Couldn't he even tell me to my face? Don't I deserve at least that? Why a divorce, Tree?"

"Baby, listen, he doesn't want you goin' through any more than you already have. I know it doesn't seem like it right now, but you will get past this."

Zakira raised her watery eyes to Tree's face and smiled.

It was killing Tree to hurt her so, but he was beginning to agree with Malik's plan. Zakira wouldn't be able to handle the coma, seeing the man she loved in such a state indefinitely. The situation was messy indeed, but Tree honestly believed it was for the best.

"It'll take me a while to draw up the papers," he said.

Zakira watched him as though he were a stranger. "There's no rush, since I don't plan on signing them."

"Z—"

"Don't, Tree. If it made Malik feel better to suggest such a thing, then that's fine for him. But I won't think about this."

Tree raked one hand through his hair. "Babe, I think the man is just trying to spare you the agony of hanging on. He wants you to be free to move on with your life, in every way…as soon as possible."

"How thoughtful of him," she whispered, moving from the sofa to pace the living room. "Tree, would you mind giving me just a little time before coming to me with this again?"

Tree smiled and stood as well. "You got it. Take as long as you need."

"As my friend, Tree, do you think I should sign those papers?"

"I think your husband is out of his mind," Tree admitted. "I hope that answers your question."

Zakira pulled him into a hug. "Thank you," she said softly.

Tree squeezed her more tightly and prayed for an end to the entire situation.

Chapter 10

"Rhonda, listen to me. I can get real bossy sometimes. So, if I'm putting too much on you, just let me
know and I'll try to cool it."

Rhonda Cooper was filling in for a seven months'
pregnant Chanel. She nodded and gave Zakira a bright
smile. "I promise. But Chanel gave me a pretty good
overview. I should be okay."

Zakira's smirk was full of humor and doubt. "Okay.
Well, holler at me anyway."

Rhonda propped her hand against her forehead in a
mock salute. "Will do," she promised as Zakira rifled
through a stack of pink message slips. Suddenly, she
snapped her fingers. "I almost forgot. Cecil and Melinda
Furches waiting in your office. They only just arrived."

"What?" Zakira exclaimed, turning in the direction

of her office. She dropped the messages to Rhonda's desk, anxious to see her old friends.

"Cecil, Melinda!" she called as soon as she burst through the door. When the Furches rushed to her with their arms outstretched, she laughed.

"Honey, we never meant to stay away so long!" Melinda cried, pulling Zakira close again.

"Oh, it's so good to see you guys," Zakira said, her overwhelming emotion giving way to tears.

"I can't believe it's been so long," Cecil marveled. "We should've been in touch before now, with everything that's happened."

Zakira nodded and tried not to let her smile fade. She didn't want to darken the joyous mood by talking about Malik and his decision to cut everyone from his life.

"So, I've heard some interesting news about you two," she smugly announced, after she took a seat behind her desk.

Cecil watched her closely. The smirk on his handsome, round, honey-complexioned face threatened to become a wide grin. "What are you hearing?"

Zakira leaned forward and propped her elbows on the desk. "I hear you're in the market to lease that warehouse. Something about terrible tenants getting tossed."

"Close," Melinda interjected.

"Close?" Zakira repeated in a flat tone.

"Close," Cecil confirmed. "We want to sell it."

Zakira's arched brows rose as the news stirred her business sense.

"So? You wanna come up?' Cecil continued. "Take a look at it?"

Zakira was excited beyond words, but she managed to remain cool. "What kind of money are we talkin' here…?"

For the next hour they discussed plans.

When Cecil and Melinda left, Zakira breathed a sigh of satisfaction and relief. *Lord, a new restaurant? How often have I thought about that lately?* she asked herself.

So many changes had taken place during the last several months. It was almost impossible to believe that she had been alone so long. The night Tree told her about Malik wanting a divorce, she thought she would never be the same. She wasn't. She was stronger. And the upcoming holiday only reminded her of the last time spent with Malik before he…left. The restaurant had become even more important to her. It had also become more successful.

Zakira relished the power and the results of her hard work and new ideas. What she loved most was the way it made her forget about Malik. She rolled her eyes toward the vaulted ceiling, a humorless smirk coming to her lips. With a heavy sigh, she silently asked herself who she was trying to fool.

Tree raised his head and smiled down at Eddie. Her eyes were shut tight, as she moaned in response to his powerful thrusts. Lowering his head, he showered her neck and chest with whisper-soft kisses. One of his large hands curled around her thigh and pulled it from against his hips. As a result, his long strokes became deeper and caressed her with unimaginable intensity.

Eddie grasped his wide shoulders and pushed her

head further into the pillow. Her lashes fluttered open and she looked across the room at the full-length mirror. Her hazel gaze slid over Tree's massive chiseled form, reflected in the mirror. She watched the movement of his body lunging forward and retreating beneath the sheets. It was such an unexpected aphrodisiac, that Eddie gasped and felt the moisture increase between her thighs.

"Dammit, Eddie…" Tree groaned, feeling the increased wetness surrounding his rigid arousal. A powerful shudder racked his large frame as he experienced a strong climax. He collapsed over Eddie and their breathless laughter filled the room.

During the last several months, the relationship had become more solid. They had grown closer and the passion had only increased. Eddie knew she had fallen in love with Trekel Grisani. She harbored feelings deeper than she ever thought herself capable of. Still, she had yet to tell him so. Tree, however, didn't mind being very vocal about his feelings.

When he caught his breath, Tree leaned across Eddie and reached for the leather trench that lay over an armchair near the bed. From the inside pocket, he withdrew a small forest-green velvet box. Bracing his elbows on either side of her, he opened the box.

Eddie couldn't breathe. Her eyes widened and slid upward to the handsome face above her. "Tree…"

"I want you with me. Just me," he said softly, lowering his head to her neck and nibbling the soft skin there. "Tell me you'll marry me."

Eddie's gaze slid over to the exquisite ring. The pear-shaped diamond sat high over a sterling silver band. "I am yours, Tree. I don't want anyone else. You know that."

Tree slid his lips up her neck and stroked his tongue along her jaw. "Then say yes," he whispered in her ear, before tugging on the lobe.

Edwina's lashes fluttered close. "I love you."

His grin was satisfaction personified. "I love you, too. Marry me, then," he added, his deep voice muffled in the crook of her neck. Finally, he raised his head, his deep-set eyes boring into hers.

"Baby, maybe this is...too soon, you think?" she stammered, her lovely light eyes staring uneasily into his penetrating dark ones.

"Too soon?" Tree repeated, a look of surprise adding a humorous gleam to his devastating features. "Well, I know we haven't been seeing each other for years, but I love you, you feel the same..."

"I just had no idea you were going to propose," she said, avoiding answering his question. Giving a nervous laugh, she raked her fingers through her short hair. "You would do this now, with me looking a mess."

His dark soulful eyes studied her face adoringly. "That's not true," he assured her.

Eddie shook her head. She didn't know what else to say.

"Can you give me a little while to think about it?" She asked, her voice barely above a whisper.

Tree kissed her cheek and slid the ring onto her finger. "Just wear this while you think and don't take too long," he ordered, giving her a devilish wink.

Eddie watched him slide out of bed, her eyes lingering on his fantastic body. When he disappeared into the bathroom for a shower, she looked back at the ring. Her eyes were clouded by sadness.

"Yeah, Z, that'll be fine. Just tell me when and where."

Zakira smiled, though a small frown formed on her face. "Glad it's not a problem, Tree. Now tell me what's going on with you."

"Nothin'. Why?" he asked, laughter evident in his deep voice.

"I don't know. It just worries me to hear a lawyer sounding so happy."

Again, Tree's rumbling laughter sounded through the line. "I just have a lot to be happy about."

"Such as? Tree!"

"Okay, okay…I asked Eddie to marry me," he finally announced, holding the phone away from his ear as Zakira squealed in delight.

"Well, when's the wedding? Do you need help with the planning? How'd you propose?"

"Hold it, Z. She hasn't given me an answer yet."

"What? Well, she's a fool if she doesn't accept. But I know she will."

"Thanks, Z."

Silence settled between them. Zakira uttered a hushed curse when unwanted thoughts intruded on the happy moment.

"What is it?" Tree softly inquired.

"Nothing. I'm—I'm very happy for you and Eddie. I just…I can't forget that my husband wants a divorce."

"Yeah, well, I've been dragging my feet on that, haven't I?"

"Malik hasn't...called or anything?" Zakira had to ask.

"No, but I'm sure he knows this is something I really don't want to be a part of."

"Do you think he'll contact another lawyer?"

"Z, no offense, but I hope he has other things to occupy his time, no matter how good an idea he thinks this is."

Zakira groaned. "Tree, when Eddie finally accepts your proposal, y'all try and remember that communication is the key to the survival of any marriage. Sex and success don't hold a candle to the power of good communication."

Tree smiled, cherishing the advice. "I'll remember, Z."

Satisfied that everything would work out between her two friends, Zakira managed a contented smile and leaned back in the white suede desk chair. "So, what do you think about my idea?" she asked.

"To open a new restaurant? I think it's great."

"Good. Well, do you think you can fit in dinner with the Furches and their lawyer tomorrow night?"

"Dinner? You know you can count me in."

Zakira chuckled. "Good, and let me know if I can help with any of the wedding plans."

It was Tree's turn to chuckle. "You'll be the first to know."

A crooked grin tugged at Tree's mouth as he shook his head. He had grown a bit more accustomed to the sight before his eyes during the last few weeks. Still, he had to admit that it all seemed unreal.

Malik was in the backyard of the small Maryland house he was renting. Music blasted from the impressive sound system in his black SUV as he pumped iron on a bench press.

"Hey, man, why don't you cool it?" Tree called to his friend, easing his tall frame into a chair and crossing his sneaker-shod feet. "It's only been a little over three weeks since you came out of the coma. Are you sure you should be doin' all this?"

Malik's full-bodied laughter could be heard even over the music. "If I'm gonna stay healthy, I need to stay in shape physically and mentally."

"Mentally, huh?" Tree parroted, grimacing a bit as he debated. "How easy is that when you're divorcing the woman you love?"

Malik's easy expression faded. "Divorcing without much success, it seems."

"You mean you still want to go through with it?"

"I mean, you didn't do what I asked." Malik clarified, sitting up on the bench. "I wanted the papers filed before I ever had that surgery. But for once, I'm glad you didn't listen to me."

"I didn't do it for you. I did it, or didn't do it as the case may be, for Z."

"Thanks anyway," Malik whispered, "I know I've got a lot to clean up, but I'm grateful to you for standing by me. Now, I've got to stand on my own," he said, lying back upon the leather bench. "I'm the only one who can fix this. I only pray I can," he said, lifting the weights with seemingly effortless repetitions.

Tree couldn't remain upset with his friend, when it

appeared he was remorseful. "You know, man, it's gonna be pretty hard to bench-press in the middle of the day when you go back to work," he pointed out, hoping to lighten the mood.

Malik sat up and added more weights to the iron bar. "Maybe so, but I'll make time. I refuse to be a workaholic ever again. Life is too short, and I plan on enjoying every minute from now on."

Tree leaned back in the blue lawn chair and toyed with the tassels at the end of his stylish, wind suit jacket. "Hmph, well now you've become totally against working and I wish you'd go home and help your wife."

The weights crashed down with a heavy clang. Malik sat up, his dark eyes narrowing. "What's wrong with her?"

"Take it easy, man," Tree advised, waving his hand toward Malik. "It's just that she works too hard. She's letting that business rule her."

Malik shrugged and reached for a towel. "That's good, then. At least, she's staying focused."

"I don't think she *is* focused." Tree argued, a frown etched between his heavy dark brows. "She's not working because she loves it, she's doing it to hide. Don't get me wrong. She's taken that restaurant to another level, but she's still shutting herself off. Mal, the woman is too young and fine to be locking herself away like she is."

"I can't see her until I know I'm in the clear," Malik explained, his voice raspy and distant.

Tree's brows rose slightly. "How much longer do you need? Your doctor gives you a shining report every time he sees you."

Malik dropped the towel to the bench and stood. "I

have a plan," he coolly stated, grimacing when he heard Tree groan.

"Man, so far, all of your plans have been stupid. You continue this plotting and planning crap and Z is gonna move on with her life and it'll be too late."

"So, are you tellin' me she's seeing someone?" Malik asked in a light voice, though his blackish-gray stare was narrowed and intense.

"Calm down, man. She doesn't have anybody new in her life."

Satisfied, Malik nodded, his confidence restored. "Well, when the time is right, she'll have me."

Chapter 11

When Zakira arrived home that evening, she settled on the living room sofa and made a call to confirm reservations at the New York hotel where she'd be staying while viewing the Furches' warehouse. After the call, she took a long stretch and pushed herself off the sofa. Upstairs, she undressed slowly, weary after such a long day.

Ever since Tree's visit to his Maryland home, Malik had had Zakira on his mind more than usual. He had already been watching her for several days and he couldn't believe how much more beautiful she was. Moreover, he was shocked by how strong his need was. He actually ached for her.

The location of the upper level master bedroom was so secluded Zakira had never heeded Malik's warnings to get covers for the small picture window that overlooked the herb garden. He never failed to mention that anyone would spy on her if they really wanted. He didn't scare her further by telling her about the clearing that offered a perfect spot to view her undressing in the bedroom. He himself had indulged in the treat on several occasions.

Malik watched Zakira, until she slipped, nude, into bed. He closed his eyes and envisioned himself there next to her, inhaling the soft, sweet scent of her skin. *Lord, things were a mess,* he thought. Of course, there was no one to blame but himself. Therefore, it was up to him to set things right again. For him, nothing had changed. He still loved his wife beyond words and knew he would do anything to get her back. However, he was fully aware of how tense things were and realized he would have to approach the situation cautiously.

Trekel pushed his key into the double-bolt lock and stepped inside the house. Zakira had called him about a week after she'd left for New York and asked if he would check on the house. As soon as he opened the heavy door, the dark pools of his eyes narrowed. There were sounds coming from the kitchen. The smells that wafted in the air triggered his appetite instantly. For a moment, Tree wondered if he had gotten the dates for Zakira's trip wrong, but he knew that wasn't the case. No, someone had broken into the house and that someone had the nerve to be cooking!

Bracing himself for the inevitable confrontation, Tree slowly walked through the house. When he arrived in the kitchen and peeked inside, his mouth fell open.

"What's goin' on, man?" Malik greeted. He moved around the kitchen as though it were perfectly normal for him to be there.

"What in the hell are you doin'?" Tree bellowed. A thunderous frown settled over his face and he couldn't remember when he had been so stunned.

"Fixing breakfast. Want some?" Malik asked, his demeanor maddeningly cool.

"Man, you are playin' a dangerous game," Tree warned, pulling his navy suitcoat away from his wide shoulders.

Malik wasn't concerned. "I know what's what. I found out about Zaki's trip from the temp covering for Chanel at the restaurant. I still have my key, our neighbors are away and I introduced myself to their house sitter who thinks I'm doing the same."

Tree could only shake his head. Malik had certainly covered his bases. Still, he thought the whole thing was just too risky. "What if someone calls?" he asked.

"The machine picks it up. Stop worrying."

Tree walked farther into the kitchen and braced his large hands against the counter. "I take it this is all part of your plan."

Malik shook his head. His dreads were shorter now; they brushed his cheeks. "No, I just wanted to spend some time in my own home, you know?"

"So, you ready to be with your wife again?" Tree asked, watching his friend nod. "How will you manage that?" he asked, listening intently as Malik shared his plan. Afterward, he could only shake his head at the intricacy of it all.

* * *

New York had been home to Zakira for one month. She had been so busy finalizing the legalities with the building, arranging for the decorating, hiring staff and getting settled in her new home that time flew by. Although "free time" was practically a dream, Zakira had made the decision to get out more. Several men she'd met had asked her out. It was flattering to discover she still "had it" and she couldn't deny she wanted to use it.

Sadly, none of her new suitors could turn on the switch inside her. Malik Badu had been able to accomplish that with little more than a look in her direction. Zakira forced herself to push those thoughts aside and just enjoy the attention.

Edwina could easily imagine the mountain of work that awaited her when she arrived in the airport lobby. She'd taken Zakira up on an invite to New York and used the time to put her own life in perspective. It was past time to get back to her Richmond practice. Her week-long trip had been extended to two weeks and though it put her way behind, it had been very much worth it.

The trip had given Eddie time to think, and she realized that all she wanted was Tree. She felt like a heel whenever she thought of the way she'd handled things following his proposal. Cowardice forced her to return his ring by express mail of all things. But she'd been too terrified to talk to him—to tell him why. It still scared her to reveal her feelings. Her fear that things would fall apart between them had been at the root of it all. Of course now, it was a chance she would gladly take. She could only hope that once she was completely honest with Tree, he would forgive her.

Snapping back to reality, she discovered that her luggage was heading toward her on the conveyor belt. Moving a bit too slowly, she just missed grabbing her overnight case. Luckily, there was someone on hand to offer their assistance.

"Thank you so much," she whispered, taking the case from the large hand that offered it. When she looked up into Tree's unsettling dark eyes, she caught her breath.

"Hello," he greeted, his deep voice very soft.

"Tree" was all she could manage.

He smiled and offered a brief nod. "I'll be seeing you," he murmured.

Eddie watched him turn to leave. Her lovely hazel stare followed him longingly. "Tree, wait!"

Instantly, he turned, almost as though he had been hoping she would stop him. His onyx stare held an expectant gleam as he waited.

"If you're not on your way out of town, would you, uh—would you like to have lunch?" Eddie asked, preparing herself for his refusal.

"Yeah, that sounds good," he accepted in a cool voice that totally belied the surprise he felt.

Since Tree had his car at the airport, they took it to one of Eddie's favorite cafés. The small family-owned establishment was located around the neighborhood she grew up in.

"Eddie Harris!" a short, plump woman called out. Her sparkling brown eyes and lovely baby-doll face seemed to radiate with happiness.

Eddie laughed, rushing forward to hug the woman. "Miss Vanessa!"

"And where have you been, little girl?" Vanessa Holmes playfully admonished the daughter of one of her best friends.

Eddie pulled the kind, older woman close again and hugged her. "I'm sorry, time just got away from me, that's all."

"Well, don't you let it happen again," Vanessa ordered, her wide eyes drifting past Edwina to the tall, handsome man behind her. "And who's this?"

Tree stepped forward and extended his hand. "Trekel Grisani."

Vanessa savored the strong handshake. "My, my, you are a good-looking thing, aren't you?"

Tree laughed, his handsome face becoming more attractive as a small wave of embarrassment washed over him. "Thank you," he managed.

"Mmm, mmm, mmm," Vanessa gestured as she appraised Tree's impressive frame. "Eddie baby, you're forgiven. With this to take care of, I wouldn't want to get out that much either!"

Between Vanessa's outrageous comments and Tree blushing heavily from embarrassment, Eddie didn't think she could stand it. "Um, Ms. Vanessa, we're gonna go get a table, all right?" she announced, her voice shaky with laughter as she took Tree's hand and led him away.

At the booth, they pulled off their coats and got comfortable. When their eyes met, laughter burst forth.

"I'm so sorry," Eddie whispered, her face alive with humor. "Ms. Vanessa isn't always so bold with someone she's just met."

Tree waved his hand. "Don't apologize. Older women tend to have good taste, so I'm flattered."

"So, um, what were you doing at the airport?" Eddie asked, once the laughter had died down a bit.

"I went to see a client who lives in Boston," Tree explained.

"Mmm," Eddie responded, as she gazed at him dreamily. Anyone who watched them closely could have detected the strong emotion between them.

"So, where were you coming from?"

"Um, I was in New York with Zakira."

Tree's long dark brows rose. "How long?"

"A couple weeks."

"That long?"

Edwina sipped from the glass of water the waitress had just placed on the table. She only nodded in response.

"Well, how is she?" he asked, scanning the contents of the menu.

Eddie picked up her menu as well. "She's better. She's dating."

"That's good," Tree absently replied. After a moment, though, his deep midnight gaze lifted and he set the menu aside. "Did you say she was dating?"

"Yeah, against my advice."

Tree hid his emotions. "Why are you against it?"

Eddie shrugged. "Don't get me wrong, I want her to get out. I just don't want her to do it on the rebound. Malik is still so much a part of her life. Whether she admits it or not."

"Hmph."

Eddie toyed with the neckline of her peach blouse. "I don't know. Maybe it is good for her."

"Good for her?"

She sensed the edginess in Tree's words and looked up at him. From the set look on his face, it was obvious he was upset by the news. "Well, I think we can both agree that she's been closing herself off. Maybe she should live a little. I mean, it's not like her husband's coming back."

Despite his concern, Tree smiled. He decided he didn't want to waste another minute talking about anyone other than him and Edwina. "So, what's good here?" he asked.

Flashing him a dazzling smile, Eddie picked up her menu. "Everything."

"Well, I'm just hungry enough to try it all," he teased. "After we finish here, I can give you a ride home if you want."

Eddie's head popped up, and she instantly nodded her acceptance.

Tree leaned back in his seat, propping his index finger along his temple. "So what'd you do up in New York?"

Eddie cleared her throat and fidgeted in her chair beneath his unsettling dark gaze. "I, um, thought— thought about a lot of stuff."

"Like what?"

"Like us."

Tree's dark gaze lowered to the table. "What about us?"

"Tree, I'm sorry that I let things end the way they did. With no explanation."

He smirked. "It's okay. I kind of guessed you were turning down my proposal when I got my ring back in the mail."

Eddie's eyes closed, and she shook her head. "Oh, Tree, I'm so sorry. I should've told you what the real problem was long ago."

"So what was it?"

"Me."

A surprised expression crept over Tree's handsome face. "What about you?"

Eddie hesitated, a combination of nerves and shame threatening to overcome her. "This is so hard…I mean, you don't know how hard it is to have practically every relationship fail. I mean, the men I've dated haven't all been jerks. The relationships never worked out. It starts to affect your self-confidence after a while, you know?"

The surprise on Tree's face soon changed to one of disbelief. "How could your self-confidence be affected?" he asked, watching Edwina give him a blank stare. "Honey, you obviously don't know how gorgeous and sexy you are. Not to mention smart and caring. You don't find combinations like that every day. Maybe all the guys you dated in the past weren't jerks, but they sure as hell were stupid."

Edwina lowered her hazel gaze to the table. "Thanks," she whispered.

"It's the truth."

"I just don't think I could handle it if we didn't work out."

Tree's deep dimples appeared as he grinned. "I don't think I could handle it either, love," he admitted. "Eddie, I can't promise anything, but I'll try like hell to keep you with me."

The phone began to ring the moment Malik stepped out of the bathroom. He had been taking a shower, cleaning up after a strenuous workout. The phone rarely rang during the time he'd been back at the house. Everyone was more or less aware that Zakira was away.

"Hi, Zakira, this is Sherry Davis." The woman's bright voice filled the room when the machine picked up.

Malik recognized their friend's voice and sat on the bed to listen.

"I got your invitation to the opening. I didn't even know you were working on another Badu's. Anyway, I see here that the date is October 20 in New York and I'm not sure if we'll be able to make it, but we'll sure try. Give me a call as soon as you can and we'll talk."

The message ended and Malik flashed a smug grin. The news was indeed interesting since Tree had yet to inform him about the opening. Already the wheels were turning as he began to adjust his plan.

The quiet swoosh of the elevator doors closing reassured Edwina. She shut her eyes, leaned back against the paneled walls and urged herself to go through with her decision. Her relationship with Trekel Grisani had gone from wonderful to even more wonderful during the two weeks since she'd returned to Richmond. They hadn't been together physically, and it was obvious to Edwina that he was trying to move slowly. It had made her love him more, but she was tired of the distance. She could only hope that when she spoke with him, she wouldn't scare him away.

It was late afternoon and the business wing of Tree's penthouse was deserted. With the exception of the soft, constant hum of office equipment, the place was silent. Still, she decided to try there first, since he might be working late.

Eddie found the office door cracked open and she peeked inside. Tree was leaning back in a huge swivel chair with his long legs propped on the desk. He seemed completely at ease as his head rested back against the suede chair. One hand covered his eyes.

Edwina's hazel gaze narrowed as she smiled. She could have watched him forever. Clearing her throat, she stepped into the office. "You look like you need to be in bed," she softly advised.

A devastating grin tugged at Tree's gorgeous mouth when he recognized Eddie's voice. "Bed isn't much fun these days," he confided without moving his hand from his eyes.

"I know what you mean," Eddie coolly replied, though her heart raced at the suggestive comment.

"Do you?" he asked, finally removing his hand. "Well, you're the sex therapist. What advice can you give me?" he teased.

Eddie smiled, then closed her eyes and begged for self-control. As much as she wanted him, she couldn't veer from her task. She cleared her throat again and walked into the office, closing the door behind her. "Tree, I need to ask you something."

The smoldering dark gaze narrowed, but Tree remained silent. He spread his hands and urged her to continue.

"May I please have my ring back?" Eddie asked simply, sweetly.

The narrowed gaze widened momentarily, before it dropped. Then, slowly, he moved his legs off the desk and pulled open a side drawer. He extracted a tiny green velvet box.

Edwina's sparkling gaze widened the moment she saw the box and she came forward. Standing behind the desk, she reached for the small piece of jewelry. Before she could touch it, Tree grabbed her hand and tugged her onto his lap. One of his large hands curled around her neck in a gentle hold. He held her in place for his kiss. Eddie moaned beneath the sharp thrusts of his tongue and returned the kiss. While the kiss became more heated, Tree pushed the ring back onto Eddie's finger. She gasped and he thrust his tongue deeper, as though he were starved for her.

Eddie moaned her disappointment when Tree broke the kiss. Her head fell back when she felt his hand beneath the raised hemline of her suede skirt.

"When?" he asked, his voice a raspy whisper.

"As soon as possible," Eddie replied instantly.

* * *

"Yes!" Zakira whispered, happier than she'd been in a long time. She stood in the middle of the room and hugged herself. A sense of accomplishment and power overcame her.

Badu's N.Y. was finally complete and ready to open for business.

She couldn't wait for the big night. Her only regret was that Malik wouldn't be there to witness his business move to the next level. Closing her eyes for a moment, she let herself envision her intense, handsome husband. She conjured images of them in each other's arms— something she had strictly forbidden herself to do.

Chapter 12

Zakira closed her eyes and snuggled deeper into the lounge chair while relishing the moments of solitude. She knew she wanted to be well rested and dazzling for the restaurant's opening.

The white cordless phone resting next to her on a small glass table began to ring. After a few moments, Zakira leaned over and picked it up. "Yes?"

"Z, it's Eddie."

"Hey, girl, what's up?"

"I just wanted to let you know we'll be there Saturday."

Zakira frowned and pushed herself up higher on the cushioned lounge. "You're coming up Saturday?"

"Yeah, I know it's the day of the opening, but we'll be there in plenty of time," Edwina assured her sister.

"I hope so, because I really need to talk to Tree."

This time, it was Edwina who frowned. "Why?"

Zakira sighed and shook her head. "I've just been having these strange feelings lately. I think I may've overlooked something…I don't know…some legality."

"Z, girl you're not making any sense."

"I know. That's why I need to talk to Tree. Eddie, Malik's been on my mind a lot lately."

"Well, honey, that's to be expected since you are opening another restaurant that bears his name."

Zakira pushed herself off the lounge, and shoved one hand into the back pocket of her denim jumper. "It's not only the restaurant. I just have a feeling he's…"

"What?" Eddie coaxed.

"Nothing. I don't know. Something just doesn't feel right."

"Z! This place is incredible!" Eddie practically screamed that Saturday as she hugged Zakira tightly.

Laughing, Zakira embraced Eddie just as tightly. "Well, it *is* a warehouse," she reminded her sister. Pulling away, she went to Tree, who held his arms apart for her. "I'm so glad you're here," she whispered.

Tree held her close and pressed a kiss to the top of her head. "You knew I wouldn't miss this," he said before looking around again. "Doc's right, this place is incredible."

"You think Malik would approve? You know how picky he always…was," Zakira asked, her wide brown eyes shimmering just a bit as she thought of her husband.

Eddie pulled her sister close as Tree squeezed

Zakira's hand. "I know he would," Tree assured her his expression tightening when one of Zakira's many male admirers whisked her away to the dance floor.

The abundance of space was not a problem. Badu's N.Y. was filled with hundreds of well-wishers, old and new friends and acquaintances. Everyone was on hand to show their support and promise their patronage. Since Zakira knew the night would determine the success of the business, she had decided to have every item on the menu prepared. There were soul food dishes, as well as African and Caribbean cuisine.

After making a few rounds to the various well-wishers in the room, Zakira ventured out to the terrace. Several small, round dining tables filled the area. At the moment, they were unoccupied. Relishing the solitude, Zakira took a few deep breaths and thought about Malik. She wished with all her heart that he could have been there with her. If only he were there now, they could have been sharing everything…together…

With a slight shake of her head, Zakira smoothed her hands over the short, black spaghetti-strapped cocktail dress. She went back into the party and found Tree at the bar.

"Do you mind telling me what your problem is?" She asked, after taking a seat on the stool closest to him at the long, mahogany bar.

Tree set his glass down and turned. "My problem?"

"It's obvious you're not in the best mood. What is it?"

Tree closed his eyes. "I'm good. I guess the place has me missing him too, you know?"

Zakira smiled then massaged his shoulder. "Yeah, I know…" she trailed away, drawing him into a hug as she spoke.

They shared a few moments of silence, until once again Zakira was escorted away by another male acquaintance.

Tree's guarded glare followed Zakira and her new dance partner. Slowly, his eyes moved past them to drift over the crowd. When he spotted a familiar face amid the swarm of people, he groaned.

"I feel like I've been dancing with you all night," Zakira said with a laugh, her wide brown eyes sparkling with happiness.

Michael Renner, the real estate broker, tugged her close. "Complaints?"

"Not one," she assured him, smoothing her hand across his cheek.

"Zaki?"

Zakira laughed again at the funny face Michael made before she turned in the direction from which her name had been called.

"Yes?" She lightly replied. Suddenly her wide smile froze.

"Zakira?" Michael whispered.

Zakira was past hearing anything. Her cocoa stare was focused on the man standing less than a foot away from her. Suddenly, she began to shake her head and back away. The expression in her gaze was fearful as she looked up and down at Malik Badu's tall, leanly muscled body.

Malik remained motionless for a long while. He let

himself enjoy the sight of her so close. When she began to back away from him, he took a step toward her. "Zaki?" he whispered.

Hearing Malik use his nickname for her, was Zakira's undoing. Her lashes fluttered close and she fainted into Michael's arms.

A couple standing nearby was the first to witness the scene. The woman cried out and alerted everyone to what was happening. The music stopped as several people rushed to that side of the room.

Michael held Zakira in a protective embrace and softly called her name. In an instant, though, Malik had knelt beside him and was taking Zakira out of his arms.

"Hold it," Michael warned, his grip tightening slightly on Zakira. "Who the hell are you?"

Malik, in no mood for questions, pulled Zakira into his arms as he stood. "I'm her husband," he announced, the tone of his deep voice brooking no argument.

Onlookers watched in amazement as the tall, intense-looking stranger left with their hostess.

Leaving the crowd behind, Malik took the stairway just off the entrance. He had already taken time to privately tour the new restaurant and knew where the office was located. Although he never expected Zakira to faint when she saw him, he was grateful for the chance to hold her in his arms.

Malik glanced over his shoulder and said a silent prayer of thanks that no one had followed them. The office door was cracked open and he nudged one wide shoulder against it and stepped inside. After kicking the door shut, he carried Zakira to the tan suede sofa in the corner of the room.

Gently, Malik set his wife down, but not before he pressed his lips against her hair. His unnerving black and gray stare traveled over her smooth dark skin as he followed the path with his fingers. Zakira shivered slightly, but did not awaken. Not wanting to disturb her further, Malik pulled off his black tuxedo jacket and placed it over her. For the next ten minutes, he simply watched her.

The pattern of Zakira's breathing changed as she slowly came out of her unconscious state. She frowned and tossed her head from side to side on the arm of the sofa.

"Zaki?" Malik called softly, tracing the line of her brow.

Finally, her lashes fluttered open and she took a moment to focus on the large figure that loomed above her. Slowly his handsome dark face came into view.

"Malik?" Zakira said, her voice barely a whisper. Raising her hand, she caressed his smooth cheek. When he turned his face into her palm and kissed it, she gasped.

Bolting upright on the sofa, her eyes widened as she stared at him. "Who are you?" she demanded.

Malik brushed her chin with his thumb. "You know who I am, Zaki," he softly but firmly assured her. He didn't attempt to offer any other calming words for he could only imagine how shocked she was.

"You're supposed to be…to be dying or…dead. What are you doing here? Why are you doin' this? Who sent you?" Zakira's voice was hushed, but her words were frantic. Her eyes were blurry with tears, but she didn't dare blink.

Malik inched closer to her on the sofa. His fingers toyed with the hemline of her dress as he watched her. "Baby, you had to think I was gone. I didn't know if I was going to make it. I—I couldn't have you waiting and…worrying about me that way. As far as I was concerned, my life was over."

Malik grew silent, allowing Zakira time to absorb everything he had said. The fingers curled around her dress, slid under the hem to trail her thigh with possessive intensity.

Zakira's lashes fluttered closed against the caress and she leaned forward. "Malik…" she groaned.

Malik could no longer wait to have her in his arms, and he pulled her small form against him. Cupping one large hand around her neck, he kissed her deeply.

Zakira felt a rush of moisture in her most intimate region. Malik's tongue assaulted the sweet, dark cavern of her mouth with slow, rapacious strokes. Zakira returned the action, gasping when he moaned in response.

Even after all the time apart, the passion was there. Their hands trailed each other's bodies with feverish intensity. They tried to rediscover what had existed in their memories for so long. Malik knew he was starved for Zakira, but he had no idea his need would be so potent. He uttered a purely savage sound and pulled her to sit astride his lap.

Zakira threw her head back as her thighs contracted around his waist. The powerful bulge of his manhood seemed far more defined than she remembered. When Malik pushed the straps away from her shoulders and buried his head between her breasts, she snapped to reality.

What am I doing? She couldn't allow this to happen, no matter how much she wanted him.

"What?" he asked, his breathing heavy and deep.

Her eyes narrowed as suspicion filled her eyes. "What are you doing here?"

Malik grinned, leaning back against the sofa as he tapped the side of Zakira's thigh. "You asked me that already."

She placed her hand over his to stop the unnerving caress. "What are you doing here *now,* after all this time?"

The grin faded from Malik's handsome face. "Think I've been gone long enough, don't you?"

"Mmm…definitely. It has been a while. Why now?"

"Zaki, I already told you—"

"You haven't told me a damn thing!"

"What do you want me to say?"

"I want an explanation for what you saw fit to put me through. I've been through hell, Malik. I'm finally getting it together and now you want to come back!"

Malik's dark eyes spewed daggers as a sinister frown clouded his face. "So, I guess my coming back is an inconvenience to you?"

"That's not the word I would use."

"Sure it is. I guess that fool I saw you hangin' all over is your new…whatever?" Malik suggested, in a nasty tone.

Zakira landed a cracking slap to the side of his face and pushed herself off his lap. "You black bastard. You're the one who just up and left. Flat out lied to me, kept me in the dark about what was really going on. And now you're going to sit there and make me feel guilty about getting my life together?"

Malik appeared to be cool as he lounged on the sofa, but his temper was raging inside. "I'm trying to get my life together too, Zaki. I want my life back."

"It's obvious you already have your life back," she coldly pointed out. "My God, you wanted to divorce me!"

"There were reasons, dammit. You know that!" Malik snapped.

Zakira rolled her eyes and turned her back on him. "Save it," she mumbled. It was killing her to know Malik had been getting his life back on track all the time she had been going crazy mourning him.

"You're still my wife, Zaki," he reminded her.

"And?" she retorted. "That's only because I begged Tree to stall with the divorce. Thankfully he didn't pressure me about it or we wouldn't even have a marriage between us. I just want to know what you expect from me."

"I expect you to act like we have a marriage between us," Malik declared as he stood from the sofa.

"You know, it's been so long I've forgotten what that means. If you think we can just pick up where we left off, forget it."

Malik pushed a large hand through his dreads and squeezed his eyes shut. "Will it be this way all night, Zaki?"

"Are you kidding me? You're lucky I don't throw your ass out of here!" Zakira raged. "Who the hell do you think you are, barging in on my life after all this time? You didn't even have enough respect for me to keep in touch, let me know what was going on or at least check to see if I was all right!"

"I knew every move you made!" Malik bellowed. "Tree told me everything that was going on here."

Zakira shook her head. Overwhelmed with hurt, anger and frustration, she lunged forward. Her small fists pounded his neck and chest. He braced himself against the blows, which bruised his emotions more than his body.

Edwina and Tree were waiting patiently outside the office. Tree had told her only that Malik was alive, leaving out the details of his own involvement. Edwina was speechless, absorbing all that had happened. It wasn't until they heard voices raised in anger and the commotion that followed that they intervened.

"Z!" Eddie called, when she and Tree rushed into the room. She reached her stepsister and pulled her away from Malik.

"I hate you!" Zakira shouted, her eyes red from crying. She struggled to break free of Eddie's embrace.

"Z, please," Eddie whispered, raising her eyes across the room toward Malik. "Honey, come on now. You need to calm down," she urged, pulling Zakira toward the door.

"You may as well go back to wherever you were," Zakira advised, her voice hoarse and surprisingly calm, "because you'll never get your hands on me or the business. Never."

A flash of something uneasy rose in Malik's dark eyes. The dark promise hung in the air like a storm cloud.

* * *

Eddie sat the mug of hot tea on the dining table and rubbed her hands together. "I still can't believe it. Are you sure that was really Malik?"

"I'm sure."

"Well, where's he been all this time?"

"Maybe you should ask your fiancé."

Eddie's eyes narrowed. "What does Tree know about it?"

Leaning against the kitchen countertop, Zakira folded her hands across her chest. "I'd say he knows a lot, since Malik has been keeping tabs on me through him."

Edwina shook her head. "Tree wouldn't…he wouldn't put you through this."

"Yes he would, Eddie," Zakira hotly corrected. "He'd do anything for Malik."

Zakira was in a terrible state and Eddie was in no condition to help. She couldn't believe Tree could be so cold, so…dishonest. Especially when he'd come down so hard on her before about not being honest with her feelings.

"Honey, I'm sorry. I didn't mean to bring you down with me."

Eddie glanced over at Zakira and smiled at her kind words. "I had to find out sooner or later. Tree never would have told me."

Zakira shrugged. "He probably would've said it was for your own good that you not know. That's the way Malik feels. It justifies his whole outlook on the situation. God, I feel so stupid!"

Eddie closed her eyes and nodded. She felt exactly the same.

* * *

"Of all the…damn crap you've pulled and I've been foolish enough to go along with, man, this has got to be the most idiotic—"

"Tree—"

"What?!"

Malik closed his eyes and massaged the back of his neck. "It's done, so we don't need to be going through this. I can't change what's already happened."

Tree braced his hands on the desk. They hadn't left the restaurant and were still in the manager's office. "Eddie probably hates me now," he groaned, his midnight eyes narrowed in anger.

"I'm sorry about that, man."

"Are you?" Tree asked, turning around to face him. "You know, Malik, if we hadn't been through so much together, I could probably hate you for this."

"I couldn't blame you," Malik told him, shoving his hands through his dreadlocks.

Tree brought two fingers to his temple and massaged the ache there. "So, uh, what are your plans now?"

Malik let out a long breath. "I just need her back, Tree."

"That's not gonna be easy."

A little smirk pulled at Malik's mouth. "I am the one she was in here beating up."

Tree shrugged. "She's gotten real tough…and real bitter."

"I'm not worried about that." Malik sighed, waving his hand.

"Well, how are you gonna play this?"

"I'm gonna match her." Malik decided. "I won't back down or quit."

Tree nodded and smoothed his hand across his wavy, black hair. "Plan on wearing down her defenses?"

"Tree, man, I think it's the only way I'll be able to get her to listen to me."

"So where are you going now?" Tree asked, watching Malik grab his jacket and head for the door.

Hand poised over the brass doorknob, Malik sent his friend a devilish smile. "I'm going to spend the night with my wife."

Eddie hated leaving Zakira after all that happened. Unfortunately, her sister's mood was too unbearable. Once she drifted off to sleep, Eddie left. It was quite late when she got back to the hotel. Not wanting to disturb Tree, who was probably asleep, she crept around the suite, shrugging out of her dress, shoes and hose. She was about to tiptoe into the bedroom when one of the living room lamps clicked on.

"Where have you been?"

Eddie shrieked as her hazel eyes slowly adjusted to the light. She saw Tree glaring at her from an armchair in the corner of the room.

"Where have you been?" he repeated, pushing his large frame out of the chair.

"I was…with Zakira," she finally told him.

Tree walked closer to Eddie, the deep frown etched on his handsome face slowly vanishing. "I figured if you were there, you would've spent the night."

"Oh, I wanted to," Eddie quickly assured him, walking into the bedroom to hang her dress. "But she's in such an evil mood, I thought she would prefer being alone."

Tree ran a large hand across his face and leaned against the dresser. "I guess she'll be that way for a while."

"Yeah, thanks to you."

Tree's smoldering dark gaze narrowed. "What did you say?"

Eddie finished with her dress and turned to face him. "I said, 'Thanks to you.'"

"What's that supposed to mean?" Tree pushed himself off the dresser.

Eddie propped a hand on her hip. "You know damn well what it means!"

"Maybe you better explain it to me," he requested, his voice raspy with anger and frustration.

"Tree, you didn't tell her where Malik was when you knew the entire time. How could you do that? How could you be so cold, so—"

"I had a job to do!"

"Oh, yeah, that's so convenient. Client loyalty. You could've refused, you know?"

The sinister glare on Tree's magnificent features belied the strong emotions coursing through him. Eddie, standing across the room wearing a skimpy, green lace bra and matching panties, both aroused and angered him. He had to shut his eyes against the sensuous image she cast. "Doc, if you think I could turn my back on Malik, you're crazy. We been through so much together. You can't even imagine."

"And that makes it okay to put Zakira through something so terrible when you had the power to stop it?"

Tree clenched his hand into a large fist, wanting very badly to vent his frustration by hitting something. Preferably Malik. Instead, he decided to drown his sorrows in a glass of something strong and headed to the door. "I need to get out of here," he mumbled, and stormed past Edwina.

The thick, navy blue comforter and matching satin sheets were tangled across the bed. Zakira had been tossing and turning since she drifted off to sleep an hour earlier.

Finally, her eyes snapped open and she sat up. She groaned and pulled her slender fingers through her tousled mane. Lord, how could things be so stable one minute and totally unglued the next? That morning, all she could think about was beginning a new chapter in her life with the business and…other things. Now, all she could think of was Malik.

When she turned and saw him standing there at the party, she had wanted to scream and run into his arms. He looked so good, so fine…so sexy. It was as though the time without him had never happened…well, almost. When he kissed her, it felt as though her insides had turned into a heavy syrup. She was completely weakened by need. All she wanted him to do was make love to her.

With a sigh, Zakira shook her head and decided to get up. A hot cup of milk would be just the thing to get her back to sleep. Without bothering to turn on the lights, she walked out of the bedroom and headed for the stairs. Over the past couple months, the sounds of New York had grown vaguely comforting. Unfortunately, tonight was no ordinary night.

Zakira reached the bottom of the carpeted staircase

and was about to leave the last step when she bumped into something or someone. Her small hands rose instantly and she found herself touching a solid wall of muscle. Instinct told her it was Malik.

Zakira pulled away, as though he burned to touch. "How'd you get in here?"

A deep dimple creased Malik's cheek when he favored her with a roguish smile. "That's my secret," he teased.

Zakira was not amused. "Yeah, you're good at keeping those, aren't you?" she noted, almost falling when he joined her on the bottom step. His hands closed around her hips and he held her to him.

"Let go," she insisted, pushing against his chest.

Instead, Malik tightened his grip and lowered his mouth to the side of her neck. "Where are you going?" he murmured.

Zakira closed her eyes and prayed for the strength to resist him. "To the kitchen...for some milk."

A wicked grin tugged at the seductive curve of Malik's mouth. His hands tightened a bit more around her hips as he towered over her. "You won't be needing it, Zaki," he assured, lifting her. He took the stairs two at a time.

Instantly, Zakira began to struggle. Her hands were curled into fists and she pounded Malik's chest and back. She fought him all the way to the bedroom. Surprisingly, Malik went directly to the room as though he had been there before. Zakira grasped the lapels of his heavy tan leather jacket when he let her go. As soon as her bare feet touched the carpet, she moved to get past him. He blocked her way. When she tried going around him on the opposite side, he blocked that path, as well.

Frustrated beyond words, Zakira raised her stormy brown eyes to his face. Determined to wipe the smug grin from his face, she laid a cracking slap against his cheek.

The grin disappeared, but Malik was far from discouraged. His unsettling gray stare narrowed and he jerked her against him. She gasped, allowing him the access he wanted. His head dipped and he pushed his tongue deep inside her mouth.

"Mmm…" they both groaned amidst the hard, passionate kiss. Once Malik released her, however, Zakira slapped him again. In response, he pulled her close to punish her with another fiery kiss.

Zakira was weakened by the desire she felt for her husband. Still, she refused to give in so easily. When he released her lips, she poised her hand for yet another blow.

Easily anticipating her next move, Malik brought her hand to his chest. "Stop fighting me," he whispered against her mouth, his tongue tracing the outline of her lips.

Zakira's long lashes fluttered closed and she practically melted in Malik's embrace. Her lips parted, allowing him entrance to the dark cavern of her mouth. A shiver ran deep through her body and almost caused her legs to buckle beneath her. "Malik, please don't do this to me," she begged, knowing that if he wouldn't stop, she couldn't.

"Baby, don't ask me that," he groaned, his fingers already going to the ties of the nightie she wore and tugging them loose. He brushed the silky material from her shoulders and eased the gown down past her breasts. It fell away to pool around her feet.

Zakira cried out softly when Malik lifted her against

him and she felt the cool leather next to her bare skin. He carried her to the tangled bed and lowered her to the middle.

For a moment, his gaze simply trailed her body. From her face, his eyes dropped to her chest where he reacquainted himself with the curve and tone of her bosom. His heated gaze was so intense, Zakira became aroused by it.

One finger reached out to trace the shape of her breasts. It dropped into the valley between them and trailed to her navel. Zakira's lashes fluttered madly as she arched her body into the caress.

Malik's own eyes closed when Zakira caught his finger and guided it to the center of her body. He caressed her there gently, his head falling to her chest when he discovered how moist she was.

Zakira's hips began to move erotically. Each stroke of Malik's fingers brought another moan from her mouth.

"Don't stop," she softly ordered, gasping at the friction of his dreadlocks against her skin.

Malik buried his face between her breasts and inhaled their soft scent. His fingers probed deeper as his lips closed around one firm nipple. His eyes were shut tightly as he savored the taste of her after so long. His tongue swirled around the hard peak, and he suckled as though he were starved.

Zakira, needing to feel his bare skin next to hers, tried to push the jacket from his back. After a moment, Malik cooperated, jerking the coat from his broad shoulders and pulling the stylish fleece sweatshirt over his head. Zakira's eyes widened as she took in the sleek, dark chiseled chest. A soft smile touched her lips as her fingers reached out to trace the unyielding surface.

Malik caught her fingers and kissed them gently. When he let go of her hand, she grasped the waistband of his jeans and tugged.

"Zakira…"

"Malik, please…"

Though he wanted the night to last as long as possible, overwhelming desire wouldn't allow him to hold out. He pushed himself off the bed and unbuckled his belt in order to unfasten his jeans.

Zakira watched, loving the way the jeans and boxers fell away to reveal his lean waist, tight buttocks and impressive masculinity. She pushed herself up and kneeled at the edge of the bed.

Malik threaded his fingers through her thick hair and pulled her head back for a deep kiss. Moaning, Zakira slid her arms around his waist, her long nails raking his wide back. The next moment, he was pushing her to the bed and following her down.

They both moaned when their naked bodies touched for the first time in so long. Malik's hands were everywhere, his lips favoring Zakira's body with thousands of tiny, wet kisses. Her embrace was tight. She never wanted him to stop.

Malik was aroused to such a fevered state, it almost drove him mad. His large hands grasped Zakira's thighs and held them apart as he plunged his throbbing maleness deep within her.

A wild cry flew from Zakira's throat when she felt the rigid length stroking her repeatedly, unrelentingly.

The fact that Malik was actually there, making love to her, brought tears to her eyes.

Malik's head was buried in the soft crook of her neck. The satisfied grin on his face reflected the happiness surging through him. None of the thousands of fantasies he'd had about Zakira came close to the true feel of her at that very moment.

The red numbers on the bedside clock read 3:00 a.m. when Malik awoke. The lazy smile on his handsome face faded when he discovered Zakira wasn't next to him. Whipping back the bed covers, he left the room to look for her.

Downstairs, he found her sitting on a cushiony chair that faced the huge bay windows in the living room. She was staring solemnly at the fantastic view of the New York City skyline.

Malik leaned against the doorjamb and watched his wife for a moment. He wasn't completely clueless and he could only imagine how unbearable the situation had been for her. Discovering her supposedly dying husband was alive and well, having a vicious fight with him and making love with him all in the same night…she must be frustrated beyond words. Malik knew he had made a terrible decision, handling his illness the way he had, but that was going to be corrected. He couldn't allow anything to stop him.

Zakira's slender fingers curled into the chair when she felt Malik's lips brush her neck. She braced herself against the rush of sensation pulsing through her body.

Malik didn't seem to notice and continued bathing

the satiny smooth column of her neck with his kisses. He was instantly aroused and needed to feel Zakira beneath him. When she pulled away and moved to the sofa, he frowned. "What's wrong?"

It was Zakira's turn to frown. "Surely you didn't just ask me that?"

Malik shrugged and crossed his arms over his chest. He stood there totally confident, though he wore not a stitch of clothing. "I don't get it. We just finished having some damn good sex and the last thing I'd expect is for you to pull away from me."

"So you expect things to be the same, just like that?" she challenged, her brown eyes wide and searching.

"Why can't it be?" Malik countered, walking closer to her. "Unless you're seeing somebody else?" He stopped before her.

Zakira couldn't stop her eyes from dropping past Malik's waist. She caught herself staring and shook her head. "There's no one serious."

Malik shrugged, even though a knowing smirk touched his mouth.

"That's only because I've been so concerned with the business. Believe me, I had no qualms about moving on with my life in every way," she assured him, hoping she sounded convincing.

Malik leaned over her on the sofa. "Sure you were," he sarcastically replied, pushing her back against the cushions. His strong, athletic form covered hers as he nibbled on the sensitive skin below her earlobe. "Well, you won't need to be so concerned with business now that I'm back," he murmured.

Zakira's brown eyes snapped to his face. She pushed Malik away with a strength she didn't know she had and get up from the sofa. She turned in the direction of the stairway. Before leaving, she delivered a parting shot. "You've proven how little you cared for me and, as for the business, you proved how little you cared for it when you dumped it in my lap. I'll be damned if I just hand it over to you now."

Malik reclined on the sofa and watched Zakira switch upstairs. His dark eyes appraised her and had to admit how tough his wife had become. He definitely had his work cut out for him.

Zakira left for the restaurant early the next morning. There was no need for her to be there at such an hour, but she couldn't be around Malik a moment longer. Even after all the drama the night before and everything preceeding that, she couldn't deny that she desperately wanted him. If she stayed home any longer, she had no doubt they would make love again.

"No!" she blurted, bracing her elbows on the desk as she held her head in her hands. "No, I'm ready to move on with my life and leave him behind," she vowed, but realized it was far from true.

The annoying buzz of the phone intruded on her thoughts. She uttered a short prayer that it not be Malik on the other end of the line.

"Zakira Badu," she curtly answered.

"Zakira, this is Mallory Harper. Food editor for *The Times*."

Zakira blinked and leaned back in her chair. "Yes? Yes, Ms. Harper. What can I do for you?"

"Well, I wanted to discuss coming in to do a write-up for my column. I'd like to do a review of Badu's before the end of the month."

Zakira was already scanning her calendar. "When did you want to do this?"

"Well, suppose I leave that up to you." Mallory said, her voice softening. "After what happened at the opening, I wasn't sure what your plans were."

"The opening?" Zakira replied, a small frown beginning to form.

"I was there last night. You seemed pretty preoccupied, but I guess that's putting it mildly."

"Very mildly," Zakira sighed, choosing not to skirt the issue. "My husband would pick last night to decide to surprise me."

"I'd heard he has cancer."

Zakira managed a nod, her eyes closing. "I'm happy to say he's recovered."

"Oh, that's wonderful news! I can see why he wanted to surprise you."

"Yes," Zakira replied, her tone revealing nothing.

Mallory cleared her throat. "So, what would be a good time for me to come in to interview you?"

Zakira suggested a few dates, but assured Mallory that any time was fine for the review.

After the call, Zakira buried her face in her hands and prayed she would survive. As if on cue, the office door flew open and Malik stormed into the room.

"You could've told me you were leaving, Zaki. I searched all over that house for you."

Zakira was instantly on the defensive. "I hope you

don't expect me to answer to you? Inform you of all my comings and goings? I didn't do that before you left and I'm not about to start now."

Malik massaged the back of his neck. "Didn't you think I'd want to be here, too?"

"Well, you're here now, aren't you?"

"Zaki, we won't get anywhere like this."

Zakira stood and pounded her fist to the desk. "Get anywhere? Where are we going, Malik? You seem to love traveling on your own."

Malik smiled, realizing that now he even relished their arguments. He strolled a bit closer to the desk. "No matter how much you hate to admit it, this place is mine too. I want to know what's going on."

Zakira stepped from behind the desk. "What's going on? What's going on is that since you've been gone, I have expanded this business. While it's too soon to boast my success, I feel good about it. What's going on is that you have done this despicable thing and now you come back expecting everything to be the same."

"Zaki—"

"Excuse me, Mrs. Badu?"

Zakira and Malik looked to the door of the office to see the restaurant manager.

"I'm sorry, I heard voices and—"

"That's all right," Zakira assured the tall, stout, honey-complexioned young man. "Justin Flowers, Malik Badu. Malik, Justin is the restaurant's manager."

Malik offered his hand. "Good to meet you, man."

Jason quickly obliged. "Same here, Mr. Badu. You got everybody around this place talking already."

"I can imagine," Malik acknowledged with a dimpled grin.

"Mrs. Badu, should I tell the rest of the staff to expect introductions today?"

"Yes, Justin, that sounds good. We'll get started as soon as we finish up in here."

"Great," Justin said, reaching over to shake hands with Malik again. "It was a pleasure."

Malik smiled before turning back to Zakira. He was impressed by how quickly she switched into business mode.

Zakira was eager to leave their conversation behind and introducing her husband to their staff seemed to be a good way of doing that. That is, until Malik began to charm everyone. When they arrived in the kitchen, he took an even greater interest. Malik was so involved with the chefs that Zakira was able to slip away without him noticing.

Later, Malik returned to the office. He couldn't deny how impressed he was with everything. And he couldn't believe how much Zakira had accomplished in such a short time.

"Well, yes considering we just opened our doors, I feel very flattered that the directors are interested in dining here. I'll connect you with our manager and he'll assist you with the reservations. We'll see you soon." Zakira said, then set the receiver down and took a seat on the edge of her desk.

Malik pushed himself from against the doorjamb where he had been watching. The ease with which she handled the caller raised his eyebrows and aroused a few other emotions. This was a new facet of her character, and it was a part of her that he wanted to know.

"That sounded important," he noted, strolling into the office with his hands hidden in the deep pockets of his saggy jeans.

Zakira smiled and offered a little shrug. "It was very important. It seems the directors from the housing committee of this district want to have dinner here the night after Thanksgiving."

Malik uttered a soft whistle. "Damn, our name has already reached the city officials? I'd like the chance to meet them."

Zakira's easy expression faded. "Well, I hope so, since you were the first person Debbie mentioned when she called. It seems your unexpected appearance last night has made you a hot commodity." She smoothed the short flaring cream skirt beneath her as she took a seat behind the desk. "Makes it very easy for you to resume control of the business."

"That's not why I did this, Zaki," Malik said, the heavy dreads brushing his cheeks when he shook his head. "The only thing on my mind was you. Us."

Zakira patted the thick braid that snaked around her head. "That's not the impression I got this morning. You seemed very eager to have me take a backseat."

Malik grinned in spite of himself. "Let's say I was reacting to what you said…about moving on with your life."

"Now I get it," Zakira whispered, her smoky brown eyes narrowing slightly. "You want to have your cake and eat it, too. First, you want a divorce so I can move on. Now, you're upset because I'm trying to do it."

"Dammit, Zaki, how many times do I have to tell you, I did that because I didn't know if I was gonna live or die? I didn't want you hanging on."

"You know what, Malik? You're so busy trying to get me to understand why you did this that you can't understand what it did to me. It's like you expect me to bow down and be grateful you're here, everything else be damned."

Malik's features were twisted into a fierce frown. "Does that mean you want things the way they were before I came back?"

"Ugggggh!" Zakira raged, her hands curling into tiny fists. "You were right when you said we're not going to get anywhere like this, so let's just end this conversation right now."

"That's the best thing I've heard today," Malik snapped before he stormed out of the office.

"Mr. Badu?"

Malik was on his way out of the restaurant after the argument with Zakira. When he heard his name, he stopped and turned toward the kitchen. "Didn't I tell y'all to call me Malik?" he teased, recognizing one of the chefs he's met earlier that day.

"Are you leaving?" Kenneth Diamond asked.

Malik massaged his jaw and glanced toward the stairway. "Yeah, I think I'm done here for the day."

Kenneth motioned behind him. "Do you have a few minutes? We want to pick your brain about some of these dishes."

"Got a menu?" Malik asked, already forgetting his aggravation.

Kenneth obliged and led the way into the kitchen. Malik spoke to the other five chefs, but his attention was more focused on the menu selections.

"Something wrong, man?" Rory Davis asked, noticing Malik's frown as he scanned the booklet.

Malik ran a hand through his dreads and shook his head. "This menu is the same as our Richmond restaurant," he noted.

"That a problem?" someone asked.

Malik laid the menu flat on the chrome counter and shrugged. "Well, not really. But a new restaurant should have a new menu. A menu is practically the voice of the restaurant, in my opinion."

"Well, what would you suggest?" Sheila Jeffries asked.

Malik tapped one finger to his chin and debated. "Got an apron?"

Zakira was on her way out when Michael Renner arrived in the lobby. Malik was leaving the kitchen when he spotted the man who wanted to become a more permanent part of his wife's life. Zakira stopped on the stairway and waited to see what would happen. She couldn't have been more surprised. The two men shook hands, and then a wave of silence settled between them.

"I, um, for what it's worth, I want to apologize for last night," Malik said, his expression sincere. "You've got nothing to do with all this drama."

Michael waved his hand. "Please, man, I know I was the last person you or Zakira were thinking about last night."

Malik gave a slow nod. "Well, I want to thank you

for helping her with all the red tape for the warehouse and for being such a good friend to her."

"It's easy to be good to such an angel," Mike said with a shrug.

"I agree," Malik added.

Mike stepped forward then. "Listen man, I know I'm probably out of line for asking this—"

"Please," Malik urged.

"How could you leave her like that? I mean, shouldn't you have wanted to spend as much time with her as possible? Especially when it looked like the end was near?"

Malik took no offense at the tough questions. "As long as I live, I think I'll regret the way I handled things," he said. "But as much as I regret it, I don't think I can ever make it up to her and I regret that even more. You can find Zaki upstairs in her office," he told Mike and headed out of the lobby.

Zakira watched him go. Then she closed her eyes to keep her tears at bay.

Chapter 13

The sexy gray business suit lay across the bed. Zakira eyed it skeptically, not sure if she should wear it or the new olive-green one she'd purchased a few days earlier. Her brown eyes darted from the bed to the closet, where the other suit was hanging. Deciding to be a bit more daring, she chose the olive-green suit. The skirt reached mid-thigh, while the coat was short and outlined her tiny waist and flattered her cleavage. She was about to head to the closet when the phone rang.

"This is Zakira."

"Hey, it's me."

Zakira sat on the edge of the bed as Eddie's slightly breathless voice drifted over the line. "Hey. What's up?"

"Are you feeling any better?" Eddie asked, sounding worried.

Smiling, Zakira took a deep breath. It seemed that so much had happened in the span of only a week, she was almost confused by Edwina's question. "I'm managing." She assured her sister. "Listen, I'm so sorry about our argument. Malik's the one who deserves my anger, not you."

"You don't need to apologize. Not for that. I know how shocked I am over Malik's return. That's why I decided to give you some space. I can only imagine how *you* must feel."

Zakira stood from the bed and took the gray suit back to her closet. "Hey, I know. Let me make it up to you, anyway. How about lunch? My treat. I know a great place."

Eddie chuckled softly on the other end. "I bet you do. And I'd take you up on the offer, if I weren't back in Richmond."

Zakira frowned. "Well, you and Tree could've at least said goodbye."

"Z, for all I know, Tree's still in New York."

"Wait a minute. What?"

"We…had a bad fight that night after I got back to the hotel. He walked out…I packed. I was gone before he got back."

Zakira closed her eyes and grimaced. "Dammit. Honey, I am so sorry. I guess I don't need to ask what you fought about?"

"It's stupid for us to be fighting over your problems, I know. But for Tree to keep that from you all this time…"

"I know, I know."

Eddie took a deep breath. "Listen, I didn't call to bring you down. I just wanted you to know I was back home."

"All right," Zakira said, walking back to her bed, "I guess I'll talk to you when I get back. Hopefully, it won't be much longer."

"Is Malik coming back with you?"

"Oh, he definitely won't be coming back with me, but he'll most likely get back around the same time I do."

"How are you going to handle that?"

"Oh, like I've handled everything else so far—in a daze."

Eddie laughed. "Well, try not to go crazy and please call if you need me."

Zakira smiled. "You know I will. Thanks, love."

"Anytime."

Zakira set the receiver back in its cradle once the connection was broken and began to get dressed. She had her under things on and was stepping into her skirt when Malik walked into the bedroom.

Malik watched his wife. His dark eyes followed the path of the skirt as she pulled it over her thighs and hips. When her hands moved to the zipper, he headed over.

Zakira felt Malik brush her hands away, before he pulled her back against him. The instant she felt his steely form behind her, she moaned. Malik's wide hands reached around to cup her breasts encased in the lacy white bra. Her nipples rose to firm buds beneath his palms as his lips tugged on her earlobe.

Arching into the erotic embrace, Zakira's arms rose

to circle Malik's neck. She gasped when his hand trailed down her stomach to disappear beneath her clothes.

Suddenly, he pulled away and smiled down at her. Obviously satisfied by the results of his teasing, he straightened Zakira's bra and zipped her skirt.

"I'll see you at the restaurant," he whispered next to her ear and pressed a soft kiss to her hair. Then he left the room without looking back.

That evening's dinner couldn't have come sooner for Zakira. She had been a mass of nerves during Thanksgiving and she prayed that Malik wouldn't suggest some emotional meal alone at the hotel suite. She'd have never survived it. She was already over the edge in response to her husband's unrelenting sexual taunts.

She smoothed her palms across the smart, chic turquoise suit she'd chosen. Her excitement was evident as she waited for the committee directors to arrive. She sent up a quick prayer that everything would go as planned and headed for the kitchen. The chefs had been instructed to prepare their best dishes and she wanted to be sure everything was in order.

Finding Malik there robbed her of her questions. She watched him wrap up his conversation with the cooks and then met him as he approached her.

"Why are you spending so much time down here in the kitchen?" she asked, her luminous brown eyes filled with suspicion.

Malik's grin triggered his dimples, and he watched her look around the kitchen before looking back at him. "It's actually one of the things I was beginning to regret about the business side of running the restaurant. I barely had any time to spend creating. Are they here yet?" he asked, before she could question him further. His dark gaze raked her petite form, loving the way the suit hugged her curves. He took her arm and escorted her to the dining room.

"We are so pleased you chose to establish your restaurant in this area."

Zakira smiled as she shook hands with one of the Better Housing Committee directors. "It seems to be a wonderful area. I loved it from the start."

Jeremy Wilcox nodded. "Well, it's made great strides. Believe me, it wasn't the most desirable part of town a few years ago."

"It's been one of our major goals to build it up and keep it up." Stephanie Hanes explained. "With this restaurant and the other establishments in the area, we hope to lure even more businesses."

"That's right. Better businesses will draw the eye of contractors and that means better housing," Shawn Robertson told them.

"Well, we hope to be here a very long time. That is, if our cooking doesn't run us out of town!" Malik teased.

"We're willing to bet that won't happen!" Brian Harris said, once the laughter softened. "What does the menu look like?"

Zakira couldn't wait to announce her selections for the evening. "I thought we'd—"

"Actually, we've taken the liberty of having some of our favorites prepared for you all," Malik was saying as he motioned for the group to head into the dining room.

"We're purchasing our seafood from a very impressive market in San Francisco. Tonight, we'll start with crab cakes in a white cream sauce, followed by scallop chowder, grilled salmon steaks, steamed vegetables and sourdough biscuits."

Zakira tried to keep her expression closed as she listened to Malik rattle off the list of unfamiliar dishes. Everyone else raved over the evening's menu, while taking their places at the table.

As their guests placed their drink orders, Zakira leaned over and tugged the sleeve of Malik's maroon jacket. "What are you doing?" she whispered, her tone fierce.

In response, Malik pressed a lingering kiss to the corner of her mouth. "Shh. Just sit back and enjoy it," he whispered back.

Zakira held a clenched fist beneath the table as her temper began to mount.

When Malik left a few minutes later to check on things in the kitchen, Zakira was right behind him and pulled him into the manager's downstairs office.

"What are you trying to do, Malik? And don't act like you have no idea what I'm talking about."

Malik's dark gaze was soft and he appeared calm. "Baby, I thought you wanted this to be something new. I just didn't think having the same menu as our Richmond place was the way to do that. We ain't a burger joint, you know."

Zakira lost some of her steam. "You're right," she conceded, massaging her neck. "Just let me know when you're going to do something like this. You can't just make decisions without including me."

Malik took offense. "I never had to consult anyone about changes I wanted to make in my restaurant, Zaki."

"Well, that was before you left the place to me," she coolly replied.

"That's a moot point now." Malik told her, slipping his hands into his trouser pockets to hide his clenched fists.

Zakira tossed a lock of her thick hair across her shoulder and fixed her husband with a firm look. "A moot point? No, it's not a moot point, Malik. Please don't make me get technical with you over this."

Malik grinned and leaned back to watch her. "Please do," he urged. "Do get technical."

Zakira looked toward the floor, before focusing on his handsome face again. "When you…left, you also left me a letter in which you stated that Badu's was mine. Remember?"

Disbelief registered in Malik's eyes. "The letter? You'd actually use that against me?" he asked, taking a step toward her.

Zakira wasn't intimidated. "I'd use it to protect myself."

"Protect yourself?" Malik asked, feeling his anger intensify.

"Badu's was my lifeline after you deserted me and there is no way I'll let you take it back. Not after all the work and time I've put into it. Now I don't want this messy, so just talk to me before you decide to make changes with the restaurant. If you can do that, everything will be fine."

Malik's dark gaze narrowed. He almost didn't recognize the woman who was his wife. His eyes followed her as she turned and left the office.

* * *

Zakira lifted a forkful of the delicious sautéed vegetables to her mouth and savored the taste. She was in the peaceful redwood-paneled dining room, sampling a new dish prepared by the chefs. From across the room, she saw Malik walk into the dining room with Tree.

"Hey, Z," Tree greeted, as he approached the table.

Zakira's gaze dropped to her lunch. "Hello," she said, only glancing at the two men.

Malik and Tree exchanged knowing looks before taking seats at the table.

"We need to talk, Zaki. I hope all this won't come as too much of a surprise," Malik said, leaning back in his chair and propping the side of his face against his palm.

Zakira set her fork aside and glared across the table. "Everything you've done has been a surprise. Please, don't stop now," she retorted.

The look on Malik's face indicated that he was furious and having difficulty keeping a lid on his temper. Uttering a heavy sigh, he looked over at Tree.

"Zakira," Tree began, pausing to clear his throat, "we're here to discuss the business."

"What about it?" she instantly asked, her eyes narrowing with suspicion.

"Well, it's obvious that Malik would want to be a part of it again. That includes making decisions without having to ask your permission."

Zakira crossed her arms over her delicate gray silk blouse. "Well, Malik should've thought about that before he decided to play this game," she countered, turning a hateful glare toward her husband.

Malik massaged his temple. "I never thought I'd be coming back, Zaki. You know that."

Zakira rolled her eyes and recrossed her legs under the table. "That's not my problem."

"Zakira…" Tree sighed.

Zakira shrugged and motioned for Tree to continue.

"Malik wants to be a part of the business again. It's to be expected, since he *is* the rightful owner. He doesn't want you out, Zakira, and that's why we're here. We need to work out an agreement that's beneficial…"

As she listened to Tree make his pitch, Zakira tried to maintain a cool demeanor. Inside, she was seething. Her hands curled into tight fists, her nails threatening to draw blood from her palms. Dammit! How could this be happening? She knew there had to be something she could do to stop Malik from just bulldozing his way back into the business she had kept afloat. Of course, she wasn't about to voice her concerns in front of the two men across the table. She decided to bide her time, until she was back in Virginia.

"Zakira…? You with us?" Tree was asking, his deep-set onyx eyes watching her intently.

"Mmm-hmm, is that it?"

Tree glanced over at Malik.

"What do you think about what I've just proposed?" Tree asked.

Zakira pushed her chair away from the table and stood. "I'm going to need time to think it over."

Tree nodded. "We can understand that, Z," he said, waiting for her to look at him. "I just want to apologize for everything that's been happening. I know it's been hard on you."

"It's fine," she assured him, with a wave of her hand. "I should've known you'd stick by your good buddy here, regardless." She sent Malik a cold look.

"Zakira…" Tree groaned.

"No, really, Tree, it's okay. I'll talk to you both after I see my lawyer."

Tree's silky black brows drew close. "Your lawyer?"

"Mmm-hmm. I think I need someone who's working in my best interest," she coolly announced.

From the look on Tree's face, it was obvious that he was hurt and offended. "I know how to keep the confidence of my clients, Z."

In spite of the almost tangible tension in the room, Zakira smiled. "It's very obvious you can keep the confidence of your clients," she told Tree. "Now, you two have a good day." She picked up her plate and left the table.

Tree muttered a frustrated curse and tossed his pen to the table. "This is going to be messy."

Malik didn't answer. His gray black stare followed Zakira until she left the dining room. Though he would be slow to admit it, he shared his friend's pessimism.

After a couple of weeks, Zakira felt the restaurant would be in good hands with Justin Flowers, the head manager. She left New York one night without any word to Malik.

The moment she arrived home and shut the front door behind her, she took a deep breath. She relished the solitude of her lovely home and couldn't wait to settle in. There was only a short time to decorate before Christmas. Was it that time already? she asked herself, unable to stop her thoughts from straying to Christmas past. She closed her eyes against the tears pressuring them. She wondered if Christmas would be synonymous with happiness again. Alone in her home she could admit how much staying with Malik in New York had affected her. She wanted to give in so badly, let him take over the restaurant and go back to the way things were. There was just one problem—she had grown used to the power of running the restaurant and couldn't give it up. A tiny part of her was actually looking forward to the fight and the chance to wipe the confident grin from his face. Pushing herself away from the door, she headed upstairs.

"Oh, it's sooo good to see you," she sighed, rushing to the middle of the room. For a moment, she stared at her wonderful, comfortable bed before she collapsed on top of it. For a while, she just lay there toying with her hair as she gazed around the room.

"What the hell…?" she whispered, a small frown forming between her brows. She noticed a few additions to her dresser that certainly didn't belong to her. Easing off the bed, she went to take a closer look. She discovered several colognes and other male paraphernalia.

Feeling her temper rising, Zakira investigated the bathroom and finally the closets.

"What the—" she breathed, discovering that the closets were filled with Malik's clothes.

Storming out of the bedroom, she raced down the stairs to see what else had been done. Her first instinct was to call Tree and find out what Malik was up to. Good sense prevailed, however, and she had just put the phone down when the front door opened.

Malik walked into the house as if nothing had happened. Zakira watched in stunned amazement as he set his bags to the floor and headed across the room to her.

Effortlessly, he lifted her from the floor while his head bowed. Zakira gasped, allowing his tongue the entrance it sought. She moaned, melting instantly against his powerful form. When she realized she was returning his kiss with wild enthusiasm, she pushed him away.

"What are you doing here?" she demanded once he set her down.

Malik smiled, enjoying the brave tone in her words while her eyes proved her unease.

"Did you hear me?" Zakira asked, taking a step backward.

Malik shrugged. "I'm home, aren't you happy to see me?" he asked, slipping his arms around her waist.

"You can't stay here," she told him.

The easy look on his dark face vanished and was replaced by a guarded one. "Baby, this isn't something you want to argue with me about."

Zakira closed her eyes against his subtle threat. His fingers had slipped beneath the tight knit fabric of her pink sweater and were stroking the bare skin at her waist. Zakira fought the wave of pleasure about to consume her from the simple touch, and managed to push him away again.

"What do you mean?"
April Winston sighed at the frantic tone in her client's

voice. "Zakira, I know this isn't what you wanted to hear. But I'm only telling you what I think is best."

"You're damned right. I've run the business by myself all this time. Now you're telling me to just let Malik come back like nothing's happened?"

"Oh, sweetie, I'm sorry but I really believe it's your best option. He only wants to be a part of the business he founded. Would it really put you in such a bad spot to let him have equal power?" April inquired, watching Zakira shake her head and shove her hands into the pockets of her stylish hunter-green coat dress. "Malik could always argue that he was acting in your best interest," she continued. "The fact that he left that letter could be viewed as something completely innocent."

"This is so unfair," Zakira argued, her high ponytail slapping the back of her neck.

April smiled, then stood and leaned against her desk. "Honey, I don't mean to make light of this. Malik could've handled this situation better, but we can't take him to court for that. I just don't think this is something worth going through a strenuous court battle over, unless…"

Zakira stepped closer to the desk. "Unless, what?"

"Well, you want to file for divorce?"

Zakira gasped at the mere mention of the word. Even after all that had happened, she still loved Malik too much to think of ending their marriage. She immediately began to shake her head.

"I thought not," April said, with a nod. "Well it's Christmastime, you know? Good will and cheer? I suggest the two of you sit down and work this out. It's a lot better than bringing your lawyers into it."

Zakira agreed and realized she'd known that all along. She reached over to squeeze her lawyer's hand. Within minutes, the two young women had wrapped up their meeting and were heading out of the office.

Downstairs, the dining room was alive with conversation and laughter. Zakira saw April out the door, before going to investigate. There, in the bar, was Malik surrounded by everyone who worked for Badu's. She leaned against the doorjamb and watched the happy scene. Seeing the gorgeous smile brighten Malik's face as he enjoyed the company of his friends tugged at her heart.

"Hey, Zakira, come on over here!" someone called and Malik's eyes immediately scanned the crowd for his wife.

Not wanting to cause a scene, Zakira tamped down her nerves and headed into the dining room. The group watched, eager to see the reunited couple in each other's arms.

The look on Malik's face told Zakira that he knew how uneasy she was. That didn't stop him from pulling her close to press a kiss against her ear.

"What are you doing?" Zakira asked through clenched teeth as she struggled to maintain her phony smile.

"You know exactly what I'm doing." Malik's soft voice drifted into her ear. "We need to have a talk."

Zakira pressed her shaking hands against his chest and she stepped away. "I'm free now."

He brushed his thumb against her mouth and smiled. "I appreciate it, baby, but I already promised to stop by the kitchen."

It was impossible to miss the desire that radiated from Malik's eyes. Zakira wanted him so much she could feel the need racing through her body. It made her so weak. Her legs were on the verge of giving beneath her.

"Baby, what is it?" Malik asked, his large hands cupping her face.

Zakira quickly pulled away, not trusting herself around him any longer. "I'll be in my office."

"Going somewhere?" Malik called out to Zakira the next morning. She had her briefcase in hand and was headed out the front door.

"The restaurant," she sang without breaking her stride.

"I've got breakfast goin'," he told her, leaning against the doorway and wiping his hands with a dishcloth.

"No thanks," Zakira declined, despite her stomach rumbling in response to the delicious smells filling the air.

Malik tossed the dishcloth over his shoulder and headed back to the kitchen. "Eddie's gonna be disappointed when she gets here."

Zakira set her leather carryall on the message desk and walked to the kitchen. "What about Eddie?"

"I invited her to breakfast."

"Why?" Zakira asked just as the doorbell rang.

Malik was opening the oven door. "That's probably her now."

Zakira left him with a curious look and went to answer the door.

"Good morning!" Eddie called, her hazel gaze sparkling when she saw her stepsister.

"Hey," Zakira called, pulling Eddie into a tight hug and rubbing her hands across the soft material of her black cotton dress.

"What's wrong?" Eddie inquired, picking up on the drawn sound in Zakira's voice. She pulled away to watch her.

Zakira shrugged. "I just found out Malik invited you for breakfast."

"Is it a problem?"

"Girl, don't be silly," Zakira replied, with a wave of her hand. "Come on in," she ordered just as another vehicle pulled into the driveway. "What's Tree doing here?"

Eddie turned and closed her eyes when she saw the man parking his vehicle. "Please don't tell me Malik's tryin' to play matchmaker?" she groaned.

"Honey, we can always leave if you want," Zakira suggested, folding her arms across the square bodice of her lime-green top.

Eddie sighed and fixed her sister with another smile. "You're crazy if you think I'll turn down Malik's cooking," she said, though her stomach churned at the thought of sitting across from Tree.

"Good morning, ladies," Tree greeted when he arrived at the doorway. His demeanor was cool and polite, though he seemed surprised to see Edwina.

"Come on in," Zakira invited with a smile as she waved him inside.

When the threesome arrived in the kitchen, Malik was in an even better mood. In fact, he appeared to be the only one in high spirits as he put the finishing touches on breakfast and instructed his guests to take their seats. When he asked Zakira to help him with something, she sighed and went over. Eddie headed toward the small round table, but then went to the

French doors that led to the patio. From there, she enjoyed the view of the backyard. Tree followed.

"How have you been?" he asked, pushing his hands into the back pockets of his loose-fitting dark blue jeans. His eyes were fixed on the yard, as well.

Eddie winced. "Fine. Considering."

"What?"

She cleared her throat. "Considering I should be married now."

"Eddie—"

"Please don't say anything." she begged, clasping her hands.

"Eddie do you think it's fair or right that our future hinge on what happens between Malik and Zakira? I love 'em, but I'm not willing to base my happiness on theirs."

Eddie ran her fingers through her hair. "How can you talk about what's right? None of what's happened has been right."

"We were right," Tree flatly replied, rolling his dark eyes away from the lawn as he looked down at Eddie. "We were very right," he added, and pressed a kiss to her temple before he walked away.

In the kitchen, Zakira was watching Malik a though she expected him to reveal his motives. "What are you up to?" she finally asked.

"'Scuse me?" he replied, rubbing his hand across the back pocket of his saggy, black denim shorts.

"Eddie and Tree seemed quite surprised to find one another here. What are you trying to do?"

Malik reached for a pot holder. "Damn, Zaki, we *have* eaten together before, you know?"

Zakira stomped her foot. "Malik Kuame Badu—"

"All right, all right," he said, chuckling as he took buttermilk biscuits from the oven. Sobering, he set the pan aside and turned to face her. "I have a lot, *a lot* to answer for. One of those things is Eddie and Tree. They're suffering because of decisions I made."

"And you think a breakfast is going to get them back together?" Zakira asked, slapping one hand to her black Capri pants.

Malik shook the dreads from his face. "No, but maybe it'll get them talking and maybe they'll listen to one another and find their way back to one another."

Zakira felt herself warming at the words he spoke from his heart. She didn't want to be affected and focused on the delicious array of food. "Only you would think a gourmet meal would solve the ills of the world," she teased, bracing her hands on the counter.

Malik walked up behind her and curled his big hands around her upper arms. "No, but my actions had consequences I never dreamed of," he whispered against her ear. "I wouldn't listen to anything except my pride. I don't believe it's possible to make up for what I did, but maybe there's a small chance I can make things right again. I'll start with Tree and Eddie, and then it's you and me."

At first, Zakira couldn't move. Soon, her entire body began to tremble as the conviction in Malik's words took root in her soul.

Chapter 14

"God, I can't take much more of this," Zakira groaned, dropping her head onto the desk. She had been in the office most of the day. The workload wasn't that heavy, but she was doing her best to avoid Malik.

Pushing herself away from the desk, she took a long stretch and stared unseeingly out the window. Lord, this situation with Malik had to give one way or the other, she told herself. The whole thing was wearing her out emotionally and physically.

"Zakira?" Rhonda Cooper called as she knocked on the door.

Zakira smiled and turned. "Yeah?"

"Malik wants to see you downstairs."

"All right. I'll be down in a minute."

Rhonda nodded and quietly left the office.

Zakira closed her eyes and took a deep breath. Malik had told her he wanted to talk, maybe now was the time. She smoothed her hands over the stylish peach cashmere dress, tossed her high ponytail and then, she headed downstairs.

The entire lower level was dark, with the exception of a smattering of candles. They flickered wildly and cast interesting, unusual patterns on the drapes and cream walls of the dining room.

"Malik?" Zakira called in a nervous voice. She cleared her throat and walked a bit farther into the room.

Malik suddenly appeared behind her. His large hands circled her waist as he pulled her back against his tall, chiseled form. "Thanks for coming down so fast," he whispered against her neck.

Zakira turned in his arms and stared up at him. "What are you doing? We're supposed to open in—"

"We're gonna be closed tonight."

"Closed?" Zakira cried, shoving her hands against his chest. "We can't just close. It's Christmas Eve, remember?"

Malik crossed his arms over his stylish burgundy shirt and waited for Zakira to end her tirade before he stepped forward. "I remember, which is why we're closing. Could I please get you to sit and be quiet?"

Zakira complied, turning to the small, round table in the far corner of the room. It had been lavishly set for two, something right out of romantic movie.

For the first few moments, the two of them filled their

plates with food and their glasses with champagne. Zakira helped herself to an abundance of the bubbly amber liquid. Malik watched her closely. Obviously he didn't care for the amount she downed.

"Oooops, excuse me," she whispered, pressing her fingers against her lips when a small hiccup escaped her.

Malik simply reached across the table and removed the glass from her fingers. Zakira immediately reached out for it, anger on her face.

"Listen, Malik," she began, pointing a finger at him, "I think I deserve something to make it through the night."

"I don't want you drunk tonight," he told her.

"*You* don't want?" Zakira asked in disbelief, her eyes wide as saucers. "I don't give a damn about what you want. After what you did—"

"Hell, Zaki, how long are you going to punish me for that?" Malik snapped.

"You just have no idea…" her voice trailed off in a defeated tone.

Malik leaned back in his chair and ran one hand across his face. "Zaki, I want you back. I want us back the way we were."

"But we've changed," Zakira cried. "When you decided to cut me out of your life, you changed everything between us and we can't go back."

"Do you still love me?"

Zakira squeezed her eyes shut tightly. "That's not fair."

"Can you answer me?"

"Malik, please, that has nothing to do with what we're going through now. You want things to be the same and they can't be. They just can't be."

"Why not?" Malik demanded, his grayish stare searching her face. "I'm alive, I'm healthy. I know you miss the way we used to be. Why can't you…" He couldn't bring himself to finish.

Zakira held her forehead in her palm and sighed. "Malik, if you're trying to repair our marriage, this isn't the way," she wearily informed him.

Malik wanted to respond, but one look at the tears sparkling in her eyes against the glow of the candlelight rendered him speechless.

Zakira headed to the office early on Christmas morning. She left Malik at their home in front of the den TV where he'd fallen asleep the night before. Unable to stand another emotional confrontation, she decided not to disturb him. At the office, she managed to dive into her work, forcing her problems to the back of her mind. Around 9:00 a.m., a knock sounded on her office door.

"Come in," she called, wondering who else would possibly think of coming into the restaurant on Christmas. When she looked up and saw Tree standing in the doorway, she was shocked. "If you're looking for Malik—"

"No, it's you I wanted to see. Do you have a minute?" he asked, watching her nod before he walked into the room.

When Tree pulled a folded piece of paper from the breast pocket of his stylish beige pin-striped suit, Zakira frowned.

"Have Eddie here today at 1:00 p.m."

Zakira scanned the contents of the paper, seeing an address. "What for?"

The look in Tree's deep midnight gaze was close to pleading. "Just have her there, all right, Z?"

"Tree, I don't know."

Tree laughed and stepped closer to the desk. "I'm not going to hurt her."

Zakira smiled in spite of herself. "I'm sorry. I know you're not. You really love her, don't you?" she asked, watching the subdued look on Tree's handsome face turn serious.

"You have no idea how much," he said.

Zakira glanced at the paper again and nodded. "I'll have her there," she promised.

The relieved smile that tugged at Tree's mouth brought a boyish gleam to his face. "Thanks, Z."

Silence settled between them. Finally Tree tried to dissolve the tension.

"Zakira, I don't want what happened to keep coming between us—"

"You know what, Tree?" Zakira interrupted as she walked from behind her desk. "All that mess is in the past as far as I'm concerned."

Tree's eyes widened slightly in surprise. "Are you sure?"

"I am. I can't fault you for trying to be a good friend. You got caught in the middle, trying to do right by us both. I'm sorry we put you there."

Unable to say anything more, Tree just shrugged. He held his hand out to Zakira, who quickly stepped forward. They hugged each other for the longest time.

* * *

"Z? What's goin' on? I thought we were going out for lunch?"

Zakira glanced at Eddie and shrugged. "I'm sure we'll have lunch."

The frown on Edwina's face grew deeper. "You're sure? Girl, where are we going?"

"We're here," Zakira announced. "Wow," she breathed, staring out over the dashboard.

Eddie turned to look out the passenger window. Her gaze widened when she saw the lovely country cottage nestled among a slew of snow-capped bushes and tall trees.

"Zakira, where are we?"

"Let's find out." Zakira suggested, getting out of the car. She felt a great deal of happiness for Eddie and Tree. Happy they would finally be together.

Eddie smoothed her hands across the gorgeous tailored lavender suit she wore. When Zakira walked by her, she grabbed her arm. "All right, Z, start talkin'. What's all this about?"

"Eddie, can we just go inside and see? Please?"

Edwina watched her sister a minute longer, then followed her up the gravel driveway to the oak door of the stone cottage.

The door was open and when the two women walked inside, they were stunned. The delightful room was cozily decorated and looked very intimate. There was a crackling fire in the brick fireplace, cushioned mauve couches were covered with throw pillows and afghans, cream-colored ceramic lamps gave off warm golden light and plants created an atmosphere right out of a fairy tale.

Zakira and Eddie exchanged glances, but before either of them could say a thing, a side door opened. A short, gray-haired gentleman in minister's attire appeared along with Tree and Malik.

It all came together in an instant for Edwina. Her crystal clear gaze grew teary the moment she saw Tree.

Zakira's heartbeat sounded madly in her ears. Her eyes were focused solely on Malik.

As Reverend Raymond Willis took his position a few feet in front of the fireplace, Tree stepped over to Eddie. Cupping her oval face in his huge hands, he kissed her mouth. "Will you please marry me now?"

Eddie smiled at the soothing deep sound of the words. "Yes," she whispered against his lips. "Yes, yes, yes…"

Reverend Willis cleared his throat. "Are we ready to begin?" he asked, a smile on his face as he watched the couple totally absorbed with one another.

Taking her hand in his, Tree pulled Edwina with him to stand before the minister. Malik and Zakira didn't speak, but took their places next to their friends. The ceremony was lovely, although quite short. Soon Eddie and Tree were pronounced husband and wife.

"Trekel, you may kiss your bride," Reverend Willis stated.

Tree wasted no time drawing Eddie's slender frame against his larger one. Dipping his head, he kissed her deeply. Eddie moaned softly, her fingers grasping the lapels of his dark suit and returning the kiss as though she were starved for the taste of him.

Reverend Willis stepped away from the couple and walked over to speak briefly with Malik and Zakira, who escorted him to the front door.

"Tree's somethin' else, huh?" Malik asked, once he closed the door behind Reverend Willis.

"Mmm-hmm," Zakira lightly agreed, turning to watch the happy couple feed each other from the buffet.

Malik's seductive stare slid over his wife's tiny form encased in the clinging powder-blue dress she wore. "It meant a lot to him for you to forgive him."

Zakira bowed her head briefly before turning to face him. "Well, I realized Tree wasn't the one to blame."

"Ah," Malik said, leaning his head back. "That would be me."

"You got it."

Malik chuckled, the dreads brushing his wide shoulders. Zakira didn't mind, since his laughter helped take her mind off the sexual tension that constantly snapped between them.

"Malik!" Eddie shouted, hurrying toward him. They hugged, and she kissed his cheek. "Thanks for being here."

"I'm glad I could be, love. You be happy, all right?" he ordered.

Eddie pulled away and looked at Tree who was standing next to Zakira. "I will," she promised. Her exquisite gaze slid to her stepsister's face and she took her hand in a firm grip. "Can I talk to you?" she requested, leaving her husband and Malik in the living room.

Eddie hugged herself in the plush bedroom, where Tree and Malik had hidden earlier with the minister. "Girl, I can't believe this! Did you know he was going to do this?"

Zakira raised her hands defensively. "I had no idea. He just told me to get you here."

Eddie was practically beaming. She rushed over and hugged Zakira. "I'm so happy," she sighed.

"You deserve it," Zakira whispered, patting her back.

"So do you."

"Eddie—"

"Z, look, I know Malik was wrong for doing what he did, but I wish you two could just get back what you had."

"I'm beginning to wonder if we'll even get close to that," Zakira admitted. She pulled away from Eddie and took a seat on the bed.

"Oh, honey, don't say that," Eddie urged, joining her sister on the bed.

"Why not, Eddie? It's the truth. Malik says he wants to set things right, but I don't think he has any idea how much he hurt me. He thinks I'm just mad and it's nothing serious. I'm just supposed to be glad he's alive—which I am. But I don't think his mission to 'set things right' involves him explaining, apologizing or something. Something to tell me how he could do this…*if* he'd do it again."

"Ah, babe," Eddie soothed, pulling Zakira close. "So that's it? Sweetie, have you told him how you feel?"

Zakira swallowed. "I can't tell him like I'm telling you."

Eddie frowned. "Why not?"

"He'll think that all this time I've just been pretending to be this great independent businesswoman when I'm the same weakling I was before."

"You were never a weakling." Eddie firmly corrected. "Honey you really need to talk to your husband about this. You know you do. Let him know how you feel or you'll never get past all this and rebuild your marriage."

Zakira smiled softly at Eddie. "You're right, I just don't know how to approach him," she admitted, and then expelled a breath. "I *do* know that I'm not gonna get you down on your wedding day on Christmas Day."

Eddie waved her hand. "Ah, girl, I don't think anything would do that."

"Now, come on," Zakira ordered, wiping a lone tear away from her cheek. "Let's get out of this room, so you can go dance with your husband."

The two stepsisters left the bedroom chattering away. They never noticed Malik standing by the door in the shadows.

The delicious aroma of spicy, bubbling lasagna and buttered French bread greeted Zakira when she arrived home the next evening. She allowed her nose to be her guide and headed for the kitchen. Her loud gasp filled the air when she found Malik there, hard at work mixing something in a huge bowl. She cleared her throat and waited for him to look up.

"Hey. Damn, I was hoping to be finished by the time you got home," he said.

Zakira waved her hand and walked closer to the kitchen island. She tossed her coat to one of the stools and smiled. "So, why didn't you ever cook like this…before? Or are you only doing this because it's Christmastime?" she teased.

Malik smiled, but didn't look up from his mixture. "I love your cooking more."

Zakira resisted the urge to toy with one of his dreadlocks. Instead, she sat at the small kitchen table. It was already set intimately for two. Malik finished his Parmesan sauce and began to set out the delicious feast.

Dinner passed quietly and quickly. The thick, gooey lasagna was cut down to only a corner. They were enjoying the flavored coffee, when the silence was finally broken.

"Zaki?"

"Mmm-hmm?"

"How could you ever believe I'd think you were weak?"

Zakira's head snapped up and she frowned across the table at him. "What do you mean by that?"

"You know what I mean," he assured her, pinning her with his unsettling gaze. "How could you ever think missing me and questioning my actions would make you weak?"

"Have you been talking to Eddie?"

Malik leaned forward and rested his elbows against the table. "No, I haven't been talking to Eddie. But I heard you talking yesterday after the wedding."

"Oh, so you were eavesdropping?" Zakira asked angrily.

"Dammit, girl, if I hadn't been there, I never would've found out anything," Malik informed her, becoming angry, as well. "Why didn't you just come talk to me?"

"Because you should've known!" Zakira snapped, slamming her palm against the table. She pushed her chair away and began to pace the checkered linoleum floor. "You should've known what your leaving did to me. It tore me apart. Sure you were sick, but I was dying, too. You didn't care about that, though. You had your plan and you were sticking to it, damn me and what you were doing to me."

Malik left the table and followed Zakira across the kitchen. "Baby, I didn't mean to make you feel that way."

"Malik, how'd you think I'd feel? Not only do you tell me that you have cancer and you're dying, but you tell me that you don't want treatment and you're going away to die. Then, I find out you've been living off somewhere for months. How did you expect this to affect me?"

"Love, I'm… I'm sorry," he told her, his intense stare filled with pain and guilt.

Zakira only shook her head. She tossed her thick curls across her shoulder, then walked over to him and poked her finger into his chest. "Do you have any idea how long it takes to build trust? I don't think men get that part of it. You want to go back to the way it was, but I'm not sure we'll ever get there again."

Malik's eyes narrowed and he tilted his head slightly. "So are you telling me you don't want to try and get past this? You expect me to just give you up? Is that what you want?"

Zakira cursed the tears that fell from her eyes. "I want— I want us to work this out, I do… But I'm so scared."

A stunned Malik pressed one hand against his chest and stepped closer to her. "Scared? Of me?"

Zakira went to lean against the oak kitchen island. She stared at the tops of her plum suede pumps and then looked up. "What if you decide it's best for you to leave again?"

Malik squeezed his eyes shut tightly. "That'll never happen."

"It happened before. I never expected it."

"Dammit, Zaki why are you doing this?" he asked, frustration tearing away at him.

"Because when you left, I felt like I had nothing. I wanted to die, cooped up in this house with all our memories. I didn't want to hear from anything or anyone. Then I realized that the business was still there and it became my life. All I could really depend on. I don't want to ever feel so helpless again. Hmph, and now you want me to hand over the only thing that kept me going…"

Malik turned away, running both his large hands through his heavy dreads. "I've been thinking about that," he said, after a long silence.

Zakira propped her hands on her hips and waited for him to continue.

"I want to spend more time in the kitchen and no time up in that office," he admitted.

"What does that mean?"

Malik grimaced and walked over to the island to sit next to her. "I always hated dealing with all those suppliers. You're a lot better at it than I ever was or ever could be. The way you deal with the business part of the restaurant is far better than I ever have."

Zakira frowned and watched him as though he were a different person. "I always thought you lived for the business part. It was like you thrived on it."

"Nah," Malik disagreed, shaking his head quickly. "I started the restaurant because I loved to cook. Unfortunately, I never counted on business taking me away from that. I think I began to resent it."

"And?" Zakira said, watching him expectantly.

Malik turned to face her, his fingers absently trailing the line of her thigh visible beneath the high hemline of her plum skirt. "Baby, I don't want our lawyers or the business to stand in the way of us getting back together. We've got a lot to work out, but I think we'll have a better chance if the restaurant isn't standing between us. We should make it legal and move past it."

"Legal?"

"You handle the business end of both restaurants completely. It's all your call. And I'll take care of the kitchens."

Zakira's large brown eyes narrowed in suspicion. "Why? Not that long ago, you and Tree were trying to sell me on the idea of giving you equal control. Or was I just imagining that?"

Malik's shoulder rose in a lazy shrug. "This is what you want. It's what you worked for. I think I knew it was for the best, but of course, I couldn't admit it at the time. Aside from all that, I love you and I'll do anything to get you back."

Zakira still appeared unsure. "Malik, I…thank you… but why do I get the feeling you're not really sold on the idea?"

Malik raised his hands. "I am. I mean everything I just said. It's just…"

"What?"

"I should probably know the answer to this question already."

"Will you please just tell me what you're talking about?"

Malik pushed himself off the island. "I've been gone a long time and even though we've been close since I came back, I know a lot has changed."

Zakira took a seat on one of the stools skirting the counter. "Like…what?"

"Your feelings," he clarified, turning to face her.

"I don't know how you can ask me that," she whispered. "We've slept together more than once since you've been back, remember?"

Malik's slow strides brought him close to Zakira. He trailed one finger down her cheek and smiled. "I'm not talking about sex, Zaki. As fine as you are, you can't tell me that a ton of men weren't trying to break down your door."

Zakira couldn't stop the tiny chuckle that escaped her. She was very pleased by the compliment, though a little embarrassed. "There haven't been a ton."

"But some."

"Business dinners, mostly. They could've escalated into something more had I taken a few of those offers. Despite my anger at you, in all honesty you weren't gone that long. There was nothing that got serious."

"Not even Michael Renner?"

"It may have become serious, had there not been another man involved," she announced, her words barely audible.

"Another man? What…other man?"

Zakira shook her head, enjoying his aggravation as she strolled out of the kitchen.

Malik uttered a short, humorless laugh and followed. Stopping her at the desk just inside the living room he braced his hands on either side of her. "Who is he?"

"You. Idiot."

"Don't tease me," he whispered, tilting back her chin with his finger.

"I'm not," she assured him, wrapping her hand around his finger. "I missed you so much. Not being able to feel you against me in bed at night, or in the middle of the day," she teased, her heart melting at the gorgeous smile he flashed. "There wasn't enough time for me to get over you—never would've been. I still love you." She ran the back of her hand across his smooth, dark cheek.

"So, where does this leave us now?" Malik asked, pressing his forehead against hers as relief washed over him.

"I don't want to argue anymore, but I can't go through this again."

Malik nodded. "I can't go through this again, either, Zaki. I talk about my pride getting in the way of my doing the right thing. But it was really my fear. You say you were afraid of my seeing you as weak. It's ironic, because that was my fear, too."

Zakira's brown eyes narrowed. "Malik…" she whispered.

He turned his face into her hand and kissed her palm. "As much as I love you, I never let you see that part of myself. I always wanted you to think of me as invincible. I did a good job of pulling it off, too, until this cancer took me down a peg. I can't promise you calm waters, Zaki, but whatever happens we'll deal with it. Together. I made a mistake, a big one, and I learned from it. It'll take you a long time to trust me again, I know that, but if you give me a chance, you won't be sorry."

"I think we can work together, but we have to share everything. *Everything,* Malik. Don't keep anything from me for my own good. I don't care how bad you think it is," she warned, her gaze steady and serious. "It's going to take a lot of talks like this, if you think you can handle it."

Malik rose to his full height and gazed down at her. "I can handle it. It'll be one of the hardest things I've ever had to do—learning how *not* to be overprotective—but there's no way I'll give up. I love you, Zaki. I love you with everything in me."

The happiness Zakira felt was intoxicating, and she hoped the feeling would never end. She was finally able to let down her guard. Her arms encircled his waist, and she smiled up at him. "At least there's one part of our relationship that won't need any work."

Malik's long, dark brows rose. "What part?"

"This part," she whispered, pulling his head down to hers.

Their lips met under a feverish kiss. Malik moaned, his tongue thrusting into Zakira's mouth. It felt incredible to have her willing in his arms. His hands wrapped around her hips, and he lifted her atop the kitchen island. He pulled her thighs apart and stepped between them to bury his head in the cleft of her breasts. One hand reached inside her blouse and freed one of the dark mounds from the confines of the lacy plum bra. His mouth sought the firm nipples, and he suckled it passionately.

Zakira threw her head back and let him have his way. She reached beneath his white T-shirt and raked her nails across the muscles that rippled in his strong back.

Their cries of arousal and desire filled the house. They reveled in the love they discovered still existed. Their every fantasy was fulfilled. Malik and Zakira held each other tightly as they lay together in their living room and watched the twinkling white lights on the tree. They each savored the journey that had brought them back into each other's arms.

Business takes on a new flavor...

SEX ON FLAMINGO *Beach*

Part of the Flamingo Beach series

Bestselling author

MARCIA KING-GAMBLE

Rowan James's plans to open a casino next door may cost resort manager Emilie Woodward her job. So when he asks her out, suspicion competes with sizzling attraction. What's he after—a no-strings fling or a competitive advantage?

"Down and Out in Flamingo Beach showcases
Marcia King-Gamble's talent for accurately
portraying life in a small town."
—*Romantic Times BOOKreviews*

*Available the first week of November
wherever books are sold.*

KIMANI™
ROMANCE

www.kimanipress.com   KPMKG0411107

The Knight family trilogy continues…

to love a
KNIGHT
WAYNE JORDAN

As Dr. Tamara Knight cares for gravely injured
Jared St. Clair, she's drawn to his rugged sensuality and
commanding strength. Despite his gruff exterior, she can't
stop herself from indulging in a passionate love affair with
him. But unbeknownst to Tamara, Jared was sent to save
her. Now protecting Tamara isn't just another mission for
Jared—it's all that matters!

"Mr. Jordan's writing simply captures his audience."
—*The Road to Romance*

*Available the first week of November
wherever books are sold.*

KIMANI™
ROMANCE

www.kimanipress.com

KPWJ0431107

The stunning sequel to *The Beautiful Ones*...

feel THE fire

NATIONAL BESTSELLING AUTHOR
ADRIANNE BYRD

Business mogul Jonas Hinton has learned to stay clear
of gorgeous women and the heartbreak they bring.
But when his younger brother starts dating sexy attorney
Toni Wright, Jonas discovers a sizzling attraction he's
never felt before. Torn between family loyalty and
overwhelming desire, can he find a way to win the
woman who could be his real-life Ms. Wright?

"Byrd proves once again that she's a wonderful storyteller."
—*Romantic Times BOOKreviews* on *The Beautiful Ones*

*Available the first week of November
wherever books are sold.*

ARABESQUE®

Love can be sweeter the second time around...

USA TODAY Bestselling Author

KAYLA PERRIN

Midnight **D**REAMS

Betrayed by her husband, Jade Alexander resolved
never again to trust a man with her heart. But after
meeting old flame Terrell Edmonds at a New Year's
Eve party, Jade feels her resolve weakening—
and her desire kindling.

Terrell had lost Jade by letting her marry the wrong man.
Now he must convince her that together they can make
all their New Year wishes come true...

"A fine storytelling talent."
—the *Toronto Star*

*Available the first week of November
wherever books are sold.*

ARABESQUE®